There was a blur before Carpo's eyes as the gun raised up and then smashed down on his head. Too late for him to flinch, too late even to blink. Just a swish of movement, a glint of steel, and then an awful pain knifing clear through his skull.

He fell to the floor, hands grabbing for his head, balls of light flaring in his eyes like Roman candles. He could taste blood seeping down the back of his throat. His face hit the floor, nostrils sucking in the fine talc. He gasped, then coughed, then choked.

The gun smashed down on his head again. Carpo put his arms up to protect himself, but they no longer responded. The light in his eyes grew brighter and brighter, and he felt himself falling inside himself, deeper and deeper, until the bright light exploded into a roaring sun.

As if from another hemisphere, Carpo heard two distinct sounds: a telephone ringing and a power tool running. The telephone was in the background, its tinkling bell eventually swallowed by the roar of the tool's engine.

It was an electric drill. It started from the side of the room and came close to him, buzzing around his face and neck . . .

Books by Mark Miano

FLESH AND STONE

THE STREET WHERE SHE LIVED

Published by Kensington Books

# FLESH AND STONE

### A Michael Carpo Mystery

# MARK MIANO

𝑘

**KENSINGTON BOOKS**
http://www.kensingtonbooks.com

KENSINGTON BOOKS are published by

Kensington Publishing Corp.
850 Third Avenue
New York, NY 10022

First Kensington Hardcover Printing: February, 1997
First Kensington Paperback Printing: March, 1998

Printed in the United States of America
10  9  8  7  6  5  4  3  2  1

*For Astrid*


*And For:*
*Mom, Dad, Nana, Uncle Lou, Andrea and Kevin*

I thank my agent, Kay Kidde, for her enthusiasm, persistence, and support. Without her, this book would still be a manuscript in the lower left drawer of my desk.

# Prologue

The smallest precinct in the New York City Police Department is located in an old brick building nestled at the back of a cobblestone parking lot. Despite a force of just one-hundred fifty officers, the precinct is responsible for one of the largest patrolling areas in Manhattan. That is because the precinct stands on the 86th Street Transverse Road—dead in the center of Central Park.

On the night of February 7, a Wednesday, the graveyard shift started like every other for Officer Gary McDonald. He was seated in the back office of the station house watching a "Honeymooners" rerun on Channel 11, his feet propped up on a cluttered wooden desk and a cigarette going in a battered metal ashtray nearby.

McDonald was a big man; for all eight of his years on the force he had reigned as the biggest cop in the Central Park Precinct. At six-feet seven inches and a weight fluctuating between three-hundred and three-hundred fifty pounds, McDonald was more than a sturdy officer when it came to patrolling the eerie darkness of Central Park alone. And that was what he did on his shift, four times a night: he piloted a small blue golf cart through the winding trails of the park.

At 11:45 P.M. McDonald flicked off the TV, buried his cigarette among the overflowing pile of butts, and readied himself for the midnight patrol of the park's northern reservoir. He bought a fresh pack of cigarettes from the vending machine in the lounge, poured a large amount of coffee into his plastic, no-spill travel mug, and ambled out to the far corner of the parking lot to warm up his police cart. The precinct owned an entire fleet of the carts, painted baby blue, with a clear plastic bubble on the top for warmth and protection. The carts were slower than the standard squad car, but they were the only vehicles suitable for the park's narrow dirt paths.

McDonald stood next to his cart while it idled, cursing the bitter cold as he smoked another cigarette. When a stream of warm air started flowing from the heater, he contorted his thick legs under the steering column and gunned the motor. The battery-powered engine provided just a trickle of heat, but, with his heavy coat bundled tightly to his body, McDonald was warm enough for the sixty-minute shift. Then it was back to the station, just in time for the "Full House" rerun on Channel 8.

McDonald circled the cart around the parking lot, pointed it up a steep, macadam ramp, and within seconds felt the wheels rumble onto the packed dirt of the reservoir. At one time, the huge lake had stored most of upper Manhattan's drinking water; now it was just a stagnant water hole protected by a thick, seven-foot chain-link fence. A dirt track followed the outer contour of the fence, the favorite running surface for several thousand joggers every day. The incredible cold that February had frozen the path to a concrete hardness, pitting its surface with footprints from runners. Over time, the prints had filled with snow and refrozen, increasing their size and creating hundreds of icy traps along the three-mile track.

"Be lucky if I make it around," McDonald grumbled, his breath fogging the windshield. The single headlight on the cart was strong enough to illuminate the space only directly in front of the cart, leaving no time for him to brace before each bone-jarring bump. One thing they did not think of when commissioning the carts was shock absorbers.

McDonald rattled slowly down the path, reaching the halfway point of the reservoir, marked by the North End Gatehouse, about ten minutes later than usual. The track grew even rougher along the second half of the reservoir, forcing him to bring the cart down to a crawl. About fifty yards past the Gatehouse, he stopped the cart, pulled out a cigarette, and lowered his head to the flame of his lighter. If he hadn't bent his head at that moment, McDonald might never have noticed the hole clipped through the bottom of the chain link fence.

"That's strange," he muttered as he cranked back on the cart's emergency brake. "Someone musta' cut through since the last shift."

He opened the cart's door and climbed from the cramped cabin, grabbing his flashlight from a holster on the door. He adjusted the billy club on his belt and felt a little farther along his waist to make sure his radio was in place. He walked a short way from the cart, took a deep, painful breath of icy air, and held it.

Nothing. No sound or movement came from the darkness around him. Slowly, he exhaled the warmed breath as he shined his torch across the track and over the bushes. Nothing. Finally, he pointed the yellow finger of light through the hole in the fence. Something reflected the light back at him, something flat against the ice. It was a shiny black spot, about fifty yards onto the reservoir; it sparkled brilliantly against the gray backdrop of weeks-old ice.

McDonald stared at the spot for a long moment before he succumbed to a fit of shivers. He pulled the radio from his belt and spoke into the handset. "Central Park precinct command. C-P command. This is radio motor patrol 316, Officer McDonald."

*"Go ahead, Officer McDonald,"* a warm, female voice said in his hand.

"Yeah, I've got a possible 10–10 here, unlawful entry on the reservoir. I'm just west of the North End Gatehouse, maybe fifty yards or so. Anyway, there's a hole in the fence, and I see something out on the ice. Was a report filed on this?"

There was a long pause from precinct command, then: *"Negative, McDonald. There's no report of a 10–10 on the reservoir."*

"Shit," McDonald said, before he pressed the button in on the radio. "Well, sometime since the eight shift, someone must've cut through the fence and gone out on the ice. I'd better check it out, so don't raise Cain if I'm late to my next station. On the other hand, don't forget I'm out here neither."

*"Officer, is this a 10–85? Are you requesting back-up?"*

"No Ma'am. But if I ain't back in a little while, don't hesitate to send some company. Over and out."

McDonald heard the handset double-click as precinct command signed off and he replaced the radio in his belt. He put both hands on the torch and flexed his fingers, trying to work blood down into the numb tips. He shined the light back toward the hole in the fence. It was a good-sized hole, covering nearly a three-foot radius, but it was low and partly concealed by weeds poking up through the snow. He noticed that most of the weeds were flattened and pointed toward the ice.

"Should've pretended I didn't see the damn thing," he complained to the icy blackness in front of him.

McDonald walked to the hole, crouched into a ball, and squeezed through the fence. On the other side was a steep, eight-foot drop to the surface of the ice. He stepped carefully down the embankment, grabbing handholds in the rocks underneath. About halfway down, one of the rocks came loose, and like the fall of a giant tree, he toppled over, landing hard on his back on the reservoir.

"Son of a bitch," he gasped, eyes watering as he stared up into the clear, still night. "I guess it'll hold though."

Actually, McDonald already knew the ice was thick enough to support his weight. The precinct charted its daily thickness and posted it in the station house so that officers would know when to watch for kids jumping the fence to ice skate. Today the ice had measured a thickness of four feet. With the wind-chill hovering at fifteen below, thin ice was the least of the big officer's worries.

McDonald padded out to the shiny black spot, his feet skidding on what appeared to be a swept area of ice leading to it.

"Musta' laid out the red carpet," he whispered while he shuffled along, taking care not to slip.

As he neared the spot, he could see it was a hole cut into the ice, about two feet in diameter and forming a near perfect circle. He felt relieved to see that the edges of the hole were smooth, meaning it probably hadn't been caused by some kid falling through the ice. It did occur to him that there were no ice chips around it. Carefully, he inched toward the edge, testing each step to make sure the ice didn't thin out near the opening.

The hole had covered over with a fresh layer of ice, but unlike the older ice, it was as clear as a sheet of glass. The black water beneath created a mirror, reflecting back the light from his torch and temporarily blinding him as he leaned out over the edge. He stared into the hole, blinking to clear his eyes, when he realized he was looking into the face of another man.

Wide, terrified eyes stared up at him just an inch below the surface. Farther down, the face was attached to a naked body, McDonald realized as he ran from the hole, legs pumping faster than they had ever carried his huge frame. But it wasn't the eyes or the naked body that would haunt him for the rest of his life—it was the face.

The face was contorted into the shape of a scream: purple lips pulled back over rows of dazzling white teeth, revealing a bloated, pink tongue and the gaping black hole of the throat. It was a scream without sound, a silent, frozen scream that mocked Gary McDonald's own screams as he fled the reservoir's ice.

# Chapter 1

Not even the coldest winter in the history of New York City could slow the pace of 42nd Street. Trucks, buses, cabs, and cars weaved slowly through the traffic, blaring horns and gray exhaust lingering in the solid, icy air. On the sidewalks pedestrians trudged, heads bent against the chill, frozen breath rising from the tops of their wrappings like smoke escaping a chimney.

High above these shivering forms were the offices of WIBN-TV, Channel 8, the city's leading independent television station. WIBN's offices and broadcast studio were lodged in the fortieth through forty-fifth floors of the Chrysler Building, the needle-shaped art deco skyscraper that graced Manhattan's skyline. The station's news department occupied the top floor, where a row of mahogany elevators deposited visitors and employees in a modern, glass-enclosed reception area with the station's bold trademark, "The Heart of New York," stenciled on the walls. The reception area offered a view of the newsroom, the tinted glass streaked by the fingers of tourists who had come to gawk at a real, working TV newsroom.

Michael Carpo worked at the back of the newsroom, his back turned to reception but his mind never quite free of the feeling that he was under observation. At twenty-eight, Carpo was considered a young and inexperienced member of the Channel 8 news staff, but he was starting to look the part of journalist. He was thin and six feet tall, with pale skin that disclosed little time spent outdoors. Carpo's hair was very dark, hanging down his forehead in a ruffled way, and his clothing was neat but uninspired—wrinkled khakis, poorly ironed blue-striped shirt, and a plastic ID card hanging from his pocket. As was customary on a Wednesday afternoon, Carpo was hunched over his desk, methodically attacking the *Times* crossword puzzle hidden beneath a pile of papers on his desk. After answering each clue, he alternated between bites off a jelly doughnut and gulps of black coffee.

"Carpo," shouted the shrill voice of an intern from across the newsroom. "Call on 4536."

Carpo swiveled quickly in his chair, punching up the numbers of the extension on his telephone pad before announcing: "Carpo here."

"Yes, hello?" a soft, male voice asked. "Is this Michael Carpo?"

"Speaking."

"My name's Frank Werner. I own an auction house uptown called Athena Galleries."

"What can I do for you?" Carpo squinted his eyes. The voice on the line was interesting, so soft it seemed transparent and tinged with a hint of a foreign accent, possibly Italian or German. He tried to imagine a face that would fit it.

"I have some information I would like to share with you, Michael. I was wondering if perhaps we might make an appointment to meet."

"What is this information about?"

"No, I am sorry, I cannot tell you that over the phone. It would not be safe. We must do this in private."

Carpo paused for a moment but didn't buy it. "I'm sorry, Mr. Werner, I'm not sure who put your call through at the Assignment Desk, but I can't help you. Let me transfer you back there and maybe they can find someone to help you."

"No, no, no," the voice pleaded, its tone hardening, the accent becoming more noticeable. "I must meet with you, Michael. It is very important. I was instructed to only speak with you. You know her. Her name is Karen Blackwell. She promised me that you would help. You do know Karen, do you not?"

It was Carpo's turn to feel his voice harden. "Yes, I know her."

"She said you would listen. She told me she knew you in college and that you were a person who looked out for victims. Well, I am a victim, Michael, and I need your help. Please."

Carpo hesitated, took a deep breath, then grabbed the daily planner from under the crossword. "Mr. Werner, what is it you want?"

"Please, call me Frank. What I want is to meet with you, sometime in the next two days if possible. By then I should have everything I need."

"I guess we could meet for lunch tomorrow, say around two?"

"Excellent. Tell me a place that is convenient."

"Let's meet at the Lantern Diner. It's on Forty-second between Second and Third. Food's not so great but we'll be able to find a quiet booth to talk in."

"That sounds perfect, Michael. I promise you will not be disappointed. This may even turn into a very big break for you."

"Don't expect it, Frank. I'll listen, but I can't promise I'll help you."

Carpo replaced the phone in its cradle and jotted down the meeting under Thursday in his planner. It annoyed him when he noticed his pen shaking as he wrote *"(Karen???)"* next to the appointment. After all, it was her name that had hooked him. Without that, Frank Werner could be some nut off the street who had found his name listed on the station's masthead in the lobby. It wouldn't be the first time something like that had gotten him in trouble.

Carpo pushed his thick black hair out of his eyes and rustled through the papers on his desk until he found the crossword.

Why would she tell him I look out for victims, he wondered before searching for the next clue.

# Chapter 2

On Thursday morning, the quiet of the small one-bedroom apartment on East 12th Street was shattered by the persistent beeping of an alarm clock. Carpo barely stirred in his sleep as his hand shot from beneath the covers, silencing the noise with an expert tap on the snooze bar.

Carpo was well practiced at this daily ritual of nine-minute sleep procrastination. Once, while a student at Georgetown University, he had struck the snooze bar twenty-six times over a four-hour period, causing him to sleep through a midterm in American Literature. In every respect, Carpo was a night owl, preferring the silent hours of night to the jarring pace of the city's mornings. These nocturnal habits had garnered him the nickname of "Batman" in college; his father called it "ass-backwards."

After a few more taps on the snooze, Carpo forced himself out of bed. It was noon, but his face was swollen with sleep, dark lines tracing the imprints of his pillow. Like a rusted automaton, he crankily started the routine that would eventually bring him to midtown for work. That routine always started with coffee.

He pulled a paper bag filled with Hawaiian Kona coffee beans from the refrigerator and measured out enough for a pot.

He poured the beans into a small grinder and chopped them to the consistency of sand, the stainless steel blades releasing a rich fragrance from the waxy brown beans.

Coffee was the one expense with which Carpo had no qualms. While he watched every dollar he put toward his meals and housing, he never thought twice about spending ten dollars on a pound of gourmet beans. He took great care in storing the beans and grinding them properly. And the best example of the money he spent on coffee occupied the only counter space in the kitchen.

It was a magnificent brass and steel Rancilio coffeemaker, imported from Italy. The machine had separate compartments for brewing American coffee and the darker roasts, like espresso. Carpo loved the machine and the whole ritual of coffee-making: sniffing the freshly ground beans as they were sprinkled into the filter, pouring the cold water into the Rancilio's well, and then listening for the inner coils to vibrate as they expanded to heat the water. When the first drops of brown liquid began seeding the bottom of the pot, Carpo walked into the bathroom to shave and shower.

By the time he returned to the kitchen to pour his first cup, his mind was awake and preparing for the upcoming day. There was the 2:00 meeting with Frank Werner, then his eight-hour shift for the nightly news at Channel 8. He was also planning to submit a sweeps series proposal about the spread of drug-resistant tuberculosis in the city's homeless shelters. He sat at a tiny desk in the corner of his bedroom and made notes on his day, an ear tuned to the news pouring from a portable radio, his hand never far from the mug of coffee. After an hour, when he could feel the caffeine pulsing through his system like an electric current, Carpo set down his pen and gathered his papers for work.

He triple-locked the door to his apartment and jogged down the six flights of stairs to the entrance. In the foyer, he peered through the slats of his mailbox, checking for any mail as he buttoned up his coat. The wind whipped specks of ice against the outside door, hard enough that it sounded like a broom sweeping broken glass. He shoved his hands into his pockets and steadied himself for the first oppressive blast of cold.

Outside, he walked quickly to the bus stop on the corner of 3rd Avenue, avoiding the oncoming pedestrians and patches of gray ice in his path. An M-101 bus took him uptown, depositing him at the corner of 42nd Street. He made his way a half-block up the street and stepped into the dimly lit Lantern Diner just a few minutes before 2:00 P.M.

Carpo ate frequently at the busy, run-down diner, partly because of its convenient location and partly because of its consistency. The Lantern served mediocre diner fare, but at least it was consistently mediocre and never disappointed him with anything worse. Carpo chose a booth facing the front door, ordered a cup of black coffee, and waited for his guest.

The clock over the register read 2:15 before he decided to go ahead and order lunch. A cheeseburger deluxe and two more cups of coffee were placed on the Formica table, consumed, and cleared, with still no sign of the mysterious caller. Finally, at 2:45, he decided to give up on Frank Werner and head to the station before the start of "morning meeting," as the staff called their first meeting of the afternoon. He paid his bill and hurried to the Chrysler Building. He arrived in the newsroom just as Channel 8's Metropolitan Editor, Major Sisco, started his review of the day's top stories.

Major Sisco was a street-smart journalist born and raised in Harlem. The nickname of "Major" stemmed from his incredibly deep, raspy voice—a voice of such unquestionable strength it snapped people to attention. But the real authority stemmed from his reputation. At thirty-eight, Major Sisco was the youngest Metro Editor in the city and one of the most esteemed names in local news.

Carpo's favorite part of the workday was Sisco's presentation of the morning meeting—a virtual performance of the news of the day. Weaving his tall, lean frame through the rows of writers' desks and reporters' cubicles, the Major emphasized his speech by waving a newly sharpened yellow pencil through the air. The effect was as if he were conducting the news, each resonant word punctuated by a hypnotic swing or menacing poke of the pencil. This afternoon, Maestro Sisco was delivering a splendid performance, pausing briefly as Carpo slid into his desk.

"Story one on the metro rundown: The city deficit. The mayor is calling it 'fiscal doomsday' down at City Hall this afternoon. The budget deficit for 1997 has reached one hundred million dollars. He's announcing a package of tax increases and cuts in city services to bring things under control."

Carpo followed his rundown as Sisco listed the various points and angles the story might cover. The stories were stacked on the rundown by order of importance. It was a hierarchy that continually changed, as the stories did, throughout the afternoon and night.

"Story two: It's the E.M.S. late issue again. Another person died last night, this time after a twenty-three-minute wait for an ambulance in Crown Heights. We have an interview with the family of the deceased. I had some video pulled from the tape library of ambulances stuck in city traffic.

"Story three: Four-alarm fire in the Red Hook section of Brooklyn. No one injured, but ten families are on the street tonight. One of our crews captured some beautiful video on this one, really amazing flames, so let's play this story up high.

"Story four: Floater in the Central Park Reservoir, and folks, I'm talking a real stiff. It was discovered around midnight by a cop on patrol. Police are labeling it a homicide, and, get this, the body was frozen into the ice, four feet thick. No ID yet on the victim.

"Story five: Sex harassment charges filed at the Twenty-third Precinct. Female cop says she's got hard proof of the abuse, including audiotapes. Let's hear what's on them and see what else she's got. We're also waiting on a statement from the police commissioner.

"Story six: Empire State Building's back on the block. That's right, the most famous building in New York City is up for sale again. With the flat economy and the depressed real estate market, this could be the white elephant of the century. I've got Graphics whipping us up something fancy to show what's going on."

Sisco was interrupted by one of the interns from the Assignment Desk. They huddled for a few minutes before he resumed his slow walk. Carpo noticed that his pencil was sketching tight circles in the air.

"All righty, listen up. There's a little more info on that floater. Seems the guy's name is Frank Werner. He's some big art dealer from the Upper East Side. Police are keeping tight-lipped, but they're swarming all over the coroner's office." The pencil stopped, its point staying straight up in the air, quivering ever so slightly. "It seems there's a rumor going around about the victim's face. Apparently, when it froze, it stayed in some sort of a scream. Ed Thomas, you're the reporter on the story. A crew's on the way down to the morgue to see if we can get a statement and a confirmation about the face. I'm moving this up to story one and I want it nailed." The Major's face melted into a wide grin. "At the very least, it'll appeal to some of our more sensationalist viewers."

Lucky for Carpo, the newsroom was a sensationalist crowd as well. At the first mention of Werner's name, he felt his palms break out in a nervous sweat. Maybe I heard wrong, he thought, all along knowing that this Werner was the same one who had called him the day before. By the time Sisco had finished giving the details on the victim's face, Carpo could barely swallow back the "holy shit" that he wanted to shout. As soon as the meeting ended, he cornered Sisco back at the Assignment Desk.

"I want on the Werner story as Ed's assistant," he announced briskly.

"Sorry Carp', no can do. We're short of writers this week, and I've been instructed by Bill not to pull anyone off the news staff."

"I'm not asking for the day to day. I'll do backgrounders, research, anything you guys need. Frank Werner called me yesterday afternoon. He told me he was in trouble and needed to meet with me. We were supposed to grab lunch this afternoon over at the Lantern." Carpo paused for a beat to let the words sink in. "Obviously, he didn't show."

Sisco's reaction was not at all what Carpo had expected. His face clouded as he snapped the yellow pencil in half, emitting a sharp crack. "Damn it Carpo, you're not a reporter, you're a writer. When are you going to learn the difference?"

The newsroom fell silent, as it did whenever the Major lost his famous temper. Carpo was shocked by the response; he struggled to think of what he'd done wrong.

"Be reasonable," he pleaded quietly. "He wouldn't let me transfer him; he said he'd only talk to me. I wasn't even going to meet him, but he mentioned the name of someone I used to know. I thought I was doing them a favor."

The Major's face lost some of its harshness. Carpo decided to take a chance. "Just let me dig around a bit, Sisco; let me try to find out why he called. I'm somehow connected to him; it might even help us break a lead."

Sisco put the pencil halves between his palms and rolled them deliberately back and forth, the wooden pieces clicking in his huge hands. He looked at Carpo and shook his head with disapproval. "You've always got an excuse, Carp'. This is already beginning to sound like the Conductor Martinez story."

Now it was Carpo's turn to show off his temper. "What are you bringing that up for? It was two years ago and I'm still sorry about it, but I'm not trying to go over you this time. Werner's call sounded personal."

Sisco reached out and squeezed his arm. "All right, all right, relax. I'll give you another shot. But this time you'd better play by my rules. You can do background research and assist Ed, but that's it. And you're still on the regular schedule, so don't fall behind with your writing." His voice dipped an octave, reverberating with a low threat. "And god help you Carpo if you hold anything back on me this time. I will not tolerate another fuck-up like the Martinez case."

Sisco didn't wait for a response. He turned and walked into the office of Bill Lipton, the executive producer of Channel 8 News. Carpo retreated to his desk, avoiding the stares of everyone who had heard their confrontation. He was stunned by Sisco's reaction, especially to something that could potentially break a story for the newsroom. And the mention of Conductor Martinez was the most shocking of all. It had been two years since the fiasco, but apparently all was not forgotten.

He grabbed the phone on his desk and dialed information. "In Manhattan, two numbers please. Athena Galleries and the Metropolitan Museum of Art, both on the Upper East Side."

As the operator read the numbers, Carpo jotted them down on a pad of paper, then he transferred them to his small, black leather phone book. He dialed the number for Athena Galleries first.

The line rang five times before an answering machine came on and a man's deep voice said: "You have reached Athena Galleries. This is Frank Werner. I'm not available to take your call, but if you leave your name and number, I'll get back to you as soon as possible." Werner's voice sounded different on the machine than it had in person. Carpo wondered if it was an indication of how agitated Werner had been before his death.

The machine beeped six times before it emitted a long tone. Carpo hung up without leaving a message. The thought of leaving his name on a dead man's answering machine left a funny feeling in his stomach. Apparently, other people didn't feel the same way since the machine's beeps indicated that there were six messages on the tape.

He stared between the number for the Metropolitan Museum of Art and the clock on the wall, trying to gauge if it would be a good time to call. He carefully pressed the numbers for the museum on the phone pad. A slow recording came on to tell him of the options available for touch-tone telephones. He listened to them all, stalling for as long as possible, until he dialed the extension he needed.

A woman with an impatient nasal voice answered the phone: "Department of Greek and Roman Art."

"Is Karen Blackwell in?" He felt his pulse pick up as he spoke her name.

"I'm sorry, she's not in her office. Can I take a message?"

"No, I'll just call—"

"Hold on sir," the woman commanded. "Ms. Blackwell just walked in."

Before Carpo could say a word, the woman put him on hold. For two tense minutes he listened to a recording of classical piano as he fidgeted with a pen. Twice he almost hung up the phone, but he knew it would only delay the inevitable. Finally, there was a click on the line and an all too familiar voice said: "This is Karen Blackwell, can I help you?"

"Karen, this is Michael. Michael Carpo." His heart was hammering so fast he felt out of breath. "I'm sorry to call you in this way. I hope I didn't catch you at a bad time."

There was a pause, and then her voice came back, steeled over and curt. "What do you want?"

"The guy you told to call me is dead. He was found murdered last night."

"What are you talking about?"

"Frank Werner, the gallery owner you had call me, the guy you said I would listen to."

This time the pause was much longer. "What do you mean? I didn't tell anyone to call you."

He filled her in on his brush with Frank Werner, starting with the telephone conversation Wednesday afternoon and ending with the discovery of his body in the Central Park Reservoir Wednesday night.

"I have no idea what you're talking about," she said when he was finished, the hardness back in her voice. "Look, I'm very busy here, Michael. I don't know why you're bothering me."

When she said his name he felt a weird sense of displacement, like it had only been yesterday, not six years, since they had last exchanged a word. If only the contempt wasn't so obvious in her words, he could almost close his eyes and transport himself to a time when she used to whisper his name.

"There must be some kind of misunderstanding," he mumbled. "I'm sorry, Karen. I'll let you go now."

Carpo hung up the phone and exhaled the tense air that had built up in his lungs. He felt exhausted, as if he had been holding his breath through the entire conversation.

It was uncanny that her voice hadn't changed a bit from the way he remembered it. He took that as a hopeful sign, as if her familiar voice meant that she hadn't changed much as a person either.

But it was six years, he reminded himself. Six long years.

# Chapter 3

"And finally tonight, an answer, perhaps, to the age-old question: Why did the chicken cross the road? Would you believe, to find a dentist? That's right, researchers at the University of California, Berkeley, say they've found a bone deposit in the mouths of chickens that is a derivative of the human tooth. So the next time you see a grumpy chicken in the road, give him a break. Maybe he's just a little long in the tooth. That's Channel 8 News for this Thursday night. For Matt Sawyer, I'm Maria Gomez. See you tomorrow night."

Carpo turned off the monitor on his desk as the screen dissolved into final credits for "The Ten O'Clock News." He packed his worn leather briefcase with his phone book, papers, and daily planner. After he saw his name roll down the screen under "Newswriters," he walked to the elevator and rode to the first floor. At the front door, he bundled up his coat, took a deep breath, and stepped into the cold.

The night was dark and still along 42nd Street, devoid of cars and pedestrians, and so cold that each of Carpo's breaths stung like a paper cut in his lungs. It was the twenty-second consecutive day of subzero wind-chill factors, transforming "the city that never sleeps" into a virtual ghost town each night. He hurried along the empty street, his leather shoes creaking as he weaved in and out of the knee-high snow banks and shimmering patches of ice. At the corner of 2nd Avenue, he stopped at a small red kiosk and bought the late editions of *The Post, The News,* and *The Times,* then he grabbed a bus heading to the East Village. The ride downtown lasted fifteen minutes, enough time for him to find a seat and browse through the headlines of the papers.

The murder of Frank Werner had topped Channel 8's telecast that evening and, as Carpo had anticipated, it appeared in all three newspapers. *The New York Post* provided the most coverage, starting with bold, three-inch lettering splashed across the front page: "Silent Scream: A Face of Death." Somehow the paper had scooped an exclusive photo of Werner's face at the coroner's office, its horrific scream stretching through the middle of the page, the throat an endless stretch of black newsprint dots. Carpo stared with grim fascination at the picture. Despite the grainy distortion from being blown up so large, the black and white photo clearly showed that the rumors of a screaming corpse were true.

Inside, the coverage of the murder consisted of a short summary of the crime, pictures of Frank Werner and the exterior of Athena Galleries, and a map of the Central Park Reservoir, with a tiny skull and crossbones marking the exact spot where the body had been discovered.

*The Daily News* also had dramatic lettering across its front page, the headline roaring: "Frozen Floater Found." There were no pictures of Frank Werner's scream, but there was an exclusive interview with Officer Gary McDonald. The policeman described how he had discovered the body, frozen solid into several feet of the reservoir's ice. Officer McDonald called his gruesome discovery "nothing much out of the ordinary these days."

Accompanying the interview was a short obituary on Werner. It detailed him as an expert of late Greek and early Roman antiquities and the owner of the highly successful, internationally renowned Athena Galleries. A small photo, courtesy of Christie's auction house, showed Werner's latest art offering: a small bust of Cleopatra VII that was scheduled to go up for auction the next week.

As Carpo expected, *The New York Times* contained the least information of all three papers—just a file photo of Frank Werner and a brief statement from the office of the deputy commissioner of public information, both appearing on the front page of the "Metro Section." The standing joke at Channel 8 was that *The Times* was useful only if you wanted to know about news going on everywhere else in the world but New York City.

When the bus pulled up to the far corner of 12th Street, Carpo stepped from the rear exit. He groaned when he heard a squeal of laughter and then the familiar chorus of, "Hey Carpy, when are you putting us on TV?"

He pretended not to hear the small group of women huddled together on the corner, but they kept at it until he broke into a smile.

"What's the matter ladies?" he said. "No Johns to pick on tonight?"

The women shrieked with mock anger. Before they could respond, Carpo ducked into Little Poland. The tiny, all-night diner was a local haunt, as popular for its excellent kitchen, which produced dozens of home-cooked Polish dishes, as for its ever-changing line-up of attractive, young Polish waitresses. He chose a stool at the end of the lunch counter as Little

Poland's owner, Devon Jacek, greeted him with a steaming mug of coffee.

"There's a fresh pirogi platter on the back burner whenever you're ready, Carpo."

"Thanks. Give me a few minutes to warm up and look over some papers."

Carpo draped his coat over the stool next to him, opened his briefcase, and pulled out a thick manila folder tied together with butcher's string. He undid the knot and removed a pile of yellowing newspaper clippings and brittle magazine articles. Each article was stamped on the top with the same black ink message: "PROPERTY OF WIBN-TV, CHANNEL 8 NEWS. FOR RESEARCH PURPOSES ONLY. DO NOT REMOVE FROM ARCHIVES."

The articles had come from Channel 8's research library, a mammoth collection of video, microfilm, newspaper, and periodical archives. "The Morgue," as it was called by the news staff, was located in a sub-basement of the Chrysler Building, a huge, climate-controlled vault where the heavy silence was disturbed only by the occasional faint rumble of trains pulling into Grand Central Terminal.

When time permitted, Carpo liked to conduct his own background searches in The Morgue. He actually found pleasure in the act of researching: checking, cross-referencing, and methodically sifting through the mass of data, clipping by clipping, in a quest for some unrealized nugget of information. Since he had been placed on part-time duty for the Werner story and was expected to keep up with his news-writing, he'd been forced to entrust the research to the library staff, composed of two full-time librarians and three college interns. Carpo had picked up the packet during his dinner break. He had ferreted it out of The Morgue by slipping it into his briefcase when the head librarian wasn't looking.

The clippings were arranged in chronological order, the earliest at the top of the pile. He grabbed the first, a crumbling article from *The New York Times* dated May 13, 1967. It was a section called "Auction Announcements," and it held an advertisement for Athena Galleries. Beneath a listing of the offerings of the gallery—a collection of Roman coins and an assortment of Etruscan tools—there was mention of "Proprietor: Frank G. Werner."

Carpo reached back into his briefcase and pulled out a pen and his reporter's notebook, a narrow spiral bound notepad with thick cardboard covers, designed for jotting down notes in the palm of one's hand. He leafed through it until he found a blank page and wrote "Werner Background:" on the top. Underneath, he scribbled, "Frank G. Werner," underlining the "G." and putting a question mark over it.

The auction announcements appeared once a week, on the same location of the same page. After a few years, they started popping up in other local papers and then on a monthly basis in all of the major art publications.

The first write-through on Werner appeared in a 1973 article from the *"Arts and Leisure"* section of *The New York Times* Sunday edition. The article reported on a unique Roman statue, called The Son of Brutus, which was expected to sell for a fantastic price when it went up for auction at Sotheby's. The marble statue had been discovered in 1957 by archaeologists digging through an underground tomb near Sperlonga, a small town on the western coast of Italy. Much of the article focused on Frank Werner and the odd case of a gallery owner deciding to sell a work of art at auction. The article also discussed the

piece of sculpture, hailed by *The Times* as "one of the most perfectly preserved statues of early Rome . . . a clear link to late
Hellenistic Greek sculpture."

Carpo scribbled onto his pad any words that didn't make
sense, starting with "Sperlonga" and ending with "late Hellenistic Greek sculpture." He also jotted down the details on
Frank Werner. The gallery owner was acting as the agent for
the statue's owner, a reclusive Italian millionaire who had fi-
nanced the 1957 expedition in Sperlonga. Over the weeks leading up to the auction, a series of articles in various publications
criticized The Son of Brutus for having an insufficient "provenance," a word which Carpo added to his list.

The day before the scheduled auction, every daily in the city
reported on its abrupt removal from the block. The statue had
been sold to an anonymous London collector. As much coverage was given to the sale of the piece, which went for an undis-
closed sum—rumors put it in the ten million dollar range—as
to the stunning insult which Frank Werner had inflicted on
Sotheby's. He had, in effect, jilted the auction house after
weeks of free promotion. The art world was outraged at the insult and reacted with swift justice; Frank Werner dropped
from mention in any publication for almost a decade.

Carpo looked up from his papers and ordered the pirogi
platter, an assortment of meat-, potato-, and cheese-filled
dumplings covered with a dark brown mushroom sauce. After
sampling a few bites, he turned back to his research.

On September 19, 1982, *The New York Times* reported on
the blitz of attention at Athena Galleries, where a high Hellenistic masterpiece, called Lady Victory, was being offered for
sale. The article was featured on page one of the Sunday *"Arts
and Leisure"* section and detailed Werner's background, including the alleged insult he had inflicted on Sotheby's ten

years earlier. Apparently, Sotheby's harbored no ill feelings toward the dealer because it offered to auction off the statue. In fact, every auction house in the city was clamoring for the right to conduct the sale, but this time Werner handled it privately.

An article in *Art News* magazine gave the most in-depth description of Lady Victory, discovered in 1863 in the Sanctuary of the Great Gods at Samothrace, a Greek island in the Aegean Sea. Werner hinted that the statue was possibly linked to the prominent statue in Paris's Louvre Museum, The Winged Victory. It was in the article that Carpo discovered what the term "provenance" meant. The magazine described the exact provenance of the statue, detailing its history of ownership. Werner claimed it had been owned for more than a century by a prominent Bavarian family with lots of royal blood but little royal cash. A week after the article, there were several articles covering the sale of the piece to a private collector in Los Angeles. *The New York Post* cited one source as saying the sale had exceeded eighteen million dollars, a price that would have set the record for highest ever paid for a Greek sculpture.

The 1987 spring edition of the *Board of Trustees Newsletter* at the Metropolitan Museum of Art carried a lengthy profile of Frank Gibbons Werner, by then considered one of the foremost experts of Hellenistic sculpture in the world. The article praised his talents for handling rare, or unknown, pieces of sculpture, and it hinted at the enormous fortune he had amassed by selling them. The article also described how Werner surrounded his works with expert opinions from top professors and curators in the field, combating faulty provenance with PhD approvals.

The museum newsletter did more than inform Carpo of Werner's middle name. He nearly spit out a mouthful of coffee when he read that Frank Werner had been named a standing member of the museum's Greek and Roman Art Department.

"Sure you've never heard of him," he whispered bitterly at the papers before him.

By the time the clippings reached the 1990s, Frank Werner was as likely to appear in a gossip column as he was in the art section. Pictures showed him dining with actors, politicians, and personalities at every benefit imaginable. His image of a society figure was reinforced every time his pudgy pink face, bushy eyebrows, and trademark bow tie appeared in a newspaper.

Much of the remainder of the file dealt with the announcement of, and background on, Werner's latest offering, The Cleopatra Bust. Carpo remembered the reference to it in *The Daily News* obituary, so he took copious notes as he read about it.

For years, legend of the bust's existence peppered scholarly art and archaeology journals. The bust was said to be the betrothal gift from Mark Antony to Cleopatra VII, the legendary queen of Egypt. Most of the articles discussed the cultural significance of the piece: critics claimed it was one of the last high Hellenistic pieces created, rivaling the head of Nefertiti; historians said it might provide clues in determining the reasons for the fall of the Greek empire; and the media followed the bust in the same way it covered a sporting event, hoping it would shatter the record for highest price ever paid for a stone sculpture. But not everyone was applauding The Cleopatra Bust.

Four months before Werner's murder, *The New York Times* ran a series of articles questioning the authenticity of the Hellenistic masterpiece. Werner claimed the piece had belonged to a wealthy Italian family, which had held it for several generations before contacting him to bring it to auction. Prominent art critics called attention to the bust's questionable provenance. Werner tried to allay their fears, and the fears of potential buyers, by commissioning several experts on Hellenistic sculpture to verify the authenticity of the bust. Werner's unease over the controversy was perhaps highlighted by his decision to sell the piece at auction, instead of handling it through Athena Galleries. He had hoped to further prove the bust's authenticity by cloaking the sale under the name of Christie's Auction House.

Carpo scraped his plate clean, sopping up the remaining globs of mashed potatoes and mushroom sauce with hunks of white bread. He signaled to Devon for the check before rustling through the remainder of the file.

The file was large enough and contained enough public information for Carpo to realize that it was impossible for anyone in the art world—much less an employee in the Department of Greek and Roman Art at the Metropolitan Museum of Art—not to know of Frank Werner.

And so, it was no real shock when Carpo came across a photograph of Werner dated two months before his murder. It was a *Daily News* photo that showed Werner toasting the director of the Met at the annual Fall Ball. What was most interesting about the photo was the elegant young woman seated to his left, smiling at Werner with a star-dazed look. Carpo tapped his fingers on the cracked linoleum counter as he considered the image of Karen Blackwell.

While he settled his bill at the register, Carpo ordered five regular coffees to go. Four of them he had Devon place in one paper bag, the single he placed into another. Carpo tucked the bags in the crook of his arm and slipped back onto the street.

He crossed 2nd Avenue and approached the group of working girls, clustered for warmth in a doorway on the corner of 12th Street. The temperature was creating havoc on them as they shivered together, their tight skirts and open shirts revealing skin that was probably close to frost bitten. He knew the four women by name, as they knew him. They were the regulars, as permanent a fixture in the neighborhood as the buzzing street lamps that flickered on at dusk.

In the summer months, the women found a steady business along 12th Street. On those warm nights, dozens of cars driven by solitary men cruised the block for a pick-up, their stopped vehicles drawing a cacophony of horns whenever the traffic light changed from red to green. On nights like that, Carpo didn't recognize half the women standing along the sidewalk outside his building, flashing skin and striking seductive poses to gain attention. He wasn't comfortable with what went on along his block at night, but he was careful never to pass judgment on the women for their unfortunate line of work.

"Slow tonight?" he mumbled as he handed each woman a coffee from the paper bag.

"Do you blame them?" asked one woman, who Carpo knew by her street name, Candi. "It's so cold out here, I don't think there's a man on the planet who could rise to the occasion."

The women giggled and looked to Carpo for a reaction. He knew they enjoyed trying to embarrass him, so he rolled his eyes with exaggerated shock before heading up the street.

"Someone was looking for you tonight," Candi called after him.

"Who?"

"I dunno. He's not from around here. And it didn't seem like he wanted you to know about it neither."

Carpo stopped. "What do you mean?"

"He was hanging out across from your place. Me and the girls thought he was checking us over, but he never bit when I walked by. Anyway, he watched your entrance for a while, then he went inside and snooped around your mailbox."

"There's fifteen apartments in my building, how do you know he was looking for me?"

"He was only looking in your mailbox, Carp'."

He pressed his arms tight to his body and allowed a quick shiver. He wasn't sure if the chill was from the cold or the thought of someone watching for him. "What did he look like?"

"Kind of creepy. He was short, but he looked muscular, kind of like a pit bull. And he was almost as pale as you, only not so sickly looking."

"Thanks for the compliment," he grumbled as the women started giggling again. "How long was he out here?"

"About a half-hour. He left after he checked out your mailbox. I think he knew we were watching him."

Carpo pulled his wallet from his pocket and fished out a business card. He found a pen at the bottom of his briefcase and jotted his home phone number beneath the printed work number. "This has my home and work phone numbers on it. If you see him around again, maybe you can give me a call, okay?"

Candi grasped the card between her thumb and forefinger and pretended to fan herself with it. "Girls, we finally got Carpo's number."

"If I get one prank call, I'm coming right to you, Candi." Carpo waved good-bye to the women and started toward his building.

The street was dark and deserted. Tall trees lined the sidewalks on both sides of the street, their brittle branches creaking like rusty hinges as the wind picked up strength, casting splintered shadows on the concrete. Carpo's building was half a block up the street, number 227. It stood on the north side;

a painted white brick building with a two-foot wrought iron gate out front.

He stepped through the gate, unlocked the front door, then unlocked the door to the building's foyer. There, he paused for a moment and stared at his mailbox on the wall. It looked completely normal. He flipped to the smallest key on his ring and unlocked it, extracting the few pieces of mail inside—Con Ed electric bill, fundraising letter from a homeless organization, and a local advertising mailer. He dropped the mail into his briefcase and steadied himself for the hike to the sixth floor.

Carpo had lived in the building for four years, but he still was not used to the stairs. The apartments on the lower floors had cathedral ceilings, meaning that several extra steps were tacked onto each landing. Multiply that by six landings and the trip to his apartment became a strenuous exertion. By the third flight, Carpo started to feel the familiar tug in his chest as his lungs sucked deeper and deeper for air. By the fifth, his thigh muscles burned with fatigue. The only incentive for living in a sixth-floor walk-up was the substantial reduction in rent each higher flight brought.

As he slid the key into the door of his apartment, the phone started ringing. He unlocked the door and hurried inside, tossing his briefcase on the couch as he picked up the phone.

"Hello?" he said into the receiver.

Instead of a voice, a series of high-pitched tones answered him, the noises so sharp that he quickly swung the phone away from his ear. He listened at a distance before bringing the phone back to his mouth. "Hello? Is someone there?"

The tones stopped immediately and no other noise came from the earpiece. Carpo shrugged and hung up the phone. He looked down at his answering machine, noticing that the message light was blinking. The red light was supposed to flash as many times as there were messages, but as he stared at the light, it never stopped flickering. Over and over it winked at him, signaling dozens of messages. A panic gripped him as he pressed the "play" button and waited for the machine to rewind. The only thing that could trigger that many messages had to be a disaster.

The first message was from an old college friend, the next three were hang-ups, and the rest were a strange combination of high-pitched tones, similar to the ones he'd just heard. He listened through most of them, each a different combination of tones, then he fast forwarded toward the end of the tape to check for any other messages.

The tones sounded like someone was pressing different sets of numbers on a touch-tone telephone's dialing pad. When he reached the end of the tape, he pressed the rewind button to erase the tones and reset the machine.

He walked into the kitchen and took a coffee mug from the cabinet, filling it with the last coffee from Little Poland. He walked back into the living room, sat on the couch, and stared at the answering machine. He wondered if the tones had been caused by a computer or fax machine calling his line repeatedly and using some type of modem language that was recorded on the tape. He leaned back against the couch, put his feet up on the coffee table, and sipped his coffee.

Suddenly, he set down the mug and grabbed the phone off the table. The numbers on the dialing pad glowed in his hand, the dial tone buzzing from the earpiece. He started pressing the keys on the phone, mimicking the various sounds his answering machine had recorded. Two long tones, pause, and two more long tones—all of the tones in different combinations. He played with the keypad for a few minutes before he realized that the tones were sounding off in succession. One–one, pause, one–two, pause, one–three. It continued like that all the way to three–nine. Beyond the progression of numbers, there was little explanation for why the machine had recorded the sounds.

Carpo hung up the phone and retrieved his coffee. He also reached for his briefcase and began to thumb through the Werner file again.

# Chapter 4

When the alarm sounded at 10:00 A.M., Carpo resisted the urge to hit the snooze bar. Instead, he flicked the buzzer off and rolled stiffly onto his back, forcing his eyes to remain open. It would have been so easy for him to bury his head back into the soft down pillow and sleep for another three hours. He contemplated that possibility as he blinked his eyes, feeling the sleep that remained under his lids.

In one quick motion he swung his legs to the floor and headed into the kitchen to make coffee. He shaved, showered, and dressed as it brewed. After it was ready, he poured himself a large mug and walked through the apartment, gathering together the Manhattan directory, a yellow legal pad, a felt tip pen, and his phone book. He piled the articles around him on the couch in the living room and moved the phone within reach.

Of all his possessions, the most important to Carpo's job was his black leather phone book. It contained, in precise and alphabetized sections, the listing of every phone number and contact he had come across during his years at WIBN. Dozens of politicians and public figures would have cringed if they had seen their unlisted home phone numbers among the smudged pages of the book. Carpo collected the names and numbers like a proud philatelist who stores away a rare stamp, content just to possess it. Most of the numbers Carpo had never used and probably never would, but he felt it was always better to have a number than to wish he had it.

In addition to the listings of the powerful and famous, the book held the bread and butter of his profession: the names and numbers for the head of every press department in the city. It was from this section that he summoned his first number and dialed the telephone.

"M.E.'s press office," said a male voice.

"Hi, this is Michael Carpo calling from Channel 8 News. Is this Dan Golden?"

"Yeah, this is Dan," the voice said, its tone lifting with surprise. Carpo smiled and made a small check next to Golden's name in his book. It was amazing how impressed people became over something as simple as remembering their name.

"Dan, I'm working on a story and I need to verify some facts. Can you spare a minute?"

"Sure, go ahead."

"In the murder of the gallery owner, Frank Werner, that autopsy is being conducted where you are, at the chief medical examiner's office, right?"

"That's correct."

"Now does that mean the chief examiner, Dr. Westlake, is doing the autopsy?"

"Hang on, let me check." Carpo could hear some papers rustling. "No, he didn't do that one."

"No?" Carpo asked, trying his best to sound shocked. "That's what I was told here. I'm glad I decided to check with you."

"Hang on. Yeah, it says here Dr. Parkes conducted the Werner autopsy."

Carpo dug his nails into the palms of his hands. "I don't suppose you'd let me talk with Dr. Parkes about the autopsy?" What the hell, he thought, it was worth a shot.

"Are you crazy? That's an active investigation. The M.E.s aren't allowed to talk to the press."

"I understand. Thanks for your help, Dan."

Carpo hung up the phone and reached for his mug. He took a drink, inhaling the steam off the coffee a split-second before swallowing so as to intensify the flavor.

When he had first started at Channel 8, making calls had been one of the most difficult things for him to do. Half the press departments in the city were designed just to keep the media in the dark about what was really going on. Even though calling for information was generally humiliating work, Carpo had quickly learned that good phone work was essential to being a good journalist. You had to be assertive, creative, and a quick thinker just to get inside the door. And once there, you had to be persistent enough to convince a voice on the line to hand over the information. It had taken him a long time to learn the tricks and pitches that could get him the information he needed.

One of the most basic tricks he used was the random dial. It worked only at large city agencies, like the chief medical examiner's office, where there were several offices on each floor. The number he had dialed for the press office was 533-1419. Carpo figured that the press office was probably located on the first floor of the building, whereas the autopsy labs were most likely located in the basement so that cadavers could be delivered underground. Since phone extensions often indicated the floor, he picked up the phone and changed one digit, dialing 533-0419.

"Good morning," said another male voice.

"Hi, Dr. Parkes?"

"No, this is Dr. Nealy."

"I'm sorry, I thought Dr. Parkes's extension was 0419. Do you know his extension offhand?" Carpo tapped his pen against the legal pad, confident he would get an answer.

Instead, the man's voice thickened with a stern tone. "Who is calling?"

"Michael Carpo," he said, trying to keep his own voice confident. Something had gone wrong, but he wasn't sure what.

"And where are you calling from, Mr. Carpo?"

"I'm from Channel 8 News."

"I thought something was wrong. Obviously you don't know Dr. Parkes, but obviously you do know that we're not allowed to speak to the press."

Carpo was stunned that his identity had been discovered so easily. He struggled to keep the conversation going. "You got me all right," he said. "How could you tell?"

"Because if you really knew Dr. Parkes, you'd know that he is a she."

Carpo apologized to the man and hung up the phone. He cursed at himself for being so naive as to assume that Dr. Parkes was a man. It was just the sort of error he had thought he was experienced enough, and sensitive enough, to avoid. He picked up the phone again and added another digit to the last number he had called. Within fifteen seconds, the number for Dr. Parkes's office was scrawled on his pad.

Three years back, Carpo would have given up after receiving a warning at the press office. A year ago, he would have surrendered after Dr. Nealy had blown his cover. But since then he had learned the importance of persistence. If they told you no at one place, there was still a chance they might say yes at the next. The trick was reaching that place.

Carpo reached for his coffee and took another drink. The hardest part was next. All he had was a name and a phone number; he needed information. To get it, he would have to change his approach entirely. On the third ring, Dr. Parkes answered the phone.

"Good morning, Dr. Parkes. This is Michael Carpo calling from Channel 8 News. I know you're not supposed to talk with me, but please give me a chance to explain why I'm calling."

The line remained silent, and for a second he thought she had already hung up. Distantly he heard her breathing over the line, so he plowed ahead with his pitch.

"I understand you're conducting the autopsy of Frank Werner. Mr. Werner called me the day before he was murdered. I think what he told me could help your investigation."

"Then, Mr. Capra, I suggest you call the police. They are the ones who handle murder investigations."

"Carpo is my last name, Dr. Parkes. I think Frank Werner knew he was in great danger when he called me. He referred to himself as a victim, and when I think back about it, it was almost like he was prophesying his own death. Please, if we could meet for lunch, coffee, anything. All I need is a few minutes of your time."

"Sorry, but you're asking me to do something that could cost my job. And for what? So you can land the big scoop of the moment? I'm not about to risk my career so you can make yours."

"You've got me dead wrong. This has nothing to do with my job. There are some strange things happening around me, and I think it has to do with the phone call from Frank Werner." Carpo broke off, realizing the pitch was not working. He was pleading with her and that rarely worked. In the split-second that he paused, he changed his approach again. "If it will make you feel better, I'll promise not to use any of the information for a news story. If it ever comes to it, I'll leave you as an anonymous source."

"That'll help me a lot when I'm standing in the unemployment line," she answered with a laugh. "Can't you see they'll know immediately where it came from? I'm the only one working on the case over here."

"But it won't get that far. I won't let it. Look, I know there's a risk for you, but if I didn't think I was in some danger, I would never have called you."

"I'm sorry, Mr. Carpo, I just don't think I can help you."

There was something softer about her voice, an apologizing tone, even a reluctance, that made Carpo believe he had a shot. Or maybe it was the fact that she had stayed on the line this long that was keeping his hopes up.

"Dr. Parkes, right now I'm just a voice on the phone. Why don't you meet me, check me out in person, and then decide whether or not you trust me? If it doesn't feel right to you, walk out. But please, give me that much of a chance."

"Did you say Frank Werner called you the day before they found his body? Wednesday afternoon?"

"About four o'clock."

There was a long moment of silence from her end. Carpo's heart leapt as he thought he had convinced her.

"I don't know," she finally said. "You're putting me in a tight situation. I need to think about it. I'm just not ready to agree to anything right now."

"That's fine, Dr. Parkes. I respect your concern. How about if I call back this afternoon?"

"No, don't call me here anymore, there are too many people who can pick up on this line. Give me your phone number. I'll call you if I change my mind."

Carpo recited his home and work phone numbers and thanked her for listening to him. After hanging up the phone, he stretched back on the couch, hand cupped over the top of the coffee mug, fingers enjoying the warmth rising from the dark fluid.

For a second he had thought she would agree; her whole tone seemed to suggest she was close to saying yes. Even so, it had gone better than he could have hoped. At least there was the chance she might call.

He walked into the kitchen and opened the door to the freezer. He felt around in the back, between the plastic ice trays and a box of frozen waffles, until his hand brushed against a light cardboard box. He pulled out the pack of Camel Lights and removed one, placing the yellow-speckled filter between his lips before tossing the box back into the freezer. He walked to the stove and turned the gas on high, dipping his head to the flame to light the cigarette.

Carpo wasn't a real smoker, but he kept a pack on hand in case someone came over who wanted a cigarette. At least, that was the excuse he made for himself. Deep down, he enjoyed the occasional smoke. It was a nice distraction whenever something stressful came about. The freezer trick he had learned at Georgetown from Karen. It was surprising how long the ice box kept a pack of opened cigarettes tasting fresh.

He drew on the Camel, allowing the smoke to pour from his lips in a lazy, meandering stream. As he smoked, it occurred to him that ice kept more than cigarettes fresh. A lot of ice could keep a body fresh.

He wondered if that was why Dr. Parkes had seemed so curious about the time Frank Werner had called him? It was the only question she had asked during the entire conversation. He wondered if she might be having trouble gauging the time of his death.

After he had smoked half the cigarette, Carpo started to feel a bit nauseous. He ran the lit end under the tap and tossed it into the trash, then he set about organizing himself for the trip to work.

# Chapter 5

When Carpo arrived in the newsroom, Major Sisco was sitting at the Assignment Desk, surrounded by the usual crowd of interns, desk assistants, and news-groupies who always seemed to be at his side. They were playing one of the favorite games at the desk: "The Sisco Stump." It consisted of people shouting out the exact street addresses of various New York landmarks to see if Sisco could guess what they were. Even Carpo was impressed when he heard the man rattle off the correct answers for the Teddy Roosevelt Museum, the Joseph Papp Theater, and the William J. Doyle Auction House.

Major Sisco had learned about the city by spending a lifetime in its streets. As he told it, his news training had started at the age of eight, when he and his friends had discovered an old, busted C.B. radio in a trash bin on the corner of 135th and Amsterdam. With a little rewiring and a fresh set of batteries, they'd gotten the radio to pick up police and fire department frequencies; the Major's career had been launched.

With the radio lashed to the basket on the front of his banana bike, Sisco and his gang had monitored the channels for any breaking stories in the neighborhood. If a big event came over, like an accident or shooting, they would tear off on their bikes, trying to beat the emergency workers to the scene. Sisco's favorites chases had been the fires.

"I loved that orange glow so much, my mom used to fear I'd turn arsonist on her," he had confessed to Carpo one day.

From this childhood pasttime, Sisco had learned the essentials of the Assignment Desk. If the scanners barked out a staticy "10–13 in progress," Sisco would say, "there's an officer in need of assistance." And his knowledge of locations went further than addresses, stretching to zip code regions, telephone prefixes, and police precinct jurisdictions. The knowledge made him a walking directory for the city. Dozens of times WIBN had scooped an exclusive story or dramatic footage simply because the Major could react to breaking news faster than anyone else in the business.

Sisco had been hired to his first job at the *Daily News* when he was seventeen. Two years later, WIBN had lured him away with promises of money, a better title, and a free ride at New York University. By the time he'd turned thirty-two, Sisco had been named the station's Metro Editor, the youngest in the city. Eight years later, he still held that distinction.

Sisco's reputation was known throughout the world of local news. He was constantly being approached with offers from newspapers and television stations in all of the major markets in the country. Every so often he would feign great interest in one of the positions and take the offer to WIBN's executive producer, Bill Lipton. Then it was up to the station to scrape together a little more money or fashion a jazzy new job title to keep the Major on their side.

Sisco was now forty, just twelve years older than Carpo, but his knowledge and experience made them seem decades apart. It was into this genius of the newsroom that Carpo often tapped, struggling to absorb the news business and make up for all of the experience that seemed to separate them.

Sisco spotted Carpo through the crowd of admirers and shouted a greeting so low it sounded like the rumblings of a kettle drum. "Look what the cat dragged in today. Mr. Carpo, strolling into the newsroom a full twenty minutes before morning meeting."

Carpo crossed the room and grasped the Major's extended hand. "I thought I'd try to stump you with a little trivia question," he said.

"Fire away, these interns can't think of anything tough."

"In Manhattan, what is at 1153 Madison Avenue."

Sisco made a face like he was insulted. "Is that the best you can do, Carp'? 1153 Madison is where our screaming little cadaver, Frank Werner, did business. None other than Athena Galleries."

He gave Carpo a pat on the back, then used the mammoth palm to guide him toward his cubicle behind the Assignment Desk. Before they reached it, the door to the executive producer's office swung open and Bill Lipton appeared.

"I want to see you two in my office," Lipton barked in his usual abrupt manner.

Sisco raised an eyebrow in Carpo's direction before he followed Lipton into the office. Carpo trailed behind them, an anxious feeling building up in his chest. A meeting in the E.P.'s office rarely signaled good news.

Lipton was a short, sandy-haired man in his forties, who always seemed gravely perturbed by something going on in the newsroom. He had served as executive producer of Channel 8 for three years, after successful stints in Miami, Chicago, and Los Angeles. He was rarely present at the morning meetings or involved in the day-to-day operations of the newsroom, but he analyzed each newscast for the slightest error or imperfection. Carpo thought of him as the strong but silent type: strong on opinions, silent on how to execute them.

Lipton's office held the coveted corner position in the newsroom; two of its walls were floor-to-ceiling windows providing dizzying views of 42nd Street and Lexington Avenue. Carpo loved that he could see the top of Grand Central Terminal, where classical architecture mixed with modern steel and glass and the statues of Roman deities romped around a bald eagle. He resisted the urge to stare down at the magnificent structure, choosing instead to sit next to Sisco on the brown leather couch that faced Lipton's desk.

Everything in the office was meticulously positioned, as if Lipton had plotted the room down to the square inch. The furniture—leather couch, coffee table, wood chair, oversized desk, and tall executive chair—was sleek, modern, and uncomfortable. Broadcasting magazines and advertising booklets sat on the coffee table, fanned out in a perfect half-circle arrangement. Even Lipton's desk seemed calculated; its polished dark wood surface held two silver picture frames at each corner, a black leather desk pad in the middle, and a gold-plated Emmy Award—Best Newscast of 1995—perched front and center.

Lipton sat in his executive chair, body perched near the edge, hands folded, forearms leaning heavily on the desk. Carpo had the sensation he was about to be pounced upon.

"Carpo," Lipton began. "I just received a call from Dan Golden, the press contact over at the chief medical examiner's office. Were you calling over there this morning?"

"Yes, I did."

"What the hell did you do that for? You know they're not allowed to talk with us."

Carpo blinked, realizing what Lipton was so angry about. "I was trying to figure out which doctor was doing the autopsy on Frank Werner. I didn't think it would hurt to make a call over there."

"Golden said you did more than call. He said you tried to get in touch with one of the doctors. Is that true?"

"Yeah, sort of. I mean . . ."

"Goddamn it, now Golden's ticked off at us. And I'm ticked off at you—real ticked, my young friend. This could hurt us when it comes time for Golden to dole out information."

"Bill, I didn't do anything wrong. It wasn't unethical to call there. I clearly identified myself and who I worked for. I just said that when they were ready to talk, I'd be ready to listen." Carpo wasn't sure if Lipton knew he had talked with Dr. Parkes and given her his phone number. *That* was unethical. He decided to leave it out.

"Next time you decide to play reporter, clear it with me. Got it?"

Carpo nodded.

"Did Golden or anyone else tell you anything?"

"Nothing."

"All the same, ask next time."

Again, Carpo nodded his head, noticing that the slower he nodded the more annoyed Lipton's face became. It was obvious Lipton was using the call to assert his authority and get some sort of upper hand.

"Now, one other thing that's ticking me off," Lipton snapped. "Why the hell didn't you tell anyone that Frank Werner called you the other day?"

"I already explained to Sisco, there was no way of knowing this guy was going to turn up dead. I wasn't even going to talk to him, but he mentioned the name of someone I used to know. I thought I was doing a favor; otherwise, I never would have taken the call."

"Who's that?" Lipton asked pointedly.

"Who's what?"

"The guy Werner mentioned that made you agree to meet him. Who did he mention?"

"It was an old friend from college. Nobody I really knew well, just a name we had in common."

Lipton grunted. Carpo couldn't tell if it meant his answers were appropriate or not. Lipton turned his glare onto Sisco and asked him to call Ed Thomas into the office.

Within a few seconds, the distinguished reporter glided in and sat in the leather chair next to Carpo. Ed was wearing a blue wool, European-cut suit, heavily starched shirt, and a lush silk tie with large red polka dots and matching suspenders. As he sat, Carpo caught an overpowering whiff of cologne. Every hair on Ed's body seemed perfectly groomed: his blond hair slicked back and combed tight against his finely boned head, face clean shaven, eyebrows brushed perfectly over his light gray eyes. Carpo had a sudden urge to reach over and smack him in the head.

In a swift, practiced gesture, Ed reached into the breast pocket of his jacket, removed a leather-bound reporter's notebook, and uncapped a gold pen. All the while, he avoided making eye contact with either Sisco or Carpo. Whether the lights were on him or not, Ed Thomas was always on stage, playing out the starring role of big city reporter.

"Shut the door," Lipton commanded once it was apparent Ed was ready. "Now, I want to coordinate how we're going to cover the Werner case. I don't want us stumbling around making stupid ass phone calls while the opposition is getting all the scoops. Got it?" Lipton glared in Carpo's direction, bringing a hint of a smile to Ed's lips.

Sisco unfolded a piece of paper and cleared his throat. "All righty, I've mapped out a tentative schedule for the Werner story for the rest of the week. Ed, tonight I'm setting you up outside the coroner's office for a live shot in the six and ten o'clock shows. You'll cover anything that develops on the story in the next few hours. Your lead is probably going to be this statue that's going up for auction at Christie's next week. It's a bust of Cleopatra that Werner was representing for some anonymous owner. Werner stood to make a pile of dough off it. Carpo's had The Morgue pull together a clipping file on Werner. It includes a lot of background on the piece. Carp', tonight you're staying on as a writer for the ten o'clock cast. There's not enough free bodies in the newsroom to spare you right now."

Sisco looked up from the paper and waited to see if anyone had a question. No one did.

"Tomorrow is Saturday and I'm bringing you both in. Sorry about the weekend and all, but something's got to give if we're going to keep on top of this. Ed, you'll take a crew down to One Police Plaza—the commissioner's scheduled a one P.M. presser. I don't expect any breaks by then, but we've got to cover it all the same. Tomorrow is also the first day of Frank Werner's wake. It's closed to the media, but I'm thinking of sending Carpo over there to poke around."

"Wait a minute, Sisco," Ed interrupted. "Any rookie can go sit at a press conference and hold a mike. Why don't you send Carpo for that? Let me go to the wake and see what I can dig up."

"That's not the way I want to handle it," Sisco said, shaking his head. "I said the wake is closed to the media. If you show up there, people are going to recognize you. Besides, if something does break in the case tomorrow, it's going to happen at the press conference. You'll go there. Carpo will go to the wake." Sisco looked around the room for any further signs of dissent before he continued.

"On Sunday, Ed, you're in again. We'll play your coverage by ear, probably do something up at the reservoir, maybe with that cop that found the body. Carpo, you're on call, but we probably won't need you unless this thing suddenly wraps up."

"Wait a minute," Ed interrupted again. "Why doesn't he work, too? I mean, I could use some help out there in the trenches. Maybe he could hold the mike or something."

Sisco lowered his head and allowed a raspy chuckle. "Ed, the last time you went into a trench, you were putting on your raincoat. You'll do just fine holding your own mike. I said Carpo would help if something breaks, but it doesn't make sense to call in another body for a seventh day."

"That's right," Lipton interjected as soon as the topic turned to overtime costs. "We don't need to spend so much on overtime. Carpo will not be needed Sunday." He stood behind his desk and brushed an imaginary fleck of dust from the polished surface. "Then we're set for the weekend. Let's reconvene Monday to map out the beginning of next week."

The men filed out of the office, Ed brushing past Carpo without a word or a glance. After he had passed, Sisco steered Carpo back into his cubicle.

"Keep an eye out for that guy," he warned as soon as they reached the confines of the tackboard walls.

"What for?"

"He called Lipton this morning to complain about you being chosen as his assistant. He wanted someone else to be put on. I think Lipton was going to change you, too, but I talked him out of it."

"It doesn't surprise me," Carpo said. "We haven't gotten along very well since the Conductor Martinez story."

"Well, start. The guy's an asshole, but he's a pretty decent reporter. I don't need internal bickering hurting us on this story."

"I've never done that."

Sisco shot him a hard glance. "Some people think you have. Now I'm not saying you haven't grown a lot since that conductor thing, I'm just warning you to watch out for him. And keep your cool. I don't want that temper of yours to cause a problem. Do your job and let me take care of Ed."

"Okay, Sisco." Carpo stood to leave, but Sisco raised a hand to stop him.

"One other thing: Be careful when you go to that wake tomorrow. Don't go sneaking around, pretending like you're one of the mourners. I want you to identify yourself to the family as soon as you get there. If they ask you to leave, then go. There's certain things we have no right intruding on."

"What am I looking for anyway?"

"I'm not sure, use your instincts. Check out the scene, see if you recognize any of the people. Listen to what people are talking about. When it's over, stop by here and report to me. I'm coming in tomorrow, too."

Carpo nodded to show that he understood. As they walked back into the newsroom, Sisco gave him a light slap on the back.

"I'm counting on you, Carpo. You've got a real good chance to make a new impression around here. Consider it like a second chance. Now, prove to them I did the right thing."

# Chapter 6

It was snowing hard Saturday morning; large, frozen flakes created a screen of blurry white along 12th Street. It muffled the noise of the street, the traffic and horns, and it coated the sidewalks, garbage, and ice in a sheet of undisturbed white.

Carpo walked to Union Square and took a number 6 train north to the Upper East Side, then headed west to Madison Avenue. Few people passed him on the sidewalk. Fewer cars passed on the street, wheels spinning with a vinyl whir as they crawled single file up the avenue. Even the sooty brick exterior of the Frank E. Campbell Funeral Home was transformed by the wet matter. It looked like a giant marble cake, its sides coated in a zebra-striped pattern of dark charcoal and bleached white.

Carpo stepped into the building, shaking the wetness from his hair as he checked his coat with a woman in the foyer. He was wearing a blue poplin suit and a dark knit tie. The suit was summer-weight, but it was the darkest one he owned. He hoped it would look in place for the Frank Werner wake. In his left hand, he carried a small bundle of red roses wrapped in clear plastic. He had bought them at the deli on his corner. His right hand was raised to his throat, tugging down on the starched collar of his shirt. It had been a long time since he had worn a jacket and tie. Long enough for him to forget how much he hated it.

"I can't wait to get this thing off," he explained to the coat check woman after he realized she was staring at his antics. "It's driving me crazy."

She smiled and handed him a ticket for his coat. "You don't look like you wear a tie very often."

Carpo made a face like he was hurt. "What are you saying? I don't fit in with the suits?"

He waited a moment while she laughed at his discomfort, then asked for directions to the Werner wake. She pointed him toward a stand in the entrance that listed the times and locations of the wakes scheduled for the day.

The Werner wake was on the second floor, in a small yellow room decorated with blue paisley curtains. The air was very warm and Carpo could feel himself begin to sweat after his brisk walk. Several rows of brown metal chairs were set up in the room. Carpo was surprised to find most of the chairs vacant, just a handful of well-dressed people sitting dutifully in the first two rows.

The chairs faced the casket, a polished ebony box that sat atop a long wooden platform. The casket appeared to float in a brilliant sea of flowers, huge bouquets that spread from one end of the platform to the other. Across many of the largest bouquets were wide swaths of red ribbon printed with block letters that spelled out the names of some of the most famous American museums, along with various short messages of condolence. It appeared that the competition for the Werner estate had already begun.

Carpo walked straight to the front of the room and wedged

his cheap bouquet among the dozens of grand arrangements. He moved to the casket, realizing for the first time that its top was open. Frank Werner rested inside, cushioned by a white scallop-cut fabric that fanned out beneath him like an accordion. Carpo moved closer, noticing a thin wooden bench placed along the edge of the platform. The aroma of the flowers, thickened by the hot room, blew over him as if he had entered a hot house. Without knowing anything about wakes, he decided to make a show of respect to the deceased. He stepped to the bench and lowered his knees to the stand. He bowed his head, as if in prayer, while he lifted his eyes for a peek at Werner's face.

Thankfully, all traces of the scream that had haunted the cover of *The Post* were gone. Carpo stared at the corpse with curiosity, for the first time placing a face to the delicate voice that had called him at the beginning of the week.

Frank Werner had been a heavy-set man, with a plump face and gray, thinning hair. At his sideburns, the hair was white and curly. He was dressed in a dark suit, a maroon bow tie knotted around his throat. Though most of his body was concealed by the rim of the casket, Carpo was surprised at Werner's size. He appeared close to six feet tall, with a large belly that cleared the edge of the casket. He was a much bigger man than Carpo had imagined from his voice. Carpo wondered what kind of impression the combination of soft voice and large body had made in person.

Despite the absence of the scream, it was obvious that Frank Werner's face had suffered some sort of major trauma. Swelling in the reservoir ice and then slowly defrosting had created hundreds of tiny rips in the flesh. The undertaker had tried to conceal these marks by applying a pancake-thick covering of makeup. It made the body look like a chalk-faced mannequin with too much rouge slapped on its cheeks. All of the makeup in the world couldn't hide the fact that Frank Werner was stone cold dead.

Carpo stood and walked to a bored-looking woman in the front row. She was wearing a simple black suit with a dark red carnation pinned above her left breast. She held a white lace handkerchief in her hand. It occurred to Carpo as he drew closer that she wasn't using the handkerchief to dab tears, she was mopping a fine layer of sweat off her brow and upper lip. She greeted him with a polite, controlled smile and introduced herself: "Leslie Greenfeld, sister of the deceased."

Carpo recited his own name and shook her extended hand. On the fourth finger of her left hand he spotted a huge diamond mounted in platinum claws. Even so, he decided to play it safe with her name. "It's nice to meet you, Ms. Greenfeld," he said.

"Yes, thank you. How did you know my brother?"

He paused for a second, remembering Sisco's order to play it straight. "Actually, I've never met Mr. Werner in person, but I talked with him recently on the telephone. I work for Channel 8 News. Mr. Werner called me the day before he died. I was hoping to come here and possibly discover why he called."

Ms. Greenfeld must have sensed his unease because she said, "Well, you needn't worry about feeling unwelcome. None of these people knew Frank either. I'm his only surviving relative and even we weren't close. Frankie was . . . difficult."

"Then would you mind if I sat here during the wake? I'd like to see the people who were acquainted with your brother."

"Be my guest. I think you'll find that the people here are mostly concerned about what the estate will do with Frankie's art collection. People liked my brother because he could get them something. People are willing to put up with a lot when it comes to art."

"Where will Mr. Werner be buried?"

The woman's face crinkled into a prunish grin. "Funny you should ask. Frankie owned a plot at the Woodlawn Cemetery, but the funeral director just informed me that they won't be able to bury him until the ground thaws. They'll have to store him until spring."

Carpo smiled back at the woman, unsure of what she found so amusing about the tidbit. "Ms. Greenfeld, do you know if your brother was in any trouble? When he called me he sounded like something was wrong."

"Frankie and I haven't spoken in, I don't even know how long, ten years maybe? He was a very manipulative man. I would not be at all surprised if he was into something way over his head."

Carpo nodded, suppressing his mind from noting just how "over his head" Frank Werner had gotten in the Central Park Reservoir.

Ms. Greenfeld turned and nodded at a couple that had just stepped into the room. "Is that all, Mr. Harpo?" she asked.

"It's Carpo, ma'am. I was wondering if there were any plans for Athena Galleries."

"Yes."

"And what is that, Ms. Greenfeld?"

"I'm selling it," she said, her voice rising as she realized she was receiving a grilling.

Carpo pressed ahead. "May I ask who you're selling it to?"

"No one yet, but as soon as I find a buyer I'm getting rid of it. Now if you'd *please* excuse me, Mr. Harpo, or Carpo, or whatever your name is. There are other people to talk to."

Carpo started to thank the woman, but she had already turned and sat in her seat. He made his way to the back of the room and chose the seat at the farthest end of the last row.

Snowstorm or not, the wake was a pitiful ceremony for a man described in the papers as a world-renowned art collector. A total of ten people dotted the chapel, and they seemed more conscious of each other than the body laid out in the front of the room.

"From fame to forgotten in a Warhol fifteen," he whispered under his breath, trying to imagine how Ed would have led into his evening "package" if he had been covering the wake.

Over the next two hours, the crowd changed but never grew much bigger. Carpo struggled to keep his thoughts within the room. The hard metal chair was starting to cut off the circulation in his legs. He twisted his body and shifted forward and back in the hope of finding a more comfortable position. There was none. It felt like the chair had been specially designed to prevent people from lingering.

Just as he was starting to think of leaving, a woman entered the chapel and walked straight to the casket. She wore a long black dress and carried a single African orchid in a red ceramic pot. She placed the orchid on the wooden bench in front of the casket. Its white, funnel-shaped flower instantly graced the dark wood. Carpo craned his neck for a glimpse of the woman, but her face was concealed behind a thick black veil. The woman sank to her knees before the body and bowed her head until it rested against the edge of the casket. She stayed like that for several minutes without moving. It was only the entrance of the funeral director, who whisked into the room to say good-bye to Leslie Greenfeld, that finally interrupted her.

The woman stood weakly, her shaking hand reaching into the casket and softly rubbing against the dead man's cheek. She moved to a chair in the first row and started searching through her purse for a tissue.

Carpo couldn't make out the woman's face through the veil,

but he had seen enough to know it was Karen Blackwell. In fact, it was the veil that had given her away. The first time he had ever set eyes on Karen, she'd been wearing something similar—a blue wool scarf wrapped twice around her face. He would never forget that first quick glimpse almost ten years earlier.

It had happened while he was a freshman at Georgetown, returning to his dorm room in Harbin Hall on a late December night during first semester finals. He had stopped in the entrance to the dorm and held the door for someone walking behind him. In the half-second that he'd paused and peered over his shoulder, he'd glimpsed a stretch of cobalt-colored fabric protecting a woman's face from the cold. There had been something about the way the scarf was wrapped, and the intrigue of a concealed face, that had seized his attention.

He'd usually taken the stairs to his room on the second floor, but on that night he'd entered the elevator with the woman. The doors had closed and the elevator carried them from the lobby. He'd stood to the side of the woman and secretly watched as she'd unwound the scarf from her face. What was hidden beneath had not disappointed. High cheekbones, wide, fawn-like brown eyes, and a regal chin had convinced him to ride past his floor to see where she lived. As they'd stood there in silence, her eyes staring up at the floor numbers, he'd openly admired her long, shiny brown hair, her exact nose, and her full, pouty lips.

On the seventh floor, she'd left the elevator. Carpo had ridden all the way to the ninth floor, then made the return trip to the second floor. A hint of her perfume had ridden with him, teasing him the entire way. Back at his room, he had pulled out the freshman face book and flipped through every picture until he'd found her name and description: "Karen Blackwell. Greenwich Country Day School. Interests: Art, Debating, and Ice Hockey Goalie."

That last one had been the clincher and had brought an instant smile to his lips. He'd tried to imagine her swathed in skates and heavy goalie pads, brazenly stopping a slapshot without concern for her beautiful face. Then and there he had sworn to himself that someday he would know this woman.

When Karen swiveled in her metal chair and looked to the back of the chapel, Carpo bowed his head and covered his face with his hands as if he were meditating. He stayed like that until he was sure she was no longer looking, then he quietly stood and left the room. He did not pause until he had retrieved his coat and was safely in the back of a taxi heading to the Chrysler Building.

# Chapter 7

Carpo had been hired at Channel 8 when he was twenty-three years old. It was his third job out of college, after a year's stint as a waiter and a few months at a large temp agency. It had taken him several months to land a position at WIBN, and he'd been happy enough to start right at the bottom, as a part-time production assistant on the weekend shift. The job entailed mostly menial tasks: rewinding and labeling the show tapes; pulling archive and file tapes for reporters; ripping scripts and running the teleprompter for the anchors; and fetching coffee, deli sandwiches, and newspapers for the producers.

While most employees dreaded working Saturdays and Sundays, Carpo had found that it provided him with opportunities he might never have experienced on a regular Monday through Friday schedule. The slower pace and quieter hours had allowed him to explore the newsroom and discover the different jobs people did there. He'd sat on the Assignment Desk during his lunch breaks and learned how the scanners worked. He'd followed reporters into the dark editing bays and studied how a package was assembled: A-roll and track, followed by B-roll. He'd also been introduced to the language of editing, words for various problems or effects with video, like dissolves, backing in video, jump cuts, and flashes.

Among the writers, Carpo had practiced working with Newsmaker, a complicated computer program that allowed him to find and read Associated Press wire copy, do basic word processing, construct a show rundown, and file scripts directly onto the teleprompter. He'd learned the proper way to order chyrons, the on-screen lettering that gave a person's name or location of the video. He'd also practiced news-writing. He'd learned the formats of the stories—package lead-ins, readers, vo's, and vo-sots—and he'd experimented with writing every type of news story, from fires and crime reports to features and kickers. When he'd finished them, he would give them to the writers and ask them to critique his work. After a while, he'd started handing them to the news editors.

Within a few months, Carpo had learned enough about the function of the newsroom that he was considered an invaluable part of the staff. His curiosity had taught him the contents of each filing drawer, the location of every archive tape, and the various commands for the Newsmaker program. He was even proficient at speed-reading a piece of wire copy and banging out a legible, and intelligible, script. His first promotion had come after eight months, to the position of full-time production associate. One year later, Sisco had asked Lipton to move him up to the Monday through Friday "A" team as a staff newswriter.

In spite of the promotions and positive feedback, Carpo had never forgotten those long hours on the weekend, learning the layout of the newsroom, practicing his writing, and struggling to develop a sense of news judgment. Back then, he had been much more naive about his profession, believing that journalism would give him the opportunity to make a difference in the world. In the five years since, he had hardened himself to the city and its many problems, sacrificing much of his idealism about journalism for a more bottom-line approach to the local news.

And the bottom-line approach was what struck him as soon as he stepped into the newsroom that Saturday afternoon. With a considerably smaller viewing audience on weekends, the newsroom staff had been cut back to a skeleton crew: just an on-line producer, two newswriters, two production assistants, a desk assistant, and a single anchor. The seven employees were expected to handle the load of fifteen employees during the weekdays. Even the hustle and energy of the Monday through Friday shift had been replaced by a library type of atmosphere. The writers talked in whispers, the young interns and P.A.s read books and magazines, and the radios and scanners at the Assignment Desk were turned to their lowest volume settings.

Carpo spotted Sisco and Ed Thomas in the newsroom. Sisco was sitting at the Assignment Desk, his feet hooked over the back of a swivel chair as he slashed through *The Post's* "Word Jumble" with one of his stiletto-sharp pencils. Ed was seated at a screening machine in the middle of the room. He avoided making eye contact with Carpo as he shuffled through a large stack of field tapes.

Carpo decided it was as good a time as any to try and smooth things over with the reporter. He walked up to him and said: "Hi, Ed. How'd it go downtown?"

"Well. It went well," Ed answered without lifting his eyes from the monitor.

"Any breaks?"

"Nope."

"Did the commissioner speak?"

"Yeah, he did."

Carpo stood in silence for a few seconds. "Yeah, things were pretty quiet at the wake, too," he offered. "Listen, maybe we can sit with Sisco for a few minutes and talk over the story."

"I'm kind of busy, Carpo." Ed's eyes lifted from the monitor and moved across the stack of tapes before locking onto his. "When you get a chance, I want you to pull these tapes." He handed him two sheets of yellow legal paper filled with the serial numbers of file tapes stored in the station's Morgue.

"What are these?" Carpo asked through a clenched jaw. He was three years and two promotions removed from pulling file tape for reporters, and Ed knew it.

"They're some stories that might have footage of Frank Werner in them. I need them for my package tonight."

"Fine." Carpo gave a tight nod. "I'll stack them in your cubicle."

"No, I want you to screen them and see if there's anything worth using."

"Great. Maybe you'd like me to do your interviews and write your package for you, too." Carpo yanked a chair around and angled it to face the reporter before sitting in it. "Look, Ed, I'm trying here, okay? I'm really trying to get along with you. But I do expect some basic courtesy. You know it's not my job to pull and screen your file tapes."

"You *would* like to report my stories, wouldn't you," Ed hissed, lips bared into a snarl, as he jabbed an index finger two inches from Carpo's nose. "You'd better start learning your place around here. You're my assistant. If I give you something to do, you'll either do it or I'll have you replaced."

Carpo stared at the finger and felt a jolt pass through his stomach. It would feel great to reach up and snap the finger, as quickly as Major Sisco had snapped his yellow pencil the other day. Easy, he thought to himself, this is not the place to lose it.

"Ed, I'd be happy to help you screen your tapes, but this list is nothing more than a wild goose chase. I'm not going to screen through every social event at the Metropolitan Museum of Art for the past two years to see if Frank Werner stepped in front of one of our cameras."

"Have it your way." Ed turned back to the screening machine and pressed the "play" button. When the tape started rolling, he turned up the volume on the monitor, making further conversation impossible.

Carpo folded the list into a tight square as he stared at the perfect blond curls hugging the back of the reporter's head. He thought about setting the list back down on the table but worried that it might trigger another exchange. Instead, he shoved the list in his pocket and walked to his desk. He started unpacking his briefcase.

Even though Carpo despised the reporter, he regretted arguing with him. It was unprofessional on both their parts. While it was highly objectionable for Ed to order him to pull and screen file tape, Carpo knew he should try and help the reporter however possible. There was just something about Ed's manner, his air of superiority, that made it impossible for Carpo to pretend he respected the man. But the anger he felt for Ed went deeper. It stemmed from the last time they had worked on a special project together, an assignment that had become known as the Conductor Martinez story.

The case had happened two years before and had nearly cost Carpo his job after Ed had accused him of holding back information. Carpo hadn't held back anything; he had merely refused to give the identity of a whistle-blower from the Metro

North Railroad, Conductor Bob Martinez. The animosity from that case still boiled in the minds of both men; Carpo knew it was affecting his handling of the Werner investigation. Already he had held back on a compelling angle in the case: Karen Blackwell's probably relationship with the murdered art dealer.

Carpo had gone to the wake that afternoon almost praying that Karen would not show up, and yet the entire time it had seemed like he was waiting for her arrival. It was inevitable. From the initial phone call from Frank Werner to the picture in the clipping file to her reaction at the wake—every sign pointed toward a strong connection between the two. And it didn't take a hardened journalist to figure out that the relationship had probably been a romantic one. Carpo knew he should be investigating that link for any sign of impropriety or misdeed. It was the single common thread he had encountered so far between him and Frank Werner. Deep down, he knew he was treating the case differently from the way he would if Karen Blackwell had been a woman he had never known, much less a woman he had never loved.

Sisco's rich baritone brought his mind back to the newsroom. "Don't you say hello anymore, Carp'?"

"You looked kind of busy with that puzzle."

"Not so busy that I missed your little spat with Ed."

Carpo nodded, angling his eyes down toward his desk. "I'm afraid I didn't handle that too well."

"No, you didn't. But neither did he. Nobody likes getting a grocery list as soon as they arrive in the newsroom. How was it at the wake?"

"Uneventful. I didn't see much of anything we can use."

"Did you recognize anyone?"

Carpo squeezed the soft foam of the arm rest but made sure the rest of his body appeared calm. "No. No one important."

"Aah heck, it was just a hunch. I'm sorry about burning your Saturday. Why don't you knock out of here and enjoy what's left of your weekend? We'll hit the trail fresh Monday, okay?"

"All right, Sisco. Thanks."

He watched the tall man turn and start for the Assignment Desk. A feeling of guilt suddenly leeched into Carpo's gut. Do it, he thought to himself. Do it now and be done with it.

"Hang on, Sisc'," he called out. "There is one thing we might want to check out."

Sisco stopped and walked back, sitting casually on the corner of Carpo's desk. "What's up?"

"I almost forgot, but there was one person I recognized at the wake. It's probably not a big deal, but maybe Ed should check her out."

"Who was it?"

Carpo took a breath. "Her name's Karen Blackwell. She's an associate curator at the Met. She showed up at the wake and seemed really upset. In fact, she was the only one there who seemed to care about Frank Werner. That's nothing criminal, but their relationship might be something to check into."

"Why do you say 'relationship'? Were they dating?"

"I don't know; it's possible. She was very upset."

Sisco wiggled his thin frame to the edge of the desk. His body had picked up an attitude of intensity. He reminded Carpo of a cat perched on a ledge, waiting for the right moment to pounce on some unwary prey.

"Did you talk to her?" Sisco asked.

"No, I didn't think it was the proper place. Besides, there's probably nothing to it."

"But if you didn't talk to her, how'd you learn her name and title?"

Carpo felt the shock register on his face. Relax, he reminded himself, don't look so guilty. Even so, his fingers dug deeper into the foam padding. He hadn't even thought of an excuse for how he knew about her.

"I was curious about her," he explained in what he hoped was a matter-of-fact tone, "so I asked some people at the wake."

"You should have talked to her. She might have told you something."

"In hindsight, yeah, I probably should have. But I don't think it's a big deal."

Sisco snorted. "But it's something, right? I mean, you must have felt something or you wouldn't have told me."

"I guess so. If you think so."

"Hell yes, I do. Why was this woman so upset? She must have been close to him. That means she might know if he was in trouble. Besides, this relationship between them sounds suspect."

"In what way?"

"For starters, what the hell are a gallery owner and an assistant curator from a museum doing so chummy?"

"Associate curator," Carpo said.

"Fine, whatever, associate curator. Obviously, you thought enough about her to get that straight."

Carpo threw his arms up in the air. "Look, Sisco, I don't know what you want me to tell you. She was crying, okay? It caught my attention. I don't know what else you're expecting from me."

Sisco reached over and gave Carpo a light punch in the arm. "What's up with you, man? Usually you're a pit bull with something like this. So much so, I always got to tell you when to let go. Now all of a sudden you're telling me no big deal?"

"Nothing's up," he said evenly. He forced his eyes to remain on Sisco's.

"Carpo, have you ever met this woman before today?"

"No."

"Never?"

"No."

"All right then." Sisco shrugged. "I'll put Ed on it."

# Chapter 8

Carpo arrived at the Metropolitan Museum of Art by cab. He paid the driver, asked for a receipt, and carefully tucked his change and the receipt into his wallet. It was Sunday, his day off, and he knew there was no chance of getting WIBN to reimburse him for the trip; but his nerves were taut, hands fidgeting, and he needed an excuse to pause before starting up the rows of stairs to the museum's entrance.

It was 5:00 P.M., less than a half-hour before the museum closed. He didn't have much time to waste. He wished it was summertime, when the crowds of tourists lounged on the warm steps, soaking in the late afternoon sunshine. He might have stopped and joined them, waiting until he felt ready to face what needed to be faced. Instead, it was winter and the empty stone steps were hard and icy. Row after row, they echoed back the sound of his cold footsteps like an acoustically perfect amphitheater. The emotion he was feeling was not nervousness, it was fear. He felt as though at any moment he would bump into Karen Blackwell; it was not how he wanted their first meeting in six years to happen.

It seemed that Carpo had been preparing for this reunion ever since he had moved to New York. So many times he had walked down a street imagining that the woman just ahead was her. A million times he'd pictured the encounter: the way he would walk over and say hello, how she would respond, what they would do. It got to the point where he was seeing Karen's face in the faces of women all over the city. He still browsed through the "Style Section" of *The New York Times* every Sunday, holding his breath as he searched under the last names that started with "B" in the wedding announcements. He also faithfully read the Georgetown alumni newsletters, searching for any information on her. When mutual friends said they had news of her, he told them he didn't care, but he listened very carefully.

It angered him that he still harbored so much feeling for her. At times he even wondered if it was abnormal to hang onto something so clearly finished. He had tried on many occasions to move on, start a new relationship, but he never seemed to have the interest or energy for it. He went on dates and had women friends he talked with regularly, but he steered clear of the sort of intense relationship—the physical and emotional commitment—demanded by a lover.

Carpo whisked through a revolving door and stepped into the museum's Great Hall. It was warm inside, which made the exposed flesh on his face feel swollen and hard. The Great Hall was an immense space, more than a city block long, and decorated with several flower arrangements perched on pedestals high above the crowd. People milled about the room with a noise and activity that reminded him of the bustle of Grand Central Terminal, but a quick glance at the marble floors, free of garbage and black lumps of gum, told Carpo that this was a place people cared about.

In the center of this energy was the information desk, a large, circular area outlined by a border of polished wood and a shiny bronze railing. Carpo approached a young man sitting within the boundary with a small sign in front of him that read, "Information."

"Hi," Carpo said. "I'm looking for an employee of the museum. Her name is Karen Blackwell. She works in the Greek and Roman Department. I think it's extension 3613."

"May I have your name please?"

Carpo started to say his name but stopped. "I'd like to surprise her. Just tell her it's an old friend from college."

The man dialed the phone and talked quietly for a few moments before hanging up. "I'm sorry, Ms. Blackwell is not in her office."

"But I'm sure she's in today. I talked to her secretary about an hour ago."

The man bent his head and peered over the top of his tortoise shell glasses, eyebrows curving high, as he stared at Carpo.

"Could you please call her office back and find out where she is in the museum?" Carpo asked. "I'll walk there. It's very important that I see her before closing."

Instead of picking up the phone, the man flashed Carpo a smug grin. "Perhaps we should have made an appointment with the person before dropping in."

Carpo's eyebrows folded together in an angry ridge, partly hiding his black eyes. "Listen pal, I didn't come here for an Emily Post lecture. I'm here to be helped. Now get back on the horn and find out where she is or I'll do it myself."

Carpo realized he was leaning far over the brass railing, practically falling into the man's lap. He straightened his body but kept his glare on the man's face. The man didn't move for a second, then he picked up the phone and dialed a number. Carpo wondered if he was calling the Greek and Roman Department or Museum Security.

"Ms. Blackwell is in the Greek and Roman Galleries right now," the man said, his voice much higher, the condescending tone absent. "I'm sorry, sir, but those galleries are not open to the public anymore on Sundays. You'll have to try back another day."

The man looked scared, and Carpo felt terrible about losing his temper. He thanked him as politely as possible for making the calls, then backed away from the desk. It was the second time in two days that he had lost his temper—first Ed Thomas, now an anonymous museum worker. He wondered who the next person would be to spark his anger. Some innocent person who bumped into him on the street? Or worse, someone he really cared for? He wondered where all of the anger was coming from, bubbling out of him like hot lava. He unbuttoned his coat and shoved his hands deep into its pockets.

He walked to a wooden bench across the Great Hall and wedged himself between an old lady clutching her purse and a young mother trying to control a pair of toddlers. The Greek and Roman Galleries were before him, an entire wing of the museum shrouded in darkness, the entrance cordoned off by a thick velvet rope and patrolled by three uniformed guards. It was now 5:15: crowds of tourists flooded toward the museum's exit. If he was going to make a move, it would have to be soon.

He crossed to the entrance of the wing and walked slowly along the velvet rope. In front were the guards, behind stretched a wide corridor of darkness. Near the back he could make out a thin band of light spilling from one of the rear galleries. He stopped next to a thick marble column that soared from the floor to the ceiling far overhead. His hand brushed against it, cool to the touch. He stared between his wristwatch and the crowds of people, hoping he looked like he was waiting for someone. His head was swimming with nervousness, heart pounding, as he watched the guards, trying to gauge the direction of their eyes, waiting for the correct moment.

It didn't take long to happen. A group of teenagers burst noisily from the coat check room. One of the kids grabbed another one's hat, and a chase began around the wooden bench where Carpo had been sitting. The guard closest to Carpo took three steps forward and ordered them to stop. By the time they had quieted down and the guard had returned to his post, Carpo had ducked under the plush rope.

He held his breath over the first twenty steps, walking purposefully into the first gallery, ears tuned for the expected cry of alarm. He didn't slow his step until he was far into the room and sure his form was cloaked in the darkness. He peered over his shoulder. The guards were there, backs turned to him, unaware that someone had crossed their velvet line of defense.

He headed down a hallway that split the galleries into sections, his head swiveling right and left as he peered through the door of each gallery. The dark rooms were filled with darker shapes—dozens of statues and busts frozen in strange positions. He pointed himself toward the band of light that came from the farthest gallery. His mind considered several possible excuses for why he was walking in the closed wing; none seemed even remotely plausible for explaining why he was tiptoeing through the darkness. He was lost? He was missing a child? He was looking for the bathroom? Carpo knew no one would believe he was looking for a bathroom or a missing child. But there, in the last gallery on the left, he did find what he had lost.

Karen Blackwell was at the far corner of the room, her figure bathed in the soft glow of a halogen spotlight mounted on the ceiling. A dozen statues were displayed in the gallery, but the spotlight was angled to capture only one of them: a pure, white marble statue of the goddess Aphrodite.

The statue was carved to life-sized proportions, standing about five feet tall, with slender arms and plump legs bent at the knees. The angle of the knees and the slightly curved back made Aphrodite appear as if she was in movement, starting to crouch or standing from the ground. It was naked and smooth. The overhead spotlight enveloped the statue so perfectly that, from where Carpo stood, the marble surface seemed to quiver like human flesh. Karen's back was to him, but he could sense that her attention was riveted on the statue, too. He squeezed his body into a dark slit between the door and the wall's molding and waited for the right moment to approach.

Karen kneeled to the floor and rummaged through a canvas knapsack at her feet. She removed a 35mm camera, lens case, and a small, folded aluminum tripod. She threaded the lens into the camera, set up the tripod, and attached the camera to its top. With the tripod slung over her shoulder, she circled the statue, silently stalking it from several different angles. Every few seconds she would halt, set down the tripod, and reel off a set of photographs as fast as the automatic winder allowed. The gallery was as quiet as a mausoleum; the only sounds Carpo could hear were the hiss of the steam heaters, the slight popping of the halogen bulbs, and the whir of the camera.

After several minutes, Karen set the camera aside and approached the statue. She was wearing a navy blue T-shirt and black jeans, the dark fabrics creating a vivid outline of her thin figure against the pure white marble backdrop. Her face was a mask of concentration, eyes squinting as they studied the curves in the marble, lips mashed together as if suppressing the urge to scream. Finally, she seemed to succumb to the desire. She moved close to the statue, raised her trembling hands, and placed them on the body of the goddess.

Carpo was confused about what he was witnessing until he remembered something Karen had told him once at Georgetown. One night, they were discussing art and she had tried to describe the feelings great works produced within her. She had called it "combustion," an actual tangible reaction that certain pieces of art spurred within her body. He had never understood what she meant by combustion until that moment, as he secretly watched her touching Aphrodite.

She shuffled around the statue, fingers tracing the lines of its body, the tips never losing contact with the marble. They ran up the hips, traced the outline of the stomach—its folds of flesh at the belly from where she leaned—then moved onto the breasts, each hand cupping the sag of the marvelous teardrops. The space between her hands widened at the shoulders, then tapered as they converged around the statue's thin neck.

Karen's face was knitted now, as if she were in pain. Beads of sweat stood out on her forehead, clinging to the dark strands of hair hanging down her face. She stopped in front of Aphrodite and slid her arms back around the neck, cradling the head like an attentive lover. Softly, she brushed her cheek against the skin of the goddess, enjoying the coolness that the marble must have been emitting.

Carpo watched in awe from the back of the room. The night Karen had described combustion to him, she had said that certain works of art actually spoke to her, conveying the thoughts and feelings that the artist had carved into stone so many centuries earlier. Carpo hadn't understood what she meant by this, and he had made the mistake of laughing at her. He still remembered the sting of her anger.

"Is there anything you don't crack jokes about," she had yelled. "You're like a child. I tell you something dear to me, something private, and you laugh."

What she hadn't realized was that he was laughing because he was trying to hide his feelings of ignorance. Growing up, he had never been exposed to art and museums. As a result, his eye was undeveloped for measuring art, his opinions unformed on matters of art history and theory. He didn't understand why people worshipped certain objects and discarded others. He also didn't understand how it could feel to be moved by an aesthetically beautiful object.

After the exchange, they had never discussed combustion again, but he had often privately wondered about it, what she'd meant by it. Now, as he witnessed it before him, he finally understood.

For close to a half-hour he stood hidden in the dark crack like a voyeur, watching and learning more about Karen than he had ever known in the years they had dated. While her hands ran smoothly over the stone, he imagined their touch, remembering the same sensation when she had caressed his own flesh. The thought of it started his heart pounding so fiercely that he feared she would hear it.

And then Carpo felt jealousy. Jealousy because a two thousand-year-old block of stone, carved with such perfection, could evoke so much passion in this woman. He was jealous of the stone and jealous of the ancient artist who had created it. He was jealous because he realized for the first time that all the love he had showered on Karen during their four years together had never come as close to pleasing her as Aphrodite did that evening.

Perhaps it was this change in his mood that altered the atmosphere in the gallery, subtly disrupting the harmony in that far corner. As his eyes watched Karen's hands, he realized they had grown as rigid as the stone they were caressing. He looked to her face and caught her expression of surprise, mouth open, cheeks flushed with embarrassment as she realized she had been caught at her most intimate and vulnerable moment. And then her face contorted with rage when she realized who it was who had caught her. She started to talk but Carpo cut her off.

"Karen, I'm sorry to bother you here," he said, walking toward her, as if his body could absorb her anger. "I need to talk with you. I think you may be in some trouble."

"What the hell are you doing in here?" she demanded, words as cold and sharp as a whip crack.

"Don't worry, I just got here. I didn't see anything. I mean, I didn't mean to—"

"No, no, no," she interrupted, head shaking from side to side, hair flailing. "No way. You don't belong here. I'm calling Security." She turned and headed toward a small orange box hanging at the opposite corner of the room.

He thought about intercepting her and trying to hold her still until she calmed down. He had a feeling it would only set her off more. "Wait, Karen, I'm serious about what I said. I think you're in a lot of trouble."

She stopped, body half turned, the option of the orange box within arm's length. "How did you get in here? Did you sneak in?"

He nodded yes and nearly panicked when she lifted the cover off the box and reached for a small black telephone inside. "Damn it, Karen, would you stop? I know you knew Frank Werner. I have proof of it. If you don't start explaining, I'm going to the police."

"Police?" She turned back to him and burst into a mocking

laugh. "You do that, Michael. Run right to the police. Tell them everything."

Carpo watched her hand move away from the phone and settle on her hip. He relaxed just a bit and walked toward her, passing the statue of Aphrodite. It was even more impressive up close, the marble losing its perfect, uniform whiteness but growing more and more lifelike as it took on the texture of ivory, the surface marred with deep veins and cracks. He forced his eyes back onto Karen.

"Look, I'm not trying to get you in trouble," he said. "I'm just trying to find out what's going on. Why didn't you tell me you knew him when I called last week?"

"Of course I knew him. Is that a crime? I was even his lover, Michael, which in your eyes probably *is* a crime."

He paused just a second before answering, but it was enough to show her that she was right. "I didn't come here to fight with you," he said quietly, suddenly feeling drained. "I want to help you."

"You haven't changed much, have you?" she said, the mocking tone still apparent. "You still think you can make a difference, save the world. Did it ever occur to you maybe the world doesn't want your help?"

Her face had returned to its normal color, but the sweat still welled on her forehead, small droplets that rolled down her face and neck, staining the top of her navy T-shirt black. She looked like an animal: wild, dangerous, yet still dazzling. Six years had done little to dim her appeal. In many ways, the added years had made her more beautiful than he remembered. Her face was sharper, muscles tauter and more defined. In spite of himself and the situation, he felt an urge to hold her.

"A reporter at Channel 8 News has learned about your relationship with Frank Werner. They're checking you out, Karen. I'm pretty sure they're going to call you."

"What did you do, tell them about me? Is that how they know?"

"I told them, but they would have figured it out sooner or later. I tried to protect you, but I had to do it. If they'd found out I was holding back on the story because of our past, I could lose my job."

She turned and slammed the door on the orange box shut, bringing a loud metallic clang. "Get the hell out of here," she hissed. "I don't want to be anywhere near you."

The words hit him as hard as a slap, and he blinked at their sting. He waited for a moment, but she had already turned her back on him, signaling that the conversation was over.

He turned and started out of the gallery, puzzling over her reaction to him. Her anger was surprising. He had expected her to be upset, especially after walking in on her, but her emotion verged on hatred. The only other time he had seen such violent emotion from her was the night they had broken up. That night she had slapped him for real, hard and right across the face. He had deserved it, too. He wondered if she still hated him for what he had done six years before.

When he reached the entrance of the gallery, he turned back. She was sitting at the foot of Aphrodite, back resting against the base, hands cupped over her face.

"Karen," he said across the space that divided them. "If you need me for anything, call me. You know where I work. I just want you to know that. To know that you can still call."

Without waiting for an answer, he left the gallery. He strode back through the darkness toward the Great Hall, suddenly looking forward to breathing the cold air outside.

# Chapter 9

Carpo still felt hollow inside when he got back to his apartment, but the feeling was as much from hunger as it was from his encounter with Karen. He had been so nervous about meeting her, he had forgotten to eat anything since a bagel that morning at Little Poland. He tossed his briefcase onto the couch and headed straight for the kitchen.

He rummaged through his cupboards, making a quick assessment of his food situation. He found a jar of peanut butter and a container of grape jelly, but he could scrounge up only one moldy heel off a loaf of bread in the refrigerator. He couldn't even remember the last time he had gone grocery shopping. Since Frank Werner had called, almost every meal had taken place in a diner or at his desk at WIBN. Finally, he came across an opened box of Ritz crackers in the back of the cupboard over the stove. The crackers were stale, but he was beyond caring. He used them to fashion a dozen miniature peanut butter and jelly sandwiches. He walked back into the living room and pressed the "play" button on his answering machine as he happily munched his dinner.

The first message was a hang-up. The second was from Major Sisco, asking him to arrive at work a half-hour early Monday for a meeting with Bill Lipton. Carpo groaned as the next two messages registered more hang-ups. He hoped it didn't mean something was wrong with his answering machine again. His mood soared on the fifth and final message when he heard a reluctant, but familiar, woman's voice.

"Michael Carpo, this is Dr. Susan Parkes calling from the M.E.'s office. Uhm . . . why don't you give me a call tomorrow? I've been thinking about our . . . conversation last week. There's something I need to tell you. I'll be in the office by eight. 533–0420. Call me anytime."

Carpo leaped off the couch and pumped his fist vigorously into the air while the message played. He was so excited, he hardly noticed when the plate of crackers fell onto the floor. It was a possible break, his first since the Werner call. He almost regretted that the meeting was confidential; it would feel great to gloat to Bill Lipton after getting chastised for calling the M.E.'s office.

He kneeled down and scooped the crackers off the floor and back onto his plate, munching a few more as he brushed the crumbs into his palm. When the floor looked clean, he sat back on the couch and turned on the television. It was just after 10:00 P.M., and he caught the opening package of Channel 8's news-cast, a live report from a fire scene in Flatbush, Brooklyn. He reached into his briefcase, pulled out his reporter's notebook and a pencil, and started making notes for his meeting with Dr. Parkes. Behind him the TV droned as the anchor, Maria Gomez, reported an exclusive story from Hauppauge, Long Island, where a baby girl had been sexually assaulted by her father and two brothers. The story was so awful that Carpo looked up from his notepad, grimacing in disgust. He went back to mak-ing notes until he heard Maria read the lead-in for Ed's live re-port on the Frank Werner murder.

The anchor threw to Ed Thomas, standing poised and cocky

outside One Police Plaza. His trench coat was unbuttoned, affording a glimpse of his fine suit, and he held the microphone off to one side so as not to block the view of his silk tie. The reporter's cheeks glowed bright red, which Carpo figured was either a product of the cold weather or Ed's confrontational reporting style. Ed's taped package started with him at a press conference firing questions at the chief of police about why there were no suspects yet in the Werner case. It was standard local journalism: lots of file tape and rehashing of the more gruesome parts of the story, mixed in with a few sound bites from police brass. Carpo figured that if no breaks developed by Monday, the story would drop from the first section of the newscast, supplanted by some more recent, sensational crime.

Carpo's ears perked up during Ed's close-up, when he reported that police were investigating several people with business or personal relationships to Frank Werner. Carpo knew enough about the story to surmise that Karen Blackwell was one of those links. He was relieved that Ed had not used her name or position at the Met during the wrap. Maybe he had done the right thing by telling Sisco to check out Karen's association with Frank Werner. He reached for the remote control and flicked off the TV before heading to bed.

For the first time Carpo could remember, he woke up before his alarm went off. It was 8:52 A.M., eight minutes before the beeping would begin. He turned off the alarm and put on a tattered blue terry cloth robe that was hanging on the back of his bedroom door. The cotton robe was full of moth holes and shredded at the sleeves, but it felt as soft as silk against his body. He made a quick pot of coffee in the kitchen, then walked into the living room and dialed the medical examiner's office. Dr. Parkes answered on the second ring.

"Morning, Dr. Parkes. It's Michael Carpo," he announced as he rubbed the sleep from his eyes. "I got your message last night. Thank you for calling."

"I can't talk right now," the doctor warned immediately, her voice lowering to a whisper. "I've been thinking about our conversation. There's something I've got to tell you."

Carpo's hand tightened on the phone. "I can meet you somewhere near your office if it would be safer."

"I've got a break coming up at 9:30. How about then?"

He peered at the clock hanging in the kitchen. It read 9:03. "That's fine," he said. "Where do you want to meet?"

"There's a coffee shop near me that's usually pretty quiet. It's a gourmet place. I think it's called The Casual Bean or something."

"The Cultured Bean," Carpo corrected. "Yeah, I know the place. It's at the corner of First and Thirty-second."

"That's the one. Now, your guarantee of confidentiality still stands, right?"

"I promise it, Dr. Parkes."

"Good, because if I don't feel right about you, I'm walking out."

"You have my word," he reassured her. "This is only for me."

Carpo thanked the doctor and hung up the phone. He glanced at the clock in the kitchen again: 9:05. Barely enough time to shave, shower, and get uptown.

It was 9:36 when Carpo strode through the front doors of The Cultured Bean. He was familiar with the shop after visiting it on a few of his gourmet coffee expeditions. The front was a small retail area with faded wood floors and a counter displaying dozens of exotic coffee blends. The place held the pungent smell of roasting coffee, mixed with the dry, sweeter aroma of English and Indian blended teas. He worked his way to the back of the store, where four small tables were set up.

Carpo checked out the people at each of the tables. The only person who seemed to fit his mental image of Dr. Parkes was a woman sitting with her back to him. She was wearing a wrinkled gray suit and nervously shuffling through some papers. He approached her cautiously, asking: "Dr. Parkes?"

The woman flashed a reluctant smile and shook his hand. She was much older than he had guessed from their two phone conversations, maybe late fifties, even pushing sixty. Her hair was straight and gray, worn pulled back in a long, neat ponytail. Her face was pleasant, thin and wrinkled in the places where she smiled. Carpo could imagine her office persona: strong, professional, and friendly. Of course, this was pure speculation since Dr. Parkes was obviously very nervous. She kneaded her hands compulsively and jumped every time the bell tinkled on the front door.

"Can I buy you a coffee before we start?" Carpo offered, hoping to break some of the tension as well as sample one of the store's blends.

She stared into her cup. "I guess I could use a refill."

He asked how she took her coffee, then walked to the front counter and ordered a regular and black cup of the Colombian house blend. He returned to the table and handed the regular to Dr. Parkes.

"Let me assure you once more that whatever we talk about will remain confidential," he said after he was seated.

"I should hope so," she sputtered. "I could get into a hell of a lot of trouble for this. Now let's get on with it. I feel like I'm about to get caught."

He thought about pulling his list of questions from his briefcase but decided it might make her more skittish. "Maybe we can start with some details on the body," he suggested. "How did Frank Werner die?"

"My report states the mechanism of death as congestive heart failure, caused primarily by dehydration. It was very difficult to pinpoint the cause of death because the body suffered considerable trauma, but dehydration definitely played a major part."

"Dehydration? Do you mean Frank Werner wasn't murdered?"

"No, the dehydration is what caused his heart to stop beating. But he was well on his way to death before that."

Carpo shook his head. "Maybe I'm not getting the terminology or something. I don't understand what you're saying."

"Do you know the difference between cause and mechanism of death," she asked pointedly.

"I guess I don't."

"The cause of death is the disease or injury responsible for death. The mechanism of death is the altered physiology and biochemistry whereby the cause exerts its lethal effect." She paused to see if Carpo understood. He shook his head again to show he didn't. "Let's put it this way," she said. "If I shoot you, the mechanism of death is exsanguination: you bleed to death. But the cause of death is still a gunshot wound."

"Gotcha."

"Good. Now, why don't I piece together what I think happened to Frank Werner. Just so you understand why I called you. It appears the victim was struck on the back of the head with some type of blunt instrument, the shape of the wound indicates a mallet or some type of small hammer. It appears he was hit two or three times and hard enough to fracture the skull."

Dr. Parkes broke off as the door to the coffee shop flew open. She darted a glance over her shoulder, then leaned in closer to Carpo. Her fingernails dug into the side of the Styrofoam cup, leaking beads of coffee through the indentations.

"What I think happened to the victim is that he was first knocked out and then lobotomized," she said, voice dropping to a barely audible whisper. "Do you know what that means?"

Carpo nodded.

"It was done here." She leaned across the table and tapped her finger lightly against the top part of his forehead, just into the hairline. "It was a rudimentary operation, performed with something like a small electric drill. The action of the bit pierced the brain and agitated it, sort of like a blender. It destroyed the function of the prefrontal lobe."

"Is that what caused the facial expression?" Carpo asked, his voice a whisper now, too.

"No, that's something entirely separate. I'll get to that in a second." She paused to take a sip of her coffee. "After the victim was lobotomized, he was basically a vegetable, clinically brain dead. This is why I called you. The victim seems to have been kept alive for at least two or three days after the lobotomy. He died after his heart failed from severe dehydration."

Carpo raised a palm into the air. "Hold on, that's not possible. Frank Werner called me the afternoon before his body was discovered. He couldn't have been a vegetable for that many days."

Dr. Parkes shook her head adamantly. "I'm very sure of it, Mr. Carpo. That's the reason I'm sitting across this table from you. The victim was brain dead for at least two days."

"How can you tell?"

"Lots of ways, starting with the head wound. The drill hole was scabbed over and already starting to heal by the time of death. That takes at least a day. There was no food in the stomach and he exhibited signs of severe dehydration. Furthermore, his body was starting to lose muscle tissue, much as we see in people on hunger strikes or suffering from anorexia. I'm quite positive, it was two, possibly even three, days."

Carpo swirled the coffee around his cup, watching the brown liquid stain the Styrofoam. "It doesn't make sense though," he said. "That would mean Frank Werner wasn't the man who called me last week."

"I don't know who called you last week, but it certainly wasn't Frank Werner."

"This method of doing a lobotomy doesn't sound like a very smart way of murdering someone."

"Think about the face," she said, tapping her fingers on her cheek for emphasis. "You've seen all the drawings and photos in the newspapers. Your news show probably even broadcast it. It was a scream, right? Well, the scream wasn't a natural one; it was created."

Carpo pushed back a bit from the table. "What are you saying?"

"The scream was carved into the victim's face—surgically carved. And it must have taken a hell of a long time. It was an amazing operation, only a surgeon could have had enough understanding of muscle and bone structure to do it. This crime wasn't done by some slasher; it was incredible, almost artistic."

She was leaning far across the table now, hands gripping its edge, face close enough for Carpo to smell the coffee on her breath. She blushed and backed off, as if she realized she was talking about the crime with a little too much passion. Carpo motioned for her to continue.

"The muscles, tendons, and ligaments of the face, all through here," she said as she mapped the area between her lower lip and the bottom of her eye sockets, "were snipped, stretched and stitched. They were manipulated until the face was pulled into the scream. The amazing thing is, it was totally done from the inside of the mouth, so from the outside it would look like a real scream. Basically, the scream was sculpted into the face."

Carpo dazed off into space for a few seconds as he tried to imagine the intricacy of such an operation. He looked back to the doctor and chuckled. "Kind of ironic when you think about Frank Werner's line of work."

Now it was the doctor's turn to look puzzled.

"You must know his occupation," he said.

"I think his sheet said art dealer."

"An art dealer who specialized in Greek and Roman sculpture. Maybe I just have a sick sense of humor, but isn't it ironic that a dealer of sculptures would end up with his own face carved."

"It was more than his face," she added, staring down at her hands. "This is another thing the media doesn't know about . . . yet."

"And won't find out, Dr. Parkes."

"Well, the victim's body was manipulated postmortem. It was shaved and his skin appears to have been ritualistically cleaned."

"What do you mean by that?"

"The body was shaved everywhere there was hair. I mean everywhere, too; there wasn't a single hair present anywhere below his scalp."

"Why was that done postmortem, while the face surgery happened while Werner was alive?"

"That I don't have an answer to. Maybe the victim died before the work was finished. I also found trace bits of cotton under the victim's nails and in places like his ear canals and nostrils."

"Any idea what it's from?"

"I'm not sure why it was done, but it seems consistent with the attention paid to cleaning the body. The entire corpse was scrubbed and inspected. I felt like I was performing an autopsy on a clean sheet of slate."

"What about the crime scene?" Carpo asked. "Who covered that?"

"I did. At least the removal of the body."

"What did you find?"

"Again, you probably already know most of the details here. The body was frozen into the Central Park Reservoir, about three inches below the surface of the ice. We're still not certain how it got in there, but the hole in the ice wasn't chiseled. There were no ice chips in the area. My guess is that some sort of torch or heat source was used to melt the ice and then the body was put into position. And whoever did it knows the area pretty well. Police patrol that reservoir every two hours. And the body was right near one of the easiest places to reach the reservoir."

"Do you put together some sort of psychological profile on the murderer?" Carpo asked.

"No, there's a psychiatric division that does that."

"Would it be possible to get a copy of their report?"

"Are you joking?" The doctor's face broke into an amused grin. "It's bad enough I'm talking with you. You're nuts if you think I'm going to start stealing documents."

"Okay, okay. How about if you put together a quick profile right now. I'm sure you've seen hundreds of murder victims. You must get some sort of feeling about the killer."

She sat back for a few seconds and took a ponderous drink

of coffee. "Let me put it this way, I don't envy the cops on this case. I don't think they're going to catch the man or woman who did this."

"Woman?" Carpo asked with obvious surprise. "Don't you think it has to be a man?"

"I don't know. It's something I've been thinking about. It's the detail, the way the victim's body was handled. It all says control to me. Someone finally got their chance to play god with Frank Werner, someone who was probably under his influence for a long time. This wasn't some random murder. It was an incredibly planned, minutely detailed act." Dr. Parkes shrugged. "Besides, the work on the face would take an awfully slim pair of hands."

"But how could a woman overpower a man? And how could she have carried the body onto the reservoir?"

"I don't know. Use your imagination. Maybe she snuck up and banged him over the head. Maybe she carted him out there on a sled or pulled him in a blanket. I'm not even saying the killer is a woman. I just don't think you should automatically conclude it's a man."

"Okay," Carpo conceded. "Can you tell me anything about the murderer's motivation?"

Dr. Parkes rolled her eyes and laughed. "Jesus, you ask some impossible questions. I will say one thing: as clean and brilliant as the surgery on the face, this was a very bloody crime. Someone out there has a lot of anger built up in them."

"Does anything else stick out in your mind, doctor?"

"That's about it. As you can tell, I have a lot of respect for the person who did this. They're smart and know about a lot of different things." Dr. Parkes glanced down at her watch. "It's after ten. Is there anything else you want to ask?"

"Yes," Carpo said. "Why did you agree to meet me?"

For the first time that morning, Dr. Parkes seemed to relax. She leaned back in her chair and stared straight into Carpo's eyes. "I don't really know," she admitted. "I've been thinking about how you said Frank Werner called you the day before his body was found. That troubled me. But you also sounded like a pretty decent guy, unlike the other jerks who call over here every day. Besides, most of my report will be public information in a few days. I just figured I'd give you a little head start."

Carpo stood and shook the doctor's hand. "Well, I can't thank you enough for your trust. You've been a great help."

"I just hope it doesn't come back to haunt me. Now do me a favor, will you, and sit back down for ten minutes or so? I want to make sure no one sees us leave here together."

With another brief handshake, Dr. Parkes moved past Carpo and left the coffee shop.

# Chapter 10

Carpo finished his coffee as he jotted some quick notes from his conversation with Dr. Parkes. At the front of the store he bought a small bag of the house coffee blend and looked over some of the fancy coffee brewers displayed on the walls. There was one machine that allowed you to roast your own coffee beans at home. Carpo was interested until he saw the hefty price tag and realized it might be difficult to find unroasted beans. When he was sure Dr. Parkes was out of the neighborhood, he stepped onto the street and plotted a course toward midtown.

The sky was clear blue and bright. Carpo tilted his face to the sun as he walked, enjoying the heat radiating from it. The angle of the sun seemed to hint that spring was not far away, as did the puddles of water from the melting snow. With still more than an hour before his meeting with Major Sisco, Carpo decided to stop into the Lantern for lunch.

He sat at the lunch counter and looked over the day's specials on the menu. The graphic discussion of Frank Werner's body had changed his appetite a bit, so instead of the usual hamburger deluxe platter, he decided to go vegetarian: grilled cheese sandwich, french fries, and a Coke. He reached back into his briefcase, took out the reporter's notepad, and continued making notes.

At the top of a fresh page he wrote, *"F.W.: Who???."* That was the question that most bothered Carpo: Who had called him last Tuesday posing as Frank Werner? His gut reaction was that the murderer, or someone working with the murderer, had made the call. But it was a strange thing for them to do, especially since there was a pretty fair chance he would eventually find out the phone call had been made after Frank Werner's death. More alarming was the fact that the caller knew enough about him to use Karen's name. The person must have known that her name would get him interested in setting up a meeting with Frank Werner.

The possibility nagged him as he waited for his food, pen drumming lightly on the lunch counter. Who could possibly know of his former relationship with Karen? And who could know that the use of her name would be enough to get him involved in the case?

On a hunch, he scribbled down the estimated time he had received the phone call from Werner: about six in the afternoon. Next to that, he put the estimated time the body had been found: sometime shortly after midnight. It was roughly a six hour difference. He figured the body wasn't even on ice at the time the phone call had been made to him.

Carpo's appetite returned once his grilled cheese sandwich was placed before him. He even recovered enough to pour a healthy amount of blood-red ketchup over his fries. He finished the meal, made a few more notes, then gathered his things and headed for the Chrysler Building.

He killed a few minutes in the lobby, browsing through magazines at the newsstand. He also watched a protest develop by a group of people in wheelchairs. They were blowing whistles and chanting slogans to protest that the building had no handicapped access. Carpo waited until he saw a Channel 8 News crew arrive to shoot some voice-over video for the evening's newscasts, then he rode up in the elevator to the News Department.

The newsroom was quiet when he walked in, just a few interns manning the Assignment Desk. Sisco, Ed Thomas, and Bill Lipton were nowhere in sight. Carpo figured they must have stepped out for some lunch. He was walking up to the desk to find out where they were when one of the interns noticed him and said: "Nice job last night, Carpo. You scooped the whole city on that Werner story."

Carpo frowned at the teenager. "What are you talking about?"

A hesitant look spread across the intern's face, as if he realized he had said something wrong. Carpo repeated the question.

"The story Ed did on the woman," the kid explained. "Karen Blackwood, or whatever her name is. The one from the museum who was questioned about the murder last night."

"I saw Ed's report on TV last night. He never mentioned a woman, especially not Karen Blackwell. What are you talking about?"

The intern blushed and looked down at a newspaper in front of him. Carpo put a hand on his shoulder and steered him around so they were face to face. "Come on," he demanded. "Tell me what you're talking about."

The kid was clearly frightened now, and all the other interns averted their eyes, as if they feared Carpo might focus his anger on them, too. "Maybe you should speak to Sisco when he gets back," the kid mumbled. "I just thought you knew about it."

"I don't know about it, but you're going to tell me."

"They went back to Ed later in the broadcast. Mr. Lipton made him move the remote outside the Met. They got some video of the woman walking to a squad car with some police detectives."

Carpo felt his palms break into a sweat. "What did Ed say about it?"

"Maybe you should look at the air check, Carpo. I wasn't really paying attention," the intern pleaded. "It wasn't anything bad. Look, even the papers had it this morning."

"Let me see." Carpo grabbed the newspapers from the intern. He started to walk away with them when he caught a glimpse of the intern's face. It was beet red, eyes glazed with fear and disbelief. The kid was probably eighteen or nineteen, still in college. Don't get mad at him, Carpo thought to himself. He's only the messenger.

"What's your name?" he asked.

"Dave Brandt."

"Listen Dave, I'm sorry about getting in your face. Okay? I'm not angry at you; I'm angry at the station. None of this is your fault."

Carpo patted the intern on the shoulder, then carried the newspapers to a free desk. He looked at the first paper, *The New York Post,* and saw exactly how bad everything was. In thick black letters, the headline screamed: "Angel of Death?" Beneath was a grainy picture of Karen being led down the steps of the museum, a pair of stone-faced detectives holding onto her arms. The photograph was of very poor quality, and Carpo realized that it had been snapped from a television screen. The source was credited to WIBN-TV.

Inside, the article softened its accusatory tone. It reported on the murder investigation of Frank Werner and discussed Karen's relationship with him. It also detailed Karen's responsibilities at the Met, which to Carpo's surprise included verifying the authenticity of some of Werner's most important works, including The Cleopatra Bust. A quote from the director of the museum, Dr. H. P. Grasso, acknowledged her verification work. He also expressed confidence that her name would be cleared in any investigation. A sidebar to the article raised the possibility of a conflict of interest if Karen Blackwell had been romantically involved with Werner while she was verifying his art. But nowhere did the story suggest a connection to his death, as the libelous headline had hinted.

Carpo finished the article and reached for *The Daily News*. The same story was buried on page eight. It had no photographs but contained the same information on Karen's verification duties. When he was done, he tossed the newspapers back on the Assignment Desk. Major Sisco was standing inside his cubicle. Before he could say a word, Sisco put a finger over his lips and waved him into the tiny office.

"Let's air this out here, away from all these ears," Sisco said immediately.

"The reports in those papers came from us. This whole angle came from us, didn't it?" Carpo said, his voice rising higher and higher. He didn't care if everyone in the newsroom heard them. "It's a load of bullshit, Sisco. I'm ashamed we did that to her. The only crime that woman committed was to cry at a wake."

"I know, I know," Sisco said, both palms up in the air, waving at him to calm down. "Last night I had Ed check out your tip. We couldn't really find much besides the fact that she'd done some verification work for Frank Werner. Ed just did a basic report. He didn't mention names or anything."

"I saw that. It was fine. Why'd we go back to him at the Met with this other stuff?"

"After the report ran, the desk got an anonymous tip that the woman was being questioned up there by police. It was still early in the newscast, so Lipton made Ed break down and move up to the museum. The story hit in the fourth section."

"Why didn't you stop them, Sisco? We never report anonymous tips. It's wrong."

"I tried to talk them out of it, but it was like a bloodlust last night. We'd been working so hard to get an angle, when it looked like we had something new we went with it."

A loud knock came from the side of the cubicle. Both men turned to see Bill Lipton standing in the opening.

"Michael," he announced briskly. "Nice work last night on the Blackwell angle."

Carpo could barely suppress the sarcastic laugh rising in his throat. "That happens to be what we're talking about, Bill. What was the deal with the second half of Ed's report?"

"What about it?" Lipton's voice rose to Carpo's challenge. "I found out from a good source that the girl was being interviewed by detectives. We already found out from you that she was involved with Werner, so I had Ed move up there for a little drama. We got there just in time to tape her being walked to a squad car."

"That's just it, Bill. She was walking to a squad car, but it wasn't a perp walk. We made it look like charges were being brought against her."

"Maybe there will be charges," Lipton yelled. "My source says she's a suspect."

"With all due respect, an anonymous tip is not a source."

"Who cares if it's anonymous or not? The desk checked out what the caller told us. It was all true."

Carpo took a deep breath and held it. The conversation was spinning out of control; he feared he would say something he might regret. "I just think it was a bad move," he said.

"You do, huh? Well, maybe that's why you fucked up on the Conductor Martinez story. Remember that one, Carpo? Sometimes you've got to push the envelope a bit, take some chances, make people feel a little uneasy. We're not in this business to make friends."

Carpo squeezed his hands into tight fists, wishing he could bury them in Lipton's throat. He glanced at Sisco for support, but the Metro Editor was preoccupied with scraping a paint chip off his desk. "I'm not going to argue about it anymore, Bill," he said. "I just think we could have shown a little more restraint."

"Listen up kid, it's time for you to grow up. You're a big boy now with a big job. If you plan on staying around here, you'd better stop asking so many questions and start finding some answers."

Before Carpo could respond, Lipton stormed out of the cubicle and into his office. The slam of his door rattled the thin walls of the cubicle.

"What an asshole," Sisco whispered a few seconds later.

"Yeah, and thanks for your support, too."

"What did you want me to do, Carp? Start another argument? Ease up, man, we're not all against you here. Why don't you go grab the aircheck and see it for yourself. It's not the end of the world."

Carpo walked back into the newsroom, fists still clenched, eyes shooting daggers at anyone who dared look in his direction. He crossed to the aircheck shelf, where copies of the station's nightly newscasts were stored, and took down the tape from the night before. At a screening machine, he fast forwarded the tape to Ed's report in the fourth section. It started with Maria Gomez reading the anchor lead-in, a "Breaking News" graphic flashing in a box over her shoulder.

"This just in to the Channel 8 newsroom: There's been a major development in the murder of Frank Werner, the art dealer whose body was discovered last week frozen into the ice of the Central Park Reservoir. We go live now to Ed Thomas, who is outside the Metropolitan Museum of Art. What's going on, Ed?"

The remote shot suddenly appeared in the small box where the "Breaking News" graphic had been. It showed Ed Thomas standing on the front steps of the museum. The box quickly expanded until Ed's head and shoulders filled the entire screen. A split-second later he started speaking, his voice breathless and two octaves lower than normal.

"Maria, tonight police are questioning a new figure in the murder of Frank Werner, and it's taking place right here on the Upper East Side, at the Metropolitan Museum of Art."

Ed's face dissolved into file footage of Frank Werner appearing at a museum fundraiser last summer.

"At the top of our broadcast tonight, I mentioned that police were investigating several people linked in business and social circles with the high society art dealer. Just minutes ago, I learned the identity of one of the people at the center of their investigation. She is twenty-eight-year-old Karen Blackwell of Manhattan. Right now she is being questioned by detectives about her ties to Frank Werner."

The file footage of Werner cut to a blurry shot of Karen walking with the two detectives toward a squad car. Carpo's stomach turned when he saw her recoil at the lights of the video camera. She tried to raise her hands to cover her face, but the detectives held onto her arms. She bent forward so that her hair fell forward, covering her face. It looked exactly like the video of every murderer and felon the cops had ever perp-walked. The video went into a slow dissolve of file tape showing homicide detectives wheeling a stretcher with Frank Werner's body off the Central Park Reservoir.

"Frank Werner's body was discovered last Wednesday, entombed in the ice of the Central Park Reservoir, a macabre scream still present on his face. Police are reluctant to comment on the involvement of Karen Blackwell in the crime. She is employed here, at the Metropolitan Museum of Art, as an associate curator in the Department of Greek and Roman Art. That, consequently, is the same department which lists Frank Werner as a standing member and consultant. Sources tell me the two were close friends, perhaps romantically involved at the time of his murder. And while detectives will neither confirm nor deny that the woman is a suspect in the case, they did tell me their investigation is proceeding. That's the latest here on Manhattan's Upper East Side. I'm Ed Thomas. Let's go back to Maria in the studio."

The screen dissolved to the bright lights of the studio, and the anchor started reading the next news story. Carpo turned down the volume on the monitor.

"Geez, I didn't realize the lighting was so bad last night," Ed Thomas said from behind him. Carpo whirled around, unaware the reporter had been watching the tape from over his shoulder. "I looked pretty awful out there," Ed added.

"It's not a beauty contest."

"What? What did you say, Carpo?" the reporter sputtered.

"Like you have any idea what I go through out there every night."

"Ed, I'm sure you go through hell out there, absolute hell."

"What's the matter? Sore that I scooped you on the latest angle?"

"Actually, Ed, I'm ashamed. Ashamed that you reported something as sensationalist as that piece of crap. What's next for you? 'Hard Copy'?" Carpo pressed the "eject" button on the screening machine and waited for the tape to pop out. He walked it back to the aircheck shelf, Ed following right behind.

"Believe it or not, I wouldn't mind a job at 'Hard Copy,' " Ed said. "At least there'd be a lot more viewers, a little national exposure."

Carpo slid the tape back into its slot on the shelf. "So then it is a beauty contest to you."

The reporter grabbed him hard on the shoulder and spun him around. Carpo looked at the hand with surprise, his pulse picking up speed. He locked his hand onto Ed's wrist and twisted it off his shoulder. "Don't touch me," he threatened. "It might make me do something we'll both regret."

"Listen up, green hand," the reporter fired back. "I don't care if you respect me or not because the people respect me. Got that? And if it means stepping on a few toes along the way, then I'll put my foot down on anyone. Even on you."

Carpo felt a veil of red dropping over his eyes. He squeezed his fists so tightly he could feel his nails bite into his palms. It was going to be bad, real bad, but he felt powerless to stop it.

It was the soothing voice of Major Sisco that cut through his murderous haze. "Don't do it, Carpo. It's not worth it."

Sisco's long arms were between them, pulling Carpo back from the abyss. Carpo glanced around him, noticing that the newsroom had filled up with the evening staff, everyone intently watching the argument. Even Bill Lipton was watching from the door of his office, a curious smile tugging at his mouth. Carpo looked to his right hand and realized it was cocked back behind his ear as if he were about to let go with a roundhouse.

"Now shake hands and get back to work," Sisco ordered. "There's no use arguing about last night's stories when we've got work for tonight."

"I'm not shaking his hand," Ed stammered through clenched teeth. "This goddamn rookie insulted me."

"Relax, Ed. He's pissed and he has a right to be. Now shake his hand or I'll shuffle tonight's reporting line-up."

The threat worked. Carpo and Ed clasped hands and gave a quick shake. When it was over, Ed stormed out of the newsroom and into the smoking lounge.

As soon as the crowd started breaking up, Sisco turned to Carpo. "What's wrong with you?" he growled. "Are you going to pick a fight every time you don't like something in the newsroom?"

"I didn't pick the fight. He walked up to me at the screening machine and it went from there."

"I've never seen you like this. You're like a goddamn time bomb. Maybe you need some time off."

"No way," Carpo said, jaw set as hard as concrete. "That's what caused the problems last night. I'm the only one here who understands the story, especially now that you all dragged Karen into it."

"Karen? Do you mean Karen Blackwell?" Sisco's eyes narrowed, a funny look coming over his face. "You holding something back on me, Carp'?"

Carpo kept his face as noncommittal as possible. "No," he said.

"That's funny 'cause you seem to get pretty antsy every time that woman's name comes up. You ever met her before?"

"We already went through this."

Sisco glanced at the clock on the wall. "I've got to start the meeting, but we'll take this up later, you hear? Now, are you going to be calm enough to work tonight or not?"

"I'm fine."

Carpo turned and strode across the newsroom, cheeks still flushed with anger. He sat at his desk and flipped open his black book, then hammered out the main number for the Metropolitan Museum of Art. There was plenty of damage control to do if he expected to ever speak to Karen again.

After two rings, a recording came on and said the museum was closed on Mondays. Carpo slammed down the phone as he cursed under his breath.

Damage control would have to wait for another day.

# Chapter 11

At 8:30 the next morning, the phone started ringing in Carpo's apartment. Every time the answering machine picked up, the caller would hang up and then call right back a few seconds later. Carpo jumped from his bed, convinced that someone had either died or was about to. He ran into the living room and snapped up the phone. No sooner did he say "Hello" into the receiver when the shouting started. It was Major Sisco.

"How could you do this to us? How?" Sisco demanded of him. The line was quiet for a second, then his voice returned, this time softer and almost pained. "How could you have done this to *me*, Carpo?"

Carpo squeezed his eyes shut, preparing himself for what was sure to be a shock. "I don't know what you're talking about, Sisco."

"Why didn't you tell me the truth? About you and the girl? I could have prevented all of this."

His head slumped into his hands. "Because it was none of your business," he said. "Not yours or anyone else's. It's been over for six years. It shouldn't have made a difference."

"Oh god, you don't even know what I'm talking about, do you? Have you seen today's *Post* yet?"

"No, I just woke up."

"You're on the cover of it Carp', a whole fucking exclusive report on you, Karen Blackwell, and Frank Werner. You're in a bind man, a real fucking bind."

"What does it say?"

"By the time I explain it, you might as well read it for yourself. But go do it fast because Lipton's hollering for your head. He's on his way into the station right now and wants a conference call with you. You've got maybe fifteen minutes, tops. I suggest you read the story and call me right back so we can think of a defense."

"I'll call your cubicle in ten," he said, already mapping out in his mind where his clothes were.

He threw on a pair of jeans, a sweatshirt and some running shoes. The fear gripped him so tightly, he felt like he was about to choke. He didn't even grab his coat; his body was so numb it would feel impervious to the cold.

He ran across 12th Street and down half a block to the newsstand. He grabbed *The New York Post* and carried it inside to pay for it, already seeing how much trouble he was in.

The front page roared: "Fatal Dis-traction—TV Newsman Linked to Murder Investigation." Worse still, his grinning face was on the cover. Somehow, *The Post* had obtained a copy of his press pass photo. It was placed next to smaller photos of Frank Werner and the blurry photo of Karen being led away from the Metropolitan by detectives.

Carpo flipped the paper upside down on the counter and paid for it, lowering his head in case the man at the register recognized him. He also bought a large black coffee and a pack of Camel Lights.

Back at his apartment, he spread the paper on his living room floor and scanned through the story, his mind racing to come up with a defense for when Bill Lipton called.

The most damaging allegation in the article was the revelation of his secret meeting with the medical examiner, Dr. Susan Parkes. Somehow the paper had found out about the meeting. It reported on the illegal nature of such a meeting and the possible repercussions within the medical examiner's office. There was also the question of whether the M.E.'s evidence would be considered tainted in a court of law if the police ever captured Frank Werner's murderer. The M.E.'s press officer, Dan Golden, was quoted in the article as saying his office was considering a lawsuit against WIBN-TV for conducting an illegal interview.

Even though the Dr. Parkes angle looked bad for Channel 8, the worst part for Carpo was the description of his former relationship with Karen. The article revealed several details about their relationship—that they had met at Georgetown and dated for four years—and even hinted at the circumstances involving their break-up. The details were so intimate and on the mark that Carpo figured *The Post* must have interviewed Karen about him. Maybe it was her way of getting even after Channel 8's report on Sunday night. The story made it sound like he was stalking his former girlfriend, using their past as leverage to investigate and humiliate her.

When he felt he had a grasp of the most serious allegations, Carpo lit a cigarette and called the station.

"Sisco here," the Metro Editor said, picking up the phone on the first ring.

"It's me."

"Make it quick. Lipton just flew in here fit to be tied. He wants you on the phone as soon as the desk can find your number. Do you have call waiting?"

"No."

"Good, it'll save us a few minutes. Now, how much is true?"

"Just about all of it," Carpo admitted, then added, "except for that fatal attraction stuff."

Sisco swore softly then took a sip of something at his desk. "So the stuff about your relationship is true? You two dated at George Washington University?"

"No, at Georgetown. But yeah, it's true."

"And is it true you've been following her around the city since Frank Werner's murder?"

"I visited her once at the Met, that was on Sunday, and I called her once last week, after I found out Werner was murdered. That's it."

"No wonder you were so upset about Ed's report. How about this stuff about harassing her? Is any of it true?"

"It's a pack of lies, Sisco. When I saw her Sunday, it was the first time in six years. I hadn't seen her or contacted her a single time before last week."

"Is it true Frank Werner used her name when he called you?"

"Yes. And I have no idea how *The Post* figured that out. I guess Karen told them."

"Damn," Sisco said. "I knew you were acting strange about this story."

"So what? It looks bad in the papers, but I haven't done anything wrong. I didn't hold back from you; I even told you to look into her relationship with Werner. I just didn't tell you that I used to date her. I sure as hell never went out of my way to nail her either."

"As soon as you learned of her involvement, you should have bowed out, Carpo. It looks bad. Right now the public thinks you sold her out; that's worse than doing something illegal. And as far as meeting the medical examiner, that *is* illegal."

"I have no idea how they found it out. The other stuff Karen may have told them, but my meeting with Dr. Parkes was totally secret. Only the doctor and I knew about it, and neither of us told anyone."

"Are you sure? Lipton found out about your phone calls over there from the press contact. Maybe the doctor told someone who decided to call *The Post*."

"I guess there's a chance, but she was so careful. She was absolutely paranoid about getting caught."

I bet she's going to lose her job."

"I feel terrible," Carpo groaned. "I just can't believe how much they know about me." Just then he remembered the message on the answering machine. Dr. Parkes had left a message on his machine Sunday night telling him to call her the next morning.

"I know how they did it," he shouted. "It was my answering machine. Somebody's been messing with my machine from an outside line. They've been punching in numbers that were recorded on my machine. They must have figured out the remote code and then picked up her message."

"What are you talking about?"

"I should have known there was a reason for those calls," he said, ignoring Sisco's question as he circled the room, the base of the phone dragging behind him. "Somebody's been keeping tabs on me from the very start. It's the only way *The Post* could have found all this stuff out."

"Gotta go, Carp'," Sisco whispered. "Lipton's at the desk."

"Do you think he's going to fire me?"

"I don't know. I really don't. Talk to you later."

Carpo hung up the phone and lit another cigarette. The answering machine had to be the way his meeting with Dr. Parkes had been discovered. All of it had to be connected; the person who had called as Frank Werner was probably the same one who had called his answering machine and been spotted watching his apartment. Then they had probably phoned it all in to *The Post*. On a hunch, he grabbed the newspaper and checked for the story's byline. It was written by Mitch McLaughlin, one of the most respected reporters on the paper's staff.

The ring of the telephone jolted him back to his most dire predicament. He took a last puff on his cigarette, crushed it out, then answered the telephone.

"Hello?" he asked evenly.

"What the fuck is going on, kid?" Lipton shouted into his ear, not even bothering to identify himself.

"I'm not sure, Bill. But someone is doing a fine job of destroying my reputation."

"Well you're doing a bang-up job of destroying the entire station's. This is a goddamn nightmare you've gotten us into, Carpo. The general manager called me at home this morning wondering why I can't keep control of my newsroom. And now I've got every TV, radio, and newspaper reporter in the city calling over here for a statement."

"I know, I know, I saw this morning's paper. But I think I know how *The Post* broke the story. I've just got to find out who's deliberately setting me up. It started with the very first phone call from Frank Werner."

"Save the story, Carp'. I don't care how the hell it happened. I care why the hell it happened."

"Okay."

"Don't bother coming in for morning meeting this afternoon. You're suspended, effective immediately. I want you in the lobby at four P.M. sharp for a meeting with the station executives."

"I'll be there," Carpo started to say but discovered he was speaking into a dead line.

He sat for a few seconds with the receiver in his hand staring off into space. He wondered what was happening. It felt like somebody out there had the reins pulled over his head tighter than a plow horse.

"McLaughlin," he muttered as he hit the button on the phone, bringing the line back to life. He thumbed through his address book until he hit "P," for *The New York Post.* He dialed the main number and asked the switchboard to transfer him to the reporter's desk.

Carpo had known McLaughlin for three years, after running into him at the scene of some stories he had field produced. They weren't friends, but somehow Carpo felt he should hold the columnist responsible for the story he had filed.

"McLaughlin," the man announced.

"Mitch? This is Michael Carpo calling from Channel 8 News."

"Hey, how're you doing, Carpo?" the man asked, his voice heavy with sarcasm.

"Not so good, considering the little number you did on me in your paper. I just want to ask you one thing: Who's feeding you all this crap?"

McLaughlin laughed over the line. "Jesus, first you sell your soul and now you expect me to sell mine. Sorry, but I don't give out my sources, Carp'. I figure you've done enough damage to the profession by ratting on that poor doctor."

"I didn't rat on her. And whoever told you that is a damn liar."

"I'll be the judge of that. Listen, while I've got you on the line, I'm working on a new tip from that same lying source who says you and Karen Blackwell broke up six years ago after you had a little problem keeping faithful. Care to comment?"

Carpo's palm closed so tightly around the phone that he nearly wrenched it out of the wall. Without answering he slammed down the receiver. He walked in tight circles around the living room, phone gripped in his fist, until he stubbed his pinkie toe on the leg of the coffee table. The pain cut through his thoughts. He plopped back on the floor and dialed the number for Dr. Parkes's office.

The phone rang fifteen times before a woman's breathless voice came on the line. "Good morning," she said.

"Dr. Parkes?" Carpo asked carefully.

"I'm sorry, Dr. Parkes has taken a leave of absence from the medical examiner's office. May I be of assistance?"

"Do you know any way I can get in touch with her?"

"If you give me your name and number, I can try and get a message to her."

Carpo thought for a moment about leaving his number but decided against it. It would be asking for more trouble if it got out that he was trying contact her. Besides, if she really wanted to talk with him—and he had a good hunch she didn't—she had his home phone number.

"No thanks," Carpo said before hanging up the phone.

He reached for the pack of cigarettes and drew another one out, its slender shape fitting neatly between his fingers. There was one more phone call he needed to make, and it was going to be the most difficult of all. He lit the cigarette and drew the smoke in, holding it until his lungs started to hurt. While he exhaled, he dialed the Metropolitan Museum of Art. Within a few seconds his call was plugged through to the Department of Greek and Roman Art.

"Is Karen Blackwell in, please?" he asked the receptionist.

"I'm sorry, Ms. Blackwell is not taking calls today," the woman stated.

Carpo figured she was running interference from all of the press calls. "This is a call I think she'll want to take," he said. "Tell her it's Michael Carpo."

The woman was obviously a faithful reader of *The New York Post.* "Oh!" she exclaimed, then added, "Wait just one moment."

The line clicked and Carpo was switched to the same classical recording he had heard the first time he'd tried to call Karen.

"Déjà vu," he said as he took another drag from the cigarette. He glanced at the clock in the kitchen. It was already 9:45. Five cigarettes in less than an hour. If the pressure kept up, he'd turn into a chain smoker.

The line clicked again and Karen was there. "What do you want, Michael?"

"Karen, we've got to talk. You've got to let me explain what the hell is going on."

"So the journalist gets a little bad press and suddenly he expects everyone to help him. Who was helping me two nights ago?"

"I understand how you feel but I can explain. At least most of it." Carpo heard the little waver in his voice grow stronger, threatening to turn into complete panic. Control yourself, he thought, stay under control. Somehow he had to keep her on the line and convince her to trust him again.

"We're both in a lot of trouble and it might get worse," he said. "A reporter over at *The Post* says he's working on a story about what caused us to break up. It sounds like he knows a hell of a lot about us. I'm wondering who told him."

"It wasn't me," she said. "That's not my style."

"Then we're being set up, and it's by someone who knows both of us very well. Listen to this, I talked with the medical examiner who did the autopsy on Frank Werner. She told me that the time of death was earlier than the time Frank called me."

"Is that the doctor you sold out to *The Post?*"

"Do you hear what I'm saying?" Carpo screamed into the phone. "The person who called me wasn't Frank Werner. It may very well have been his killer. That's the same person who used your name to get me interested in the case."

Her sarcastic tone evaporated. "So what can I do?"

"Meet me. As soon as possible. Before this person gets a chance to do more damage."

"I don't know, Michael. I'm in a lot of trouble here. There's a chance they're going to curtail some of my duties in the department."

"Karen, I just got suspended from my job. Later on today I have a meeting with the station's executives. There's a good chance they're going to fire me. If you don't help me clear this up, my career is finished."

She started to say something, then stopped. When her voice came back, the words were hesitant: "I'm not sure if I trust you."

"I've got no one else to turn to, Karen. It's pretty obvious that you're the common link with everything happening."

"But what do you want me to do?"

"I already told you," he said. "Meet me."

"I've got a busy day here. I can't just leave to go see you."

"Then I'll come to you."

Carpo heard some papers shuffling. "I guess I could see you here around two," she said. "But it can't be for long."

"That's fine. I have to be back at Channel 8 by four anyway.

That's when the executives are planning their roast for me."

"Then I'll see you here at two?" she asked, her tone rising at the end of the sentence like an agonizing question.

Or was it the sound of hopefulness? Carpo's heart leapt at the possibility of her being excited to see him, but he knew better than to get his hopes up. Their common past no longer meant anything in their present predicament. They needed each other now, not for intimacy but for survival.

"Be careful, Karen. Don't speak a word of this to anyone," he said. "I'll see you at the museum at two."

Carpo hung up the phone and reached for another cigarette.

# Chapter 12

Carpo approached the museum from 82nd Street. He crossed 5th Avenue, then cut through the double line of taxis that idled outside the museum, waiting for passengers.

It was starting to snow again, and the rush of small flakes created a near white-out, concealing the ends of the huge building. The flakes clung to his black hair, penetrating the top layers with a fine mist. He didn't mind the snow as much as the cold, and thankfully, the temperature was no longer wedged in the below zero range.

She was waiting in the Great Hall when he entered. They exchanged a stiff hello, and there was a brief, awkward moment when he leaned over to kiss her check but instead grabbed her extended palm for a quick handshake. She was wearing a black cashmere sweater and a charcoal gray skirt, a dark red scarf tied loosely around her neck. She handed him a small metal button and told him to fasten it to his collar. Then she grabbed him at the elbow and steered him toward the rear of the museum.

They passed a security point, where a uniformed guard eyed his metal button and nodded at Karen's laminated employee pass. They moved down a long hallway lined on both sides with glass display cases full of various decorative pieces.

Carpo followed closely behind Karen, his head darting from side to side as he tried to glimpse the objects they were passing. In all his years in New York he had visited the museum twice, both times on stories for Channel 8. He suddenly regretted that he had never returned during his free time to roam the endless galleries and quiet corridors, crammed full of humankind's finest treasures. They walked through part of the medieval collection, where dusty wood carvings of saints hung on the walls. They turned right and passed through the Hall of Armor, the tooled armor polished and poised as if ready to mount a steed and ride off to battle.

At the end of the gallery, Karen pushed through a metal door with an "Authorized Personnel Only" sign painted in the middle. It opened to a wide, artificially lit corridor that ended at a steep flight of stairs. They walked up them and passed through a second metal door, this one with a printed cardboard sign taped to it reading: "Department of Greek and Roman Art." Beyond was another long hallway doubling back over the way they had walked two flights below. The walls of the passage were lined with bookcases holding hundreds of reference books. Carpo strained to read the covers of the books, most were in French, German, and Italian. Every few feet the shelves ended at the doors of an office. At the last opening on the right, Karen unlocked the door and guided him into her office.

It was a small room, about ten feet square, cluttered with a wooden desk, leather couch, and several metal stands holding more reference books. In the spaces between the stands hung framed posters announcing various past major exhibitions held by the museum. Karen pulled the chair away from the desk and turned it to face the couch. She sat and motioned for Carpo to do the same on the couch.

It was nearly 2:30, the afternoon light filtering into the room from two large windows over the desk. From where Carpo sat, the windows provided a commanding view of Central Park—the wide expanse of trees and the white ice of the reservoir up front, the gray forms of buildings on the Upper West Side popping through in the back. The sight of the reservoir brought his mind to their predicament.

"Thanks for meeting me, Karen," Carpo said. "I really need your help. Someone is toying with me, Karen, toying with my life. I've got to put a stop to it before they destroy everything I've worked for."

"I'm in trouble, too, Michael, unless you've forgotten that nice little story your station did on me."

"I had nothing to do with it. I told the reporter to look into your connection with Frank Werner. I had no idea it was going to turn into that. But that's why we need to work together. It's no coincidence—from Frank's call to the newspaper stories to the tip Channel 8 got that the police were questioning you. This is all proceeding according to somebody's sick plan."

"What do you mean?" she asked, her face turning pale. "Do you think someone knew they could get you to investigate me?"

"Yes, I do. And I also think they knew that if I looked into you, I'd find out about your ties to Frank Werner and probably even do a story on you. I already told you it wasn't Frank who called me last week. The autopsy report shows he was dead by the time the call was made. I should have figured it out a long time ago, too. The day I found out Werner was murdered, I called over to Athena Gallery. I got a recording on the answering machine with his voice. It sounded nothing like the man who called me."

"But who would go through all of this trouble to hurt my reputation?"

"I don't know, but it must have something to do with your ties to Frank." Carpo avoided her eyes at the first mention of her relationship with the art dealer. Deep down, he was more than a little curious about their connection, but he sensed it would be a mistake to push for it. "It might help if you tell me about him," he said gently.

"I don't know if there's much to tell," she said. "Yes, I was seeing Frank, for about three years, but we were friends more than anything else. I mean, that's not to say we weren't inti-mate, but I knew him for so many years, I . . ." She stopped talking, face flush with embarrassment.

"Don't think, Karen, just tell me about it," he said. "All of it. How you met him, how you started dating. Everything."

She settled back into her chair, brushed a strand of hair from her forehead. "I met Frank about three and a half years ago. It was during a preview party at his auction house, Athena Galleries. Of course, I'd heard of him before that, seen him around the museum a few times, but I'd never met him. Then one day, out of the blue, I receive an invitation to this preview party.

"I went to the party and it was amazing. Here was this world famous art dealer who's suddenly interested in me. But he wasn't just interested in how I looked; he was interested in what I knew, about art." A hint of a smile appeared at the cor-ner of Karen's mouth, creating a tiny dimple in her cheek. "We talked a long time that night. He ignored everyone else at the party, and there were some real big names there. Right away people said he was hitting on me, but he wasn't. At least, he wasn't aggressive about it. We just talked about art, what it meant to us."

"When did you see him again?" Carpo asked.

"About a week later. You see, at the time, my career wasn't

going so great here at the museum. It wasn't bad, but this business is filled with wealthy old men and I was starting to wonder where I fit in. A few days after the party, the director of my department called me into his office. He said that Frank had personally requested me to do the verification work on one of his pieces. It was totally unheard of for someone at my level. I did the project and it was a success. Frank and I worked great together. He requested me for another project, and pretty soon I was verifying all of his pieces. It might not sound like much, but here was the greatest dealer in my field bringing me his top, top pieces and asking for my expertise. Suddenly, it's like the whole art world knows I do Frank Werner's statues. I started getting contracts from all over the country. That's when the museum started promoting me, too. From Curatorial Assistant to Associate Curator, in just two years time. It was flattering."

She looked straight into Carpo's eyes for a long moment. He noticed the hazel color of her pupils, as wide and reflective as the eyes of a cat. She reached over and touched his arm for a brief second, as if she were steadying him for what was to come next.

"So along came this older man—famous, wealthy, and very, very brilliant," she said carefully. "He swept me head over heels, completely off my feet. He became my best friend, my mentor, and, finally, my lover." She paused in her story, eyes probing Carpo's face for a reaction. He forced his eyes to remain locked on hers, fighting every impulse in his body to look away. "But it was more than that, Michael," she said, smiling. "It was his passion. He was the first person I ever met who was as passionate about art as I was."

"Don't tell me he used to fondle naked statues, too," Carpo joked, hoping to crack some of the tension.

Karen blushed and shook her head. "No, nothing like that. But he did know about those desires I have. He even encouraged it. I sometimes wonder if he didn't spy on me at the museum and if that was what made him invite me to his party."

"Why? Has anyone ever caught you?"

"You mean besides you?" She flashed an annoyed smile. "Once someone from the Conservation Department walked in on me. I don't think he saw anything, but it was a little awkward. Besides, it's not like I lose control and start panting over the statues. I just like to know how they feel."

"You said that you and Frank were broken up by the time of his murder," Carpo said. "What happened?"

She leaned forward in her chair and gathered her hair at the back of her head, curling it around her neck like a fur wrap. "I guess what first drew me to Frank is what eventually drove me away," she said. "Frank was a dealer, and that means, first and foremost, he was a salesman. I'm not saying that's bad—we tend to look down on it a bit here—but it's a necessary part of the business."

Karen's hands returned to her lap. She stared out the window, considering the leafless trees of the park, the wide white reservoir, the falling snow. He noticed the pale color of her skin and the way she held her arms tight against her body, as if she were cold.

"But Frank wasn't just selling art," she continued, voice as detached as her eyes, "he was selling stories. He knew his pieces like you or I know an old friend. He knew their history and significance. He made them sound exciting and dramatic, like each piece was vital to understanding the history of man. It was creative and entertaining and . . . and it was wrong."

"Why was it wrong?" Carpo said.

"Because every piece had a story, a story so incredible and

so fantastic, the truth never seemed to matter anymore." She
turned and locked her eyes back onto Carpo's. "It started really bothering me about six months ago. I was verifying Frank's
latest piece, a bust of Cleopatra the Seventh that's going up for
auction. Frank claimed the piece was the lost betrothal gift
from Mark Antony to Cleopatra. That's a nice little piece of his-
torical significance when you want to sell a statue, isn't it?"

"What's the bust like?"

"It's magnificent. As aesthetically perfect as any statue
I've worked on. But obviously, there was a lot of skepticism surrounding the story Frank was telling everybody. Not to mention that the bust already had a questionable provenance. Do
you know what that means?"

"I think so. It's the history of an art work all the way back
to its creation."

"That's right. It's an important tool we use to prove the
ownership and authenticity of a piece. The Cleopatra Bust has
no concrete, verifiable provenance. Frank claimed the Nazis
had stolen the piece from an Italian collector. It was then stolen
in turn by a Russian soldier after the defeat of Germany. The
soldier carried his treasure back to the Soviet Union and died
a few years later. Over the decades, the soldier's family kept
its possession of the bust a secret. Then two years ago, the soldier's son moved to the United States and approached Frank
about selling the piece."

"Sounds pretty fantastic," Carpo said. "How do you check
a story like that?"

"That's where the museum and my work come into play. I
wasn't too interested in all of the thefts in the twentieth century. My job was to verify the work as coming from the period
when it was supposedly carved, late Hellenistic period, around
30 B.C. That's when it's generally acknowledged that Antony

presented Cleopatra with the bust. If I verified that, the value of the piece would soar because it would mean that Frank's story was possible. And people really wanted to believe in it."

"Did you?"

"I didn't really have an opinion on it. It's important for me to approach each piece with an open mind, no matter how fantastic the story sounds or how concrete the provenance appears. I had my doubts, but my job isn't to say whether or not the story is true; it's only to determine the time period the piece comes from. Besides, Frank didn't care if I believed the story or not; he just wanted the museum's stamp of approval."

"Did he get it?"

"Yes and no," Karen said. "That's why we finally broke up."

Carpo noticed the strain on her face, eyebrows furled together, lower lip tense. "Karen, you don't have to do this now if you're not up to it," he offered.

"No, you should know everything," she said. "The bust was handed over to the Conservation Department first. They ran some scientific tests on it to see if it checked out."

"On stone? What can they test?"

"They do things like magnify the exterior of the stone to see how it's weathered. There are certain marks that appear under magnification, like root marks and burrows, that help judge the age of the stone. The bust passed right through the department. They said it appeared to come from the late Hellenistic period."

"So the piece was approved?"

"No. After the scientific tests, it was sent to me for the final verification. I didn't pass it. It didn't make sense to me."

"What do you mean?"

"It was wrong, stylistically inaccurate for the period. It

was out of character for a piece supposedly coming from the high Hellenistic era."

"What was wrong with it?"

"The hair was carved in a style that would never have appeared in that day. It had to be at least two hundred years younger, maybe even more."

Carpo shook his head in disbelief. "And no one else recognized this?"

"It's not something that just leaps out at you, like Cleopatra had a perm or something. There are very small nuances in the styling, the way the hair is tooled, the depth of the curls. You'd have to see it in person and be able to reference other works from the same period to understand me. And even with the inaccurate styling, it's not to say the piece is worthless. I already told you, it's one of the most artistically perfect pieces I've ever encountered. And usually a piece that's dated older would mean it's worth a lot more money."

Carpo nodded, understanding her point. "But that would mean the piece lost the Werner story," he said.

"Exactly, Michael. It no longer had the single aspect that set Frank's pieces apart from everyone else's—the amazing history."

"I can imagine what happened next."

"When I refused to approve the bust, Frank went berserk. It was as if all his interest in my art background and expertise suddenly meant nothing to him. He threatened me, said my approval meant nothing, that he would proceed without my signature."

"When was this?"

"About a month ago. I'll never forget it, Michael. It was terrible. We were arguing at his gallery, and Frank started getting physical with me, shoving me around and slapping me. I fell down, and he grabbed my neck so hard I thought he would break it. He said he hoped I was safe with my position at the museum because he would personally make sure I never verified another work in New York City. That was the last time I saw him. We never even spoke again. Two weeks later, you called me and told me he was dead." Karen looked up at Carpo. Her face was stained with muddy trails of mascara and tears. "I know there are a lot of people who think I had something to do with it. The cops have already been here twice. It's not true, Michael. I swear, it's not true."

Carpo leaned forward until his face was a few inches from hers. "I believe you, Karen," he said. "I really do. Let me just ask a few more questions and we'll stop. Where's The Cleopatra Bust now?"

"It's at Christie's," she said. "It goes on the block tomorrow afternoon."

Carpo recoiled with shock. "But you said it didn't pass the verification."

"Frank found another expert here who verified the work. It was enough to let the sale go on."

"But doesn't everyone know that you turned it down?"

"Some people know, but it doesn't really matter. It's a personal view. It's almost like getting a second medical opinion. If you can find someone else with a title to verify it, then the piece still has value."

"Well that's good then," Carpo said, settling back against the couch, face breaking into a wide smile.

"Why is that good?"

He put his hands gently on her face, using his thumbs to rub the stains from her cheeks. "Because I have a feeling that if we follow that bust, it's going to solve a lot of this mess we're in." He pulled a business card out of his wallet and scribbled his home phone number on it. He set the card on her desk, then stood and held his hand out, helping her from the chair. "Karen, I've got to get to the station. Why don't you call me tomorrow morning. Maybe we can go to the auction together."

She shook her head. "I wasn't planning on going."

"Why not?"

"I don't know, I think it might be a little awkward there, considering the circumstances."

"You think people will recognize you?"

"Of course they will, Michael. I dated him for three years."

He touched her shoulder. "Think about it, okay? I'm going to go, and it might be helpful if you came, too. You might recognize someone I wouldn't."

"All right, I'll think about it."

Carpo turned back to the couch and grabbed his overcoat, then swung it heavily over his shoulder. As he moved past the desk, something blue caught his eye through the window. He stopped and looked for it as he slid his arms into the coat. It appeared again, a solid piece of blue moving very slowly. He could barely follow it as it appeared and disappeared, threading among the thick layer of trees. It wasn't until the blue spot hit an open area that he realized what it was.

It was a small blue police cart circling the jogger's track around the Central Park Reservoir. He watched it roll along as he buttoned up his coat, something bothering him about what he was seeing. It was the view of the park provided by the window—a bird's eye vista of the north end of the reservoir. He racked his brain to remember where he had seen it before.

When Carpo remembered, it took every muscle in his face to keep looking calm as he followed Karen out of the office.

He had seen that section of the park in a drawing in *The New York Post* on the day he had discovered Frank Werner was murdered. It was a map that had shown the northern part of the reservoir. The windows in Karen's office afforded an unobstructed view of the area on the map where the black skull and crossbones had appeared.

It was the spot on the reservoir where Frank Werner's body had been discovered entombed in the ice.

# Chapter 13

Carpo left the museum and walked down 5th Avenue, following the outer sidewalk that marked the border of Central Park. The fresh snow was already melting on the cobblestone walk, creating tiny streams of water that trickled toward the gutters. When he spotted a bus coming down the avenue, he walked to a stop and put together enough odd change to make up the $1.50 fare. Tired and very confused, he looked forward to the long ride to midtown.

The bus halted before him, belching a thick black exhaust, which lingered heavily in the air. He paid his fare, took a transfer from the driver, and moved to an open seat in the back. He looked out the grimy window and watched as the Central Park landscape moved past.

Central Park. Everything since the Werner phone call seemed to draw him to this dark, mysterious place. He stared at the dense, wet trees and allowed his eyes to unfocus, his mind coming up with a dozen different reasons why Karen could not have been involved in the murder of Frank Werner.

First off, Carpo couldn't believe it was in her character. In the four years they had dated, she had never shown any tendency toward crime, much less murder. Secondly, even if she did have it in her to kill someone, what would her motivation have been? Was she angry about being spurned by her former lover? Did she feel physically threatened by him? Did she believe he was going to destroy her reputation in the art world? None of these motivations seemed plausible to him. On a more practical level, Karen was physically too small to pull off the murder alone. Despite what Dr. Parkes had told him about keeping an open mind about the crime, Carpo could not imagine her overpowering a man as large as Frank Werner, then dragging his body onto the ice and entombing it there.

But for every excuse he came up with, Carpo still could not counter the startling view from her office. Dr. Parkes had noted how much planning had gone into the crime: The body had been placed in a spot that was easily accessible from the jogging path; plus, it had occurred at a time that fell between the police patrols of the reservoir. The view from Karen's office would have solved both of these logistical problems.

But why had she invited him up there? If she was somehow involved, wouldn't she have realized he might recognize the view from her office? In fact, if she was guilty of something, why would she agree to meet him and answer his questions in the first place? Carpo held onto that thought, rolling it over in his mind and coveting it. He desperately wanted to believe in her innocence.

The bus roared down 5th Avenue, squeezing the smaller trucks and cars out of its lane. In the sixties, it passed the red brick buildings of the Central Park Zoo. Lines of shivering schoolchildren threaded from the sidewalk through the main entrance. In the fifties, there were the flashy stores of the shopping district, and then, in the forties, the brimming sidewalks of the Diamond District.

When the bus pulled outside the New York Public Library,

just below 42nd Street, Carpo exited from the rear door. The library courtyard was snowbound and deserted, a far cry from summertime when tourists crowded around the coffee bars on either side of the main steps. The only familiar sight in the bleak courtyard were the twin lions guarding the building's entrance, their gray stone manes dusted with snow.

Carpo walked to the opposite side of the street and used his transfer on the crosstown bus. He chose another seat near the back of the bus and waited until it pulled up outside the Chrysler Building. He lingered for a while at the newsstand in the lobby until his watch read ten of four, then he boarded the elevator and rode up to the forty-fifth floor.

When he stepped into the newsroom, Carpo felt like the bearer of the plague. People openly stared at him and whispered to each other, some even moved away from him, as if his bad luck might be contagious. He guessed they knew of his predicament, especially since rumors flew faster in the newsroom than the urgents that came over the A.P. wires.

Sisco spotted him from his cubicle and walked over. "Carpo, it's good to see you," he announced a little too eagerly.

"Thanks, Sisco. Thought maybe I was branded with the scarlet letter, the way everyone's staring at me."

"Not at all." Sisco wrapped a bony arm around Carpo's shoulder and whisked him into his cubicle.

"Let's cut the bullshit," Carpo said, taking a seat. "How much trouble am I in?"

"Put it this way, you ever heard of a meeting between a newsroom employee and the top four executives at the station?"

"Do you think they're going to can me?"

Sisco scratched the stubble on his chin. "I'm not sure, but

I don't think so. They've been holding meetings all morning to decide what to do with you. They even asked what I thought they should do."

"What did you say?"

"I said they should fire your sorry ass." Sisco broke into a raspy chuckle.

"I'm glad one of us finds this amusing."

"Aw, come on, Carp'. If you go in there looking all defeated, they will fire you. You didn't really do anything out of the ordinary for this place, you just got caught."

"What should I tell them?"

"The truth, that's for damn sure. Tell them everything you know about the phone call, the woman, even the medical examiner. You don't want to get caught in any more lies."

"None of the other stuff was lies either; it just wasn't anybody's business."

The phone on Sisco's desk rang and he picked it up. After a few short words, he hung it up and turned to Carpo. "They're waiting for you in the conference room."

Carpo got up from the chair and stretched his legs. Sisco stood with him and grabbed his hand, gripping it tightly in his huge palm.

"Good luck, Michael," he said. "I really mean it."

Carpo did a double-take when he realized the man had used his first name. It was the first time he had ever heard him use it. "Christ, Sisco, you sound like I'm being sent to the electric chair."

He left the newsroom, cut through the glass reception area, and walked past the bank of elevators to the far side of the building. The section held the station's executive offices and conference rooms, an area Carpo had visited just a few times in his career. The walls were decorated with glossy promotional photos of the station's most popular sitcom reruns: "Full House," "Cheers," and "Seinfeld." The first two conference rooms Carpo passed were empty. The third held the top four executives of WIBN-TV.

The station's general manager, Martin Pinkney, was seated at the head of the table, his back to the door. Pinkney was a short, handsome man, widely considered to be one of the top television executives in the business. At the age of forty-three he had taken over WIBN, raising it from the city's number three to number one independent station within four short years. To his right sat Kate Brimley, nicknamed the "Ice Princess" by the newsroom employees. As another young, successful executive, she ruled Channel 8's Public Affairs Department with an iron fist. She had once fired a guard because he'd left his post at the front desk to get a drink of water from a fountain ten feet down the hall. On the left side of Pinkney sat Felix Arroyo, WIBN's news director. Arroyo was the only minority in an executive position at any television station in the city. His handsome face was used regularly in Channel 8's public relations campaign. Arroyo had reached his position after serving fifteen years as executive producer of the evening news. Despite his prominence on bus and subway billboards, he was about as hands-off an administrator as there existed in the business. Next to him sat Bill Lipton, staring at his watch in a perturbed way.

Carpo took a seat in the only vacant chair in the room. It was placed at the far end of the table, the four executives facing him like a firing squad. Reinforcing that perception was the small black tape recorder placed conspicuously between them in the center of the table.

As soon as Carpo was settled, Lipton stood and addressed the room. "This meeting was called at the request of Martin

Pinkney and Kate Brimley. It is in regard to certain activities many of us consider inappropriate for an employee of the Channel 8 News team." Lipton sat and shuffled his papers until he found a yellow legal pad. He pulled a ballpoint pen from the breast pocket of his jacket, uncapped it, and sat at the ready.

Carpo watched Lipton's preparations, then stared at the rest of the executives. They sat in a protective horseshoe, all of them staring intently across the table as if he were some newly discovered creature plucked straight from the wilderness. After a minute of silence, Carpo cleared his throat. "Is there something I'm supposed to say?" he offered.

The sound of his voice chipped away the final piece of civility that remained in the room. All four executives began speaking at once, some shouting orders, others posing questions, and Lipton repeatedly demanding, "We want the truth! We want the truth!"

After several seconds, they began to quiet down according to seniority, until Martin Pinkney was the only one talking: ". . . of this irresponsible behavior, our newsroom has become the laughing stock of the city. How do you respond to that?"

Carpo shook his head from side to side. "I'm sorry, Mr. Pinkney, I couldn't hear what you were saying."

"That's exactly the attitude I'm talking about, Marty," Lipton yelled, the tip of his pen stabbing the legal pad. "This kid is always being obstinate toward authority."

"Obstinate?" Carpo asked. "I was being serious. I couldn't hear what Mr. Pinkney asked me."

"Then let me repeat it for you, Mr. Carpo, and I do suggest that you listen," Kate Brimley said, her words mouthed precisely, as if she were reprimanding a naughty child. "How do you defend your actions regarding the murder investigation of

Frank Werner? Can you give us one, single reason why your employment here should not be terminated?"

"Actually, I can give you several reasons why I shouldn't be fired," Carpo said. "But maybe the best way to do it, is to just explain what's been going on."

"Then why don't you do that, Mr. Carpo," Brimley said icily.

Carpo cleared his throat again as he chose his words. He realized what he was about to say would determine his future at Channel 8. "About a week ago, I received a phone call in the newsroom from someone who claimed to be Frank Werner. The person said he needed to meet me; he said he was in a lot of trouble. I know we're not supposed to take these calls, but the man used the name of a woman I used to date while I was a college student."

"Is this the woman from the Metropolitan Museum of Art?" Brimley asked.

"Yes, it was—Karen Blackwell. This man said he knew her, and he told me that she had said I would help him. I agreed to meet him the next day for lunch at the Lantern Diner. He never showed up. A short while later, I discovered that Frank Werner had been murdered. I went straight to Major Sisco and told him about the call and the meeting."

"Is that when you asked to be placed on the story?" Arroyo asked.

Carpo nodded. "Yes sir. It seemed that I might have an inside track on the story, so I asked Sisco to put me on it as Ed Thomas's assistant."

"Did you volunteer because of the woman?" Pinkney asked.

"It wasn't the only reason," Carpo said. "I think I might have volunteered if she wasn't involved, but I was definitely curious about her."

"And is this when you started harassing her?" Brimley asked.

"No, ma'am, I never harassed her. Over the next several days I tried to make contact with her, but she made it clear she wanted nothing to do with me. I did visit her at the Metropolitan, but I left when she made it clear she didn't want to talk to me. After I established a definite link between her and Frank Werner, I told Sisco that Ed Thomas should look into it. At no time was there a fatal attraction episode or anything like what *The Post* alluded to this morning."

Brimley tapped a bright red fingernail on the table, creating sharp little clicks. "It sounds like harassment to me. I mean, you didn't report her until you were rebuffed."

"Ms. Brimley, I know it looks bad, but I didn't harass her. I went to Major Sisco with the lead because I was afraid it would look like I was holding back on the story because I once dated her."

"Before, you said the man who called you *claimed* to be Frank Werner," Martin Pinkney said. "Why did you say that?"

"As you probably know from the story in *The Post,* I had a meeting with the medical examiner who performed the autopsy on Frank Werner. It was supposed to have been a confidential, off-the-record interview for my own personal use, but it somehow got leaked to Mitch McLaughlin at *The Post.* This M.E. told me that Frank Werner was dead at the time the phone call was made last week. That means the person who called me was not Frank Werner; he was impersonating him."

Carpo waited for the next question, but none came. He stared among the executives' faces, looking for some sign of encouragement, but he was unable to gauge their thoughts.

"There's more, too," he said. "I now believe that the person who called last week is the same person who leaked my meeting with Dr. Parkes to the press *and* leaked the second half of Ed Thomas's exclusive story on Karen Blackwell Sunday night."

"Of all the cockamamie nonsense," Lipton yelled. "That phone call was checked out by our desk. It provided us with reliable information."

"I don't mean to contradict you, Bill," Carpo said, "but I was told in the newsroom that it was an anonymous tip."

"Anonymous or not, we checked it out and it was good information."

"I'm not going to argue about whether or not the tip was correct. What I'm saying is that someone is controlling a lot of things in my life. My answering machine has been accessed, my apartment is being watched, my—"

"How do you know that?" Brimley interrupted.

"Know that my apartment is being watched?" Carpo asked. Brimley nodded. "Well, there's a prostitute who works on my street who keeps an eye out for strangers. A few nights ago, she told me a strange guy was hanging around outside my apartment."

A second after saying it, Carpo realized it had been a mistake to mention Candi. Brimley shook her head in disgust, eyes squeezed tight, as if he had just told her that he'd propositioned the woman.

"I think we've heard enough, Mr. Carpo," Pinkney announced sternly.

"But there's more, Mr. Pinkney. These events are all tied together. It's got to be the same person, or persons, who are responsible for all of these things. I believe, now, that the person who called me last week is either Frank Werner's murderer or somehow linked to him."

"As I just said, we have heard enough." Pinkney's voice was

lower, more threatening. "Over the past week, you have brought embarrassment and disgrace to your newsroom and the entire station. Your actions are not ones I would characterize as acceptable for a journalist. Instead of finding news, you're making it."

Pinkney looked around the table at his co-executives, turning the focus of his speech from Carpo to them. "Now, Major Sisco says he's done some solid work here—he worked on two Emmy-winning features and he won a Folio for us last year on the Long Island hurricane damage. But we mustn't forget this matter of the Conductor Martinez story, for which we almost suspended him two years ago. I, for one, do not believe Michael Carpo should be fired."

Carpo felt a rush of relief, thinking Pinkney was about to reinstate his job.

"However, I do recommend a full suspension of two weeks without pay and one year of probation, and I want his employment records to reflect such. Mr. Carpo, do you have any further questions?"

"No, sir," he mumbled.

"Then this matter is ended." Pinkney pushed his chair back from the table and stood. "Kate, if you'd please prepare a press statement for immediate release concerning the suspension."

The words registered slower with Carpo, almost as if he were hearing them at a different speed from everyone else. "Suspension," he whispered. Even though it could have been much worse, Carpo felt shocked.

Pinkney and Brimley huddled for a moment by the door to decide on the exact wording of the press release. Carpo stood shakily from his chair and brushed past them.

"Now, let's not make a big scene when we get back to the

newsroom," Lipton said from his side. "Just gather your things and get out."

Carpo nodded and continued walking, hoping to put some distance between him and the executive producer.

"I'm going to have to ask for your card key, Carpo," Lipton said. "You can get it back when you return."

He reached into his wallet and withdrew the plastic card that unlocked the doors at the station. He handed it to Lipton.

"And your press shield," Lipton added.

"It's at home," he lied. The credential was tucked safely in his other pocket. Without his press shield, he was powerless if he wanted to speak to an official, enter a crime scene, or just prove that he worked at Channel 8.

"Then drop it off in the lobby tomorrow morning. Otherwise, I'll have it reported as stolen."

"Okay."

They entered the newsroom together. Carpo felt his cheeks go hot when he came face to face with his co-workers.

"One more thing, Carpo," Lipton said, his voice loud enough for the entire room to hear. "You're off the Werner case. If I hear of you making so much as one phone call on the story, you're never coming back. Got it?"

"Okay," he said again.

He walked straight to his desk and sat down, burying his head in his hands. He exhaled, the stress making him feel nauseous. He began going through the drawers of his desk, checking for anything he might need over the next few weeks.

Sisco tapped him on the shoulder. "What happened?"

"Two week suspension, one year probation. And it all goes on my permanent employment record."

"Damn them, Carp'. I didn't think they'd do it."

"It could have been a lot worse. Pinkney brought up the Conductor Martinez thing. They really were thinking of firing me."

Sisco clucked his jaw angrily. "So what are you going to do?"

"I dunno, I guess lay low for the next two weeks. I'm off the Werner story. Lipton says I'm canned if I do any more work on it."

"Yeah, I heard the little announcement."

"Carpo, I thought you'd left already," a woman announced from behind him.

Carpo turned and found Mary Snow, a fellow newswriter, standing with a piece of paper in hand. "Don't worry, Mary. They'll be kicking me out of here soon enough."

"A call came through for you about fifteen minutes ago," she said. "Here, I took down the number. It's from some woman named Candi. She says it's an emergency."

"Thanks." Carpo grabbed the piece of paper and dialed the number on his phone. While the line connected, he motioned for Sisco to wait.

The phone rang for a long time before Candi's voice came on. "Hullo?"

Carpo could tell from the background noise that she was speaking from a street phone. "Candi? It's Michael Carpo."

"Carpo, oh thank god it's you," she shouted excitedly. "Get your ass down here, man. The guy's back, sure as I'm talking to you."

"What guy?"

"The one I told you about last week."

"You mean the guy who was watching my apartment?"

"It's him. I'm looking at him right now."

"I'm on my way, Candi. Don't let that son of a bitch out of sight." Carpo slammed down the phone.

"What's up?" Sisco asked.

Carpo scooped his briefcase off the desk and grabbed his jacket from the back of his chair. "The guy who's been screwing with my life is standing outside my apartment as we speak."

"But I thought you said you were off the Werner story?"

Carpo flashed him a hard look. "Who said anything about Frank Werner?"

# Chapter 14

When Carpo got down to 42nd Street, he stood on the corner of Lexington Avenue and watched as yellow cab after yellow cab passed him by, all occupied. He tried flagging down a few of them anyway, waving a twenty dollar bill in the air to entice a passenger to give up their ride, but every car seemed to carry a businessman totally unimpressed by the money. Finally, Carpo ran for the subway.

Grand Central Station was crowded and noisy, commuters rushing in every possible direction like the denizens of an ant farm searching for their respective tunnels home. Carpo wasted another ten minutes standing in line at the token booth before he caught a number 4 express train down to Union Square, six blocks north of his street. When he emerged from underground, darkness had fallen. It was a mixed blessing; he hoped it would provide him with some measure of concealment, but it also meant that it had taken more than a half-hour to get downtown.

He mapped out in his head the phone booth from which Candi had called him. It was on the northeast corner of 12th Street and 2nd Avenue—the same block as Little Poland. He crossed over on 13th Street, hoping to talk to her before approaching the man outside his building. He pulled the lapel of his coat tightly against his face, as much to protect his face from the raw wind as to shield his identity. He spotted Candi as soon as he reached 2nd Avenue. She was standing at the phone booth, talking to someone on the telephone. Even from a block away, Carpo could see that she was shivering violently. The phone booth, open on its bottom half, and her skimpy clothing offered virtually no protection from the elements.

He slid into the booth next to hers and picked up the phone like he was making a call. Casually, he peered around the side of the booth. The street was too dark to see anything. After a few seconds, he reached over and tapped Candi on the shoulder. She looked at him with surprise, before a crooked smile appeared on her chattering mouth.

"Carpo, baby, how long've you been standing there?" she asked into her phone.

He winked at her and twisted away, speaking loud enough for her to hear him. "I just arrived. Is he still there?"

"No, he left about ten minutes ago. You sure took your sweet time getting down here."

"I'm sorry, I got caught in rush hour. How long are you going to be on the phone?"

"On this? Naw, there's no one on the other end. I'm just trying to look busy."

"But if he's not here, why are we pretending to talk on these stupid phones?" he said, hanging his up. "Let's go to Little Poland and warm up. You look like you could use a cup of coffee."

She hung up her phone, and they headed a few doors up the block to the diner. Once inside, Candi was overcome with a barrage of shivers. Carpo threw his coat over her shoulders and rubbed her back.

"Ooh, that's better," she chuckled through purple lips. "It's damn cold out there."

"You should have waited for me in here."

"I was too afraid he'd get away. I was trying to see if I could get a better look at him."

"Did you?"

"Not too good. Just his general size."

"And what's that?"

"Short. He's real short. And he's got some nice threads. Nice and warm. He had this big red coat and one of those furry hats that wrap around your ears. I could use one of them."

A waitress pointed them to a booth near the front door and took their order. Carpo asked for black coffee; Candi ordered a hot chocolate.

"Tell me how you spotted him this time," he said after they were alone again.

"It was like the last time. Me and the girls was working the street and I noticed this guy kind of slinking around the cars across from your building. I thought he was some regular John who was a little shy, so I walked over and asked if he was looking for a date. He was spooky, Carp'."

"In what way?"

"Like I said, he was small, but he was built, you know? Kind of like a man trapped inside a child's body."

The waitress stopped back at their booths and deposited the hot drinks and a basket of steaming corn bread on the table. "Compliments of Devon," she said when Carpo started to say they hadn't ordered it.

Candi reached for one of the buttery breads. "Boy, you sure get the royal treatment around here."

"Devon still thinks I'm going to send the station's restaurant reviewer down here. That's the last thing I'd do. Before you'd know it, there'd be limos out front and Devon would be taking reservations."

"I'm still waiting for you to do a story on us girls. You could call it 'The Ladies of 12th Street.' "

"It doesn't look like your business needs help either. Back to this guy. If you saw him again, do you think you could recognize him?"

"If he was wearing the same hat and coat, I could."

"What did he do after you asked if he was looking for a date?"

"He waved me off like this." She flapped a skinny hand up and down, as if she were shooing away a fly. "By that time I recognized him, so I kept after him. He turned away from me real fast so I couldn't see his face. Then he shouted at me to go away."

Carpo leaned forward, trying to recall the voice of the man who had called him. "What did his voice sound like? Did he have an accent?"

"I don't know, maybe a little one. The only thing I remember is that his voice was high."

"How high?"

"Mariah Carey high. No, even higher. Like, Michael Jackson high." Candi giggled.

"So you went and called me at the station. Then what?"

"I waited by that phone booth until you called back. He stood by the cars for a while, then he went and peeked in the door of your building. After a while, he took off up the street."

"Shit," Carpo muttered into his coffee.

"I'm sorry, Carp'. I screwed up, didn't I?"

He looked up from his mug, surprised to see a hurt look on

her face. He quickly shook his head. "No, Candi, you did exactly what you were supposed to." He reached into his shirt pocket and pulled out the twenty dollar bill that he had used to try and flag down a cab. He pressed it into her palm. "Here, I want you to take this for your time."

She unrolled the bill slowly, her face cracking a wide smile when she recognized Andrew Jackson's face on the front.

"You don't have to do this, Carpo," she said, eyes sparkling as brightly as if he had handed her a five carat diamond.

"And you didn't have to call me or stand out in that cold for so long. I wish I had more than that on me. You deserve it."

Candi folded the bill into a tight square and slipped it into a pocket on her leather vest. They sat quietly as they finished their drinks, neither rushing to head back outside. The wind was picking up strength on the street, gusts whistling sharply under the front door of the diner. In almost a gut response, Candi closed her eyes and permitted a small shiver.

"You're not planning on staying out there anymore tonight, are you?" Carpo asked.

"Girl's got to make a living."

"What do you say we walk up to the ATM on 14th Street. I'll get you another twenty so you can go home."

"Naw, you've been nice enough already."

He paid for their drinks and picked up his coat, helping Candi put on her jacket. He fingered the fabric of the jacket, a fake lightweight fur, and decided to offer help again.

"Come on, Candi, this coat's too light for this weather," he said more forcefully. "At least let me run up to my apartment and get you an old sweater."

Whether it was the draft sweeping under the front door or the remnants of the earlier chills, Candi squeezed her arms against her body and succumbed to one big shiver. Weakly, she opened her eyes and said: "Okey-dokey, Carp'. If it's no problem, I'll borrow a sweater."

He held the door for her and allowed her to hook her arm through his as they rushed back across 2nd Avenue. He could imagine what Kate Brimley would think if she could see them walking together now. When they reached his building, he unlocked the front door and held it open for her. He moved to the second door and unlocked it, too.

"You want to come inside?" he offered.

"Now, Carpy, if I didn't know better, I'd say you was hitting on me." She flashed him another wide smile. "But I'm a lady, so I'll stand right here in the vestibule and wait for you, thank you very much."

Carpo laughed heartily as he passed through the second door. He started up the stairs, two at a time, until he felt the familiar burn spread through his chest and thighs. The final two flights he tackled at a slow walk. Inside his apartment, he rummaged through a closet until he found a heavy old wool sweater. He left his apartment unlocked and bounded downstairs, three steps at a time, until he reached the first floor. At the door to the foyer, he stopped dead, amazed to see that Candi had disappeared.

"Well, I'll be," he muttered as he opened the door leading to the front entrance.

Candi was there, crouching on the floor, head ducked below the bottom-most window.

"What the hell are you doing, Candi?"

"Get down!" she hissed urgently. "It's him. Right across the street. The guy leaning against the van."

He dropped to his knees beside her and peered through the

window. Sure enough, there was the outline of a man crouching between a tree and a white van on the opposite side of the street.

Anger exploded within him, blotting out any sense of fear or reason. "Wait here," he commanded, tossing the sweater at Candi.

He burst through the door and charged straight across the street. The man spotted him coming and stood upright, then bolted from his hiding place. Carpo sprinted down 12th Street after him, Candi's shouts echoing from behind: "That's him, Carp'! Get him! You get the son of a bitch!"

The man was built like a bull—short, thick, and exceptionally quick, even with the thin layer of ice spread over parts of the sidewalk. Carpo could see the man's thick arms pumping as they raced west down the block. Carpo's own shoes were leather-soled and provided little traction. At the corner, he slipped and fell hard to the concrete. He was up in an instant, gasping for breath, as he crossed 3rd Avenue against the light, dodging the oncoming traffic.

The man continued along 12th Street heading for the west side, about a half-block ahead. Carpo shifted from a sprint to a steady run, trying to make up for the slower pace by extending his stride and taking advantage of his longer legs. He bobbed in and out of ice patches, garbage bins and pedestrians. The pace felt good to him, his energy fueled by a searing anger.

When the man reached 5th Avenue, he hesitated for a second, then turned and headed downtown, aiming for the distant darkness of Washington Square Park. Carpo gritted his teeth and forced his pace back to a sprint. The cold air made each breath feel like a gut punch. He ignored the pain and concentrated on swinging his arms and legs as hard as they would go.

If he was going to catch the man, it would have to happen before they reached the park.

The gap closed quickly, twenty-five yards to fifteen to just ten yards ahead. He could see the bright red color of the man's jacket, even the blue lining of its collar. They were both moving much slower, the cold air taking its toll; Carpo had the sensation they were actually running in slow motion. The man's fur cap blew off his head, rolling on its edge along the sidewalk until it came to rest in the gutter.

The man reached the park just a few steps ahead of Carpo. He ran straight through the big arch at the entrance, then veered left onto a narrow pathway. Carpo saw the change of direction and stepped quickly to the left, hoping to use the angle to cut the man off. It was too sharp for his speed. His foot came down on an ice patch, knee buckled, then he crashed head first into a line of shrubs along the path. He struggled to his feet, slipping again before he got back on the path. He whirled in circles, searching the darkness for movement. The man seemed to have disappeared.

Carpo ran blindly forward along the path, street lamps lighting the way every ten yards or so. He slowed his pace and gave a cry of anguish, frustrated and exhausted, his breath coming now in convulsive gasps. By the time he reached the far end of the park, he was hyperventilating. He leaned against a car parked on the perimeter of the park as he strained to heat the gulps of icy air that were being forced into his lungs.

"Are you all right?" someone asked from his side.

He coughed up a little phlegm and wiped it off with the back of his hand. He looked up at a young woman standing back from him, arms wrapped across a bundle of textbooks. One of the books had a bright blue NYU sticker on the cover.

"I'm okay," he said.

She stared at him in the scared sort of way New Yorkers do when they feel like they're getting involved. "Look, I don't really know what's going on here, but if you were chasing that guy in the red jacket, he ducked into the library."

She pointed at a mammoth building on the southeast side of the park. It was the New York University Library; the huge structure, with its ugly red sandstone exterior, glowed like a lantern in the darkness.

"Thanks," he shouted as he half-jogged, half-stumbled across the street. He pushed through a revolving door into the library's entrance, a glass atrium that soared the entire height of the building. A row of turnstiles blocked his path to the library, each turnstile guarded by a uniformed guard in a tiny plastic booth. The guard in the last turnstile was standing in his booth, shouting into a telephone as he looked into the library. Carpo ran to the booth and rapped his knuckles on the plastic barrier until he got the guard's attention.

"Did a guy in a red jacket just run through here?"

"Yeah, he jumped my turnstile about a minute ago."

"Which way did he go?"

The guard pointed at a pair of double doors across the atrium. "Straight into the Main Reading Room."

Carpo put one hand on top of the turnstile, the other on the circle in the plastic barrier the guard was speaking through. In one clean movement, he vaulted the arm of the turnstile. The guard tried to stop him by reaching his hand through the small opening, but Carpo shrugged away from him.

"Hey! You're not allowed back there either!"

Carpo raced across the wide atrium, shoes clicking on the polished marble, and burst through the double doors, headlong into the silence of the Main Reading Room. As if on cue, dozens of young student faces snapped up in unison. He came to a stop and looked around the room, trying to spot the man. Within a few seconds, most of the students lost interest in him and looked back down at the books, magazines, and newspapers lying on their desks. Carpo moved to the first desk and tapped a large kid on the back. The guy looked about eighteen years old. He was wearing a ripped T-shirt with the NYU slogan printed on it like it was a beer can.

"Did a guy in a red jacket run through here about a minute ago?" Carpo demanded of him.

The kid's pale, pimply face shook back and forth, no.

Carpo moved to the next desk and asked the same question of another student, who also shook his head no. He moved onto the third, fourth, and fifth tables, all of the students giving him the same answer. No one had seen a man enter the room in a red jacket. His questions were starting to gain attention; several student heads bobbed back up to watch him.

"For Christ's sake," he shouted in frustration. "Did anyone see a short guy in a red jacket run through here?"

His question was met with a chorus of "ssh" noises. But a blonde girl sitting at the table closest to him said, "A short guy ran through here about a minute ago, but he wasn't wearing a red jacket."

A loud commotion came from the entrance to the room. Four guards rushed in, walkie-talkies blaring out instructions.

"Which way did he go?" Carpo asked the girl.

"There, into the stacks." She pointed to the left of the room, at the first in a long row of bookshelves.

Carpo sprinted for the stacks, hearing the guards shout behind him. He reached the opening to the stacks but he was too tired to make it any farther. The first guard to reach him was a bulky football-type, who tackled him low in the knees, knocking him headlong into the books. Carpo pushed the man off and made it to his knees before he was gang tackled by the other three guards. Within seconds, the bulky guard had his arms pinned behind his neck in a double nelson, pushing his nose deep into the all-weather carpet.

"Keep struggling and I'll snap your neck," the man shouted. To prove his threat, he cinched down on the back of Carpo's neck, until his chin was planted in his chestplate. The pain was unbearable. Carpo saw spots flash in his eyes; the ligaments in his neck crackled grotesquely.

"Okay, okay. Uncle. I give," he gasped through his contorted throat.

The guards lifted him off the ground like he was a rag doll. They carried him out of the room and across the atrium, tossing him up against the plastic booth he had run past. The guard was still inside, talking on his telephone. Someone grabbed Carpo by a handful of his hair and shoved his face against the booth.

"No, that's the second one," the guard in the booth said. "The first one was a lot shorter. And he was wearing a red jacket."

Carpo leaned his head back, trying to get the bulky guard to loosen up on his hold. "He's not wearing a red jacket anymore," Carpo said. "He must have discarded it somewhere between here and the Reading Room."

"How the hell do you know?" the bulky guard demanded, cinching down on his neck again.

"Would you lay off for a second?" Carpo shouted. "Reach into my back pocket, the left one, and check my ID. I work for Channel 8 News. I was covering a story in the neighborhood when I spotted that guy mugging an old lady in the park. I wasn't trying to break in here, I was just trying to catch him."

One of the guards felt through his pocket and pulled out the press pass. "Ease up on him, Jim," the guard told the man holding his neck. "He's telling the truth."

Bulky Jim reluctantly released his grip. The guards passed the ID among themselves, comparing Carpo's face to the picture on the shield.

"Who's the guy you were chasing?" one of them asked.

"How should I know? I told you, I saw him knock over an old lady in the park. The guy could be dangerous."

"Wait a second," Bulky Jim said suddenly. "How do we know this ain't a fake ID? I think we should call Channel 8 and make sure this guy really works there."

"Go right ahead," Carpo bluffed. "But I wouldn't all stand here while that mugger is still running loose in there."

The guards looked at each other until the one in the booth spoke up. "He's right, you guys had better look around. Give me that ID. I'll call this guy's station and make sure he's telling the truth."

One of the guards handed the press pass through the small window, then the group of them jogged back in the direction of the reading room.

"What's the number for your station?" the guard asked through the partition.

"221–2211," Carpo said, watching as the guard set the ID on top of the small desk in the booth. He looked toward the front door, a mere ten feet away, and thought of making a run for it. The only thing that kept him from bolting was his press pass. Either way, if Lipton caught wind of this, he was finished.

"Yes, hello, this is Stan Daniels from the Pinkerton Guard Agency. I'm calling to confirm that a . . . Michael Carpo is an employee of Channel 8 News."

Carpo felt a sinking feeling in his gut. He wondered what the chances were that the person at the Assignment Desk would just answer yes to the question then not tell anyone else in the newsroom about the call.

"No, sir," Stan continued, "I'm asking because he broke into the student library at New York University. He claims he was on a story in Washington Square Park when he witnessed a purse snatching. He rushed into the library and we had to make a stop on him."

Carpo put his hand over his eyes and massaged his temples. He was finished.

Stan nodded his head a few times, then said, "Okay, sir, I just need your name as a reference for any report I might have to fill out. Say that again? With an 's' or a 'c'? Okay. Thank you, Mr. Sisco." The guard looked up at Carpo and nodded. "Yes, he's right here. Hold on."

The guard passed the phone through the hole in the partition. "A Major Sisco would like to talk with you," he explained.

"Hello?" Carpo said sheepishly into the phone.

"Chasing purse snatchers into the NYU Library, are we now?" Sisco asked maliciously. Carpo managed a shaky laugh, despite the pain shooting through his neck. "What's next for you, little brother? You going to start mugging people, too?"

Carpo turned his back on the guard. "You know what's up, Sisc'," he whispered. "I chased that son of a bitch from my apartment all the way down here."

"Any luck?"

"I don't know. A bunch of guards are searching the building for him."

"May I make a little suggestion? If you're going to run around the city chasing people, stop flashing that press shield around. If Lipton finds out you're using it, he'll have your head."

"I know, I know."

"And try keeping a little lower profile. If any of those papers catches wind of this, you'll be back on page one."

"I promise, I'll be more careful."

"Now, why don't you put that nice guard back on the phone so I can confirm that you're the indentured servant of Channel 8 News."

Carpo handed the phone back through the partition. The guard talked to Sisco for another couple of seconds before he hung it up and tossed the press card back. Carpo shoved the card into his pocket as the four guards reappeared in the atrium. Bulky Jim was at the head of the pack, carrying a bright red jacket in one hand.

"No luck, huh?" Stan called from inside the booth.

"Nope," Jim said. "He left this in a trash bin around the corner. A student says he saw a guy slip out the fire exit in the alley."

"Did you check the pockets for anything?" Carpo asked.

"Not yet," Jim said. His face contorted into a mean frown. "Hey, Stan, is this guy kosher?"

"He's cool."

Jim patted around in the pockets of the jacket. All of them were empty. Carpo took a step closer, noticing that the label on the jacket said "Bogner." It was the label of a major ski apparel manufacturer—American, he thought, but not something he could check out easily.

"Check the inside pocket," he suggested, pointing to the inside breast pocket. "In there."

The guard reached inside and unzipped the small pocket.

"Here's something," Jim murmured, his hand pulling out a piece of white paper folded into quarters. He unfolded it and read it, a puzzled look weighing down his face.

"What the hell is this?" he asked, passing it on to the other guards. Carpo strained to get a look as they took turns reading its contents.

"Can I take a look?" he chirped from the back of the crowd.

Jim handed him the paper. Several strange words were printed on it in light, swirling script. Foreign words. The top two were *Dactylopius coccus*, with the word *opuntia* written underneath. At the bottom of the paper was a telephone number with an area code unfamiliar to Carpo: (505). Carpo copied the words on the back of one of his business cards before he handed the paper back to the guards.

"If it's okay with you guys, I'd like to head home," he announced.

The guards conferred for a moment before asking him to print his name and phone number on a blank sheet of paper.

"You think you could fill out a description on this guy if we needed it?" Stan asked.

"Nothing more than his height and the red jacket. He was wearing a fur cap, but it fell off while I was chasing him."

"Then I guess you can go," Stan said. "But I suggest you stay away from this library for a while. We're not going to take it too kindly if you come running through here again."

"Don't worry." Carpo rubbed his neck as he flashed a wink at Bulky Jim. "I'll keep my distance."

He walked out of the library and retraced his steps north toward his apartment. He took his time as he crossed the park and cut up 5th Avenue. His neck ached horribly. He concentrated on keeping it still, which made things difficult whenever he came to an intersection. His right knee felt sore, too, from either the spill he took on 12th Street or the one in the park. The image of the man running ahead of him played over and over in his mind. He gritted his teeth, wishing he had run faster, just a few steps faster, and caught the man.

As he trudged forward, he repeated the names they had found inside the man's jacket: *Dactylopius coccus* and *opuntia*. They were strange words, obviously foreign. Something about them reminded him of Latin words, perhaps medical or scientific terms.

On 10th Street, Carpo spotted the man's fur hat laying in the gutter. He walked over and picked it up, dusting off some of the snow it had picked up from rolling down the sidewalk. The fur was gray with silver ends. He was no expert, but he guessed it was made from the pelt of some type of fox or wolf. There were no labels inside, no indications of place of manufacture or even hat size. He pulled the hat over his forehead, noting that it was a perfect fit. Size ten and a half. The man he was chasing had a pretty large cranium for being so short, Carpo mused.

While he still had no better idea who the man was, he felt he was at least putting together a picture of him. He was someone who wore Bogner ski jackets and foreign-made fur caps. Expensive items. The kind of clothes a person buys when they have enough money, and enough time, to shop in boutiques, instead of department stores.

He tugged the hat off his head, amazed by how soft and warm the fur was. He rolled the hat into a ball and shoved it into the pocket of his jacket.

He turned onto 12th Street and broke into a grin when he spotted Candi standing outside his building, waiting for his return. His wool sweater hung all the way down to her knees, hiding the leather vest, faux-fur coat, and even her tight mini. He wet his lips and started whistling a little tune as he walked, despite the stiffness spreading through his joints.

Candi would be disappointed that he hadn't caught the man. But at least she would have a nice fur cap to keep her head warm for the rest of the winter.

# Chapter 15

Carpo woke up the next morning feeling as if his neck had been ripped clear off his shoulders. The pain was so great, he could barely roll out of bed and get to the medicine chest in the bathroom. He downed three ibuprofen before he slumped back to bed, staying there, in a state of motionless semiconsciousness, until the phone started ringing at eleven. Stiffly he moved from the bed to the living room, left hand massaging the back of his neck as his right scooped up the phone.

"Hello?" he said hoarsely.

"Good morning, Michael."

It was Karen. Her cheery voice brought a reluctant smile to his face. He lowered himself to the edge of the couch. "Hello," he said again.

"You sound terrible. What's the matter?"

"I had a bad night."

"What happened?"

"Where should I start? Channel 8 suspended me from work for the next two weeks. Then, I spotted that guy who was watching my apartment last week. I tried to catch him but he got away."

"I'm sorry about Channel 8," she said carefully, as if unsure of what to say. "What happened with the guy?"

"I chased him all the way down to Washington Square Park. I lost him when he ducked into the NYU Library. The guards there thought I was the bad guy, so they tossed me around a bit."

"Are you okay?"

"I'll be fine." He switched the phone to his other ear. "So . . . today's the big day. Are we going to the auction?"

"We are if you want a final look at The Cleopatra Bust."

"What time does it start?"

"The preview started an hour ago. The auction begins at four."

"Let's meet at three-thirty."

"It's going to be a mob over there, Michael. If you want a good look at it, I think we should meet at two."

"Two it is then."

"The auction house is Christie's. It's at Fifty-ninth and Park. I'll meet you inside the front door. And don't take offense, Michael, but it's a pretty ritzy crowd. You'd better wear a jacket and tie."

"Thanks," he grumbled.

"I'll see you then."

Suddenly he remembered the slip of paper the guards had found in the jacket last night. "Wait, don't hang up yet, Karen. I need to ask a question. Can you hang on?"

He put down the phone and ran into his bedroom, grabbing his pants off the floor. He removed his wallet from the front pocket and withdrew the business card on which he had jotted down the strange words.

"Do the words *Dactylopius coccus* or *opuntia* mean anything to you?" he asked, spelling both sets of words.

"No, I've never heard of them. Did you check the dictionary?"

"Yeah, I looked them up last night. Nothing under *dactylopius*, but a *dactyl* is a prefix for a finger or toe and a *coccus* describes a type of bacteria."

"What about the other one? *Opuntilla?*"

"No, *opuntia*. There was a definition for that. It's a type of cactus or prickly pear. It doesn't say where from."

"The *coccus* part sounds kind of familiar," Karen said. "I had a friend once who came down with something called *streptococcus*. I remember, it was a fairly serious illness."

"There was also a phone number, area code five-o-five. Do you know where that is?"

"No, but why don't you call the operator to find out?"

"That's what I'll have to do," he said. "Sorry to keep you on the phone."

"What are the words from, Michael?"

"They came off a piece of paper I found in the jacket of the man I was chasing last night. I thought maybe they were connected to Frank Werner."

There was a long pause from Karen's end. "They don't ring a bell with me. If you want, I can try asking around here to see if anyone knows what they mean."

"That might be helpful. I'll see you at two."

Carpo returned the phone to its cradle and leaned back against the couch, cushioning his neck between two pillows. He closed his eyes and thought about all of the places that ached on his body. His right knee was swollen and had two nasty purple and yellow bruises on either side of the knee cap. His shoulders, back, and chest hurt even when he sat motionless, the nagging reminder of Bulky Jim's effective wrestling hold. Even his voice had not escaped unscathed. It was scratchy and hoarse; he figured he could do a pretty decent imitation of Major Sisco.

He reached for the phone and dialed zero. When the operator came on, he asked where area code (505) was located. It was for New Mexico. He held the phone in his lap for a few seconds, came up with a quick little story, then dialed the full number from the piece of paper. The line clicked a few times before it started to ring. On the fifth ring, a woman with a Southern twang to her voice came on the line: "Hell-oh?"

"Hi, I found your number on a scrap of paper, and I'm trying to figure out who I'm calling."

"You're calling Insect Warehouse, sir."

"Insect Warehouse? What's that?"

"We're the largest wholesale dealer of quality insects in the southwest United States."

"You mean, you sell insects? The crawling ones?"

"Crawling, climbing, hopping, flying, swimming. That's correct, sir. We raise more than two-hundred and fifty different types of Insecta, as well as a few other types of arthropod, such as arachnids and myriapods."

Carpo scratched the stubble on his cheek. "You'll have to excuse my ignorance, but what do people want them for?"

"Oh, sir!" the woman exclaimed in a shocked voice. "There are literally thousands of uses for Insecta in our daily lives. Insects are one of god's most maligned and misunderstood creatures. Dozens of companies rely on our hatching services for many different and very crucial industrial products. Not to mention that we cater to the smaller insectariums and individual collectors as well."

Carpo smiled, enjoying the woman's sales pitch. "Well, maybe you can help me with something. Next to your phone number, there were several words I didn't understand. Maybe you know what they mean."

Carpo read the words to the woman, spelling each one out carefully. He could hear the click of keys from the woman's keyboard as she entered the information on a computer.

"No, I'm very sorry, sir, but my files show no listing for a *Dactylopius coccus,*" she said. "But you are in luck. My supervisor just walked in the office. He's one of the leading entomologists in his field. Let me put him on the phone; his name is Dr. Karl Tibbs."

The woman's voice was replaced by that of a man, who talked so quietly that Carpo had to strain to understand him. "This is Dr. Tibbs," the man said. "What can I do for you?"

"Dr. Tibbs, my name is Michael Carpo. I'm trying to find out what a *Dactylopius coccus* and an *opuntia* are."

"Ah, yes, *Dactylopius coccus,*" he said, the words rolling expertly off his tongue. "That would be the Latin name for the cochineal insect. It comes from the Dactylopiidae family, found here in the southwest U.S. and in Mexico. I'm not sure if you've ever seen the cochineal, but it's a scaly insect with a distinctive bright red color. Really beautiful, actually. The *opuntia,* I believe, refers to the *Opuntia coccinellifera.* It's a type of cactus that the cochineal feeds upon. If you'll give me a moment to look it up, I can provide some more details on the insect's derivation and breeding habits."

"No, that's okay," Carpo said. "I'm wondering if Insect Warehouse sells this insect."

The man chuckled a bit. "Cochineal used to be one of our most popular insects, especially the females, but industry has come up with some good, cheap artificial alternatives."

"What type of industry?"

"All kinds. Any that need a durable, dark red dye. You see, the bodies of the female cochineal are dried and pulverized, then the red powder is used as a coloring agent in all types of products."

"Can you name a few of them?"

"Oh, I think they use the powder in food dyes, stone and fabric dyes, even in cosmetics."

"That's very interesting," Carpo said, wondering how the insect fit in with the man watching his apartment. "There's one more thing I'd like to ask, Dr. Tibbs. I found this piece of paper with the Latin name for the insect and *opuntia* written on it, and I'm afraid someone is probably going to want it back. Does Insect Warehouse keep records of people who buy cochineal insects?"

"Let me put Mary Lou back on the line. She handles most of our mail orders."

Mary Lou's chirpy voice returned to the line and began to extol the various degrees and honors held by Dr. Tibbs. Carpo cut her off as politely as possible and asked her about finding a listing for cochineal insect orders.

"Dear, that would be quite an undertaking. The cochineal is still a popular breed. I just wouldn't know where to begin. Several dozen companies place orders for it each month."

"I think this guy might be an independent collector of it. Do you keep separate listings for people who aren't affiliated with a company?"

"Yes, sir, we do. However, I won't be able to help you with that. Insect Warehouse guarantees complete confidentiality to our customers."

"Confidentiality? For insect buyers?"

"That's correct, sir. You'd be shocked at how our society stigmatizes the insect collector. People can be so very ignorant and cruel."

"Then, may the good lord forgive me," Carpo mumbled just loud enough for Mary Lou to hear.

"What's that, sir?"

"Nothing. Well . . . it's just . . . I feel so sorry for the man who dropped this slip of paper. You should have seen him, carrying it all excited in the subway when it fell out of his hands just as the train doors shut. I held it up as he started moving out of the station and this horrible look came over his face, like I was waving his first born right there before his eyes." Carpo winced, wondering if he was laying it on a bit thick. "I so wanted to do a good deed today."

Mary Lou sounded genuinely moved by the story. "What a good Samaritan you are, sir. Maybe I could look through my computer, just to see what comes up under cochineal. Where are you calling from?"

"I'm in New York City."

"We don't characterize orders by city, only by state. But I can check for New York State. Would you mind holding for a couple of minutes?"

"Not at all, Mary Lou."

She was gone for fifteen minutes, long enough for him to start wondering if she had forgotten about him. There was no recording on the line, no way of knowing if they were even still connected. He was just thinking of hanging up the phone and calling her back when she returned to the line.

"Sir, I looked through the computer files and found ninety-six listings for cochineal insect orders in New York State last year."

"Ninety-six?" he said, a frown spreading over his face. "That sounds like a lot."

"That's right, sir. Most of those went to university and college science departments. A few were also mailed to some of the bigger companies in your state. However, for independent collectors, there were twelve listings."

"Terrific," he said, trying to stop the corners of his mouth from tugging into a smile.

"If you have a few minutes, I can read them to you."

"That would be great, Mary Lou. You've given me so much help today, I think you're the one who deserves the title of good Samaritan."

"Why thank you, sir. Thank you very much."

It took Carpo ten minutes to copy down the names and addresses for each person. As he did, he made little check marks next to the names that seemed most promising. He tried to do it according to his theory—that a well-dressed man was probably pretty well-off.

Two names came from New York City: one in Astoria, Queens, the other on East 57th Street in Manhattan. The Astoria address was a possibility, but Carpo was intrigued by the East 57th Street address. The area was known as Sutton Place, one of the most exclusive sections in the entire city.

Three other orders had been placed from Westchester, the region to the north of the city. Carpo had never visited the area—the towns listed were Scarsdale, Pelham, and Rye—but he knew parts of it had expensive homes for suburban commuters, as well as a few posh estates.

There were several listings around the state about which Carpo had no idea—big cities like Albany, Buffalo, and Syracuse and smaller ones like Cooperstown, Monticello, Binghamton, and Corona.

Twelve names in twelve different parts of New York State.

It seemed to Carpo a small step toward finding the identity of the man.

He didn't want to consider the chance that the man might live outside New York State, right over the border in Connecticut or New Jersey.

Or, worse still, the possibility that the man was an employee at one of those eighty-four other large corporations or universities Mary Lou had mentioned.

# Chapter 16

After a quick lunch at Little Poland, Carpo rode the 3rd Avenue bus to 59th Street, across from Bloomingdale's, then cut across two avenues to Park Avenue. He was dressed in the same combination of white shirt, dark suit, and dark knit tie he had worn to the Werner wake. Thankfully, Karen had not seen him there and would not recognize his clothes.

As he strode along the even pavement of Park Avenue, he could feel his black hair absorbing the mid-day sun. His winter coat was slung over his shoulder, the buttons on his suit jacket open. On both sides of the street, the gutters looked like miniature riverbeds, their rough concrete sides funneling streams of melted snow to the sewers. It was hard to imagine that a day earlier the temperature had been below freezing.

He arrived at Christie's a little before two. Several stretch limos were discharging passengers on the curb—from the corner of 59th down to Delmonico Hotel—and throngs of well-dressed men and women made their way through the entrance of the auction house. A glass case along the outer wall of the building contained a large banner that announced: "The Sale of The Cleopatra Bust." The case contained several large photos of the statue taken from different angles. Underneath, smaller italicized lettering called the work "*a testament to his-*

*tory's greatest love affair."* Carpo smirked when he noticed the wide black lettering at the far right of the advertisement: "Offered posthumously by Frank G. Werner." It seemed everyone was cashing in on the murder of the week.

Karen was waiting inside the front door. She looked intense and business-like, dressed in a black suit and white silk blouse, a luxurious red silk scarf knotted at her neck. Her hair was down, its shimmering brown color rivaling the glossy sheen of the scarf. He leaned over and placed a soft kiss on her cheek, a gesture that broke the tension between them and afforded him a whiff of her perfume. Its light fragrance, and the memories it resurrected, brought a momentary rush of emotion to him; he struggled to get past the polite greeting without appearing speechless. She curled her arm through his and led him up the front stairway toward the exhibition room.

"Are you limping, Michael?" she asked when she noticed him wince on one of the steps.

"It's okay. My knee's a little bruised from last night." He suddenly realized they had passed by the white-gloved attendant without so much as a nod. "Don't we need to buy tickets?"

"Auction previews are open to the public, Michael, and I have seats reserved for us in the bidding gallery." She flashed him a curious smile. "Is this your first auction?"

"My very first."

"Good. I think you'll enjoy it. Especially since the bidding should go very high."

On the second floor, she steered him straight into the heaviest part of the crowd, surging toward a dark room at the end of the landing. In the center of the room, raised above the heads of the onlookers, was The Cleopatra Bust. It sat atop an oiled mahogany pedestal, about seven feet off the ground, and was bathed in the glare of spotlights. They pressed into the crowd, moving slowly forward, watching as The Cleopatra Bust drew closer and closer, until they were standing at the foot of the pedestal.

His first impression of the bust was its proportion, scaled almost exactly to life size. He had expected it to be much larger, rivaling the size of the statue of Aphrodite he had seen Karen touching. But even with his untrained eye, Carpo could understand why the piece was garnering so much attention.

The bust was constructed, with simple curves and soft features, a composition that relayed both beauty and charisma. The marble held a reddish hue, a coloring that must have come from the centuries of dust and pollution which had eventually penetrated the porous stone. The hair was ornately tooled, each delicate strand revealed layer atop layer of precise curls. Beneath the hair was a wide forehead, a lazy curve that melted into the ridge of the eyebrows. Most stunning were Cleopatra's eyes, two almond-shaped slits that looked almost Asian. The eyes gave way to an exact nose and smooth, delicate cheeks. The lips appeared to close with a hint of pressure, forming a sensual crease, almost as if Cleopatra was pouting.

Carpo stood in front of the statue for several minutes, ignoring the pressure of the crowd at his back as he admired the details and expression of the face. It was a while before he realized that Karen was staring at him, eyes twinkling with amusement. He shrugged at her and shook his head, as if to say he couldn't help himself.

"She's beautiful, isn't she?" Karen said.

"Absolutely stunning. I never quite grasped what you meant about art moving you; now I think I understand. I have an urge to carry on a conversation with her."

"Would you like to hear a little about her background? It's a fascinating story."

"I'd love to."

She slipped her arm through his and scooted next to his body, close enough that he could feel her warmth and softness.

"The bust is a life-sized rendition of Cleopatra the Seventh, the legendary queen of Egypt. Everybody's heard of Cleopatra because she supposedly had a voracious sexual appetite. That's the only story that ever gets told about her, from the poetry of Shakespeare and Chaucer to that awful Liz Taylor movie. But the truth is, Cleopatra was a brilliant leader. She ruled as queen of Egypt for twenty-one years, transforming her country into a nation rivaled only by the enemy to the north, the Roman Empire."

"But I thought the bust was presented by Mark Antony," Carpo said. "Wasn't he a Roman?"

"That's what makes their relationship so incredible, that the leaders of two rival empires could actually fall in love. Mark Antony commissioned The Cleopatra Bust in the spring of 34 B.C. It was done to celebrate a military victory, the capture of King Artavasdes of the Armenian Empire. He presented it as a betrothal gift during a triumphal parade through the streets of Alexandria, where he crowned Cleopatra the 'Queen of Kings.' "

"That must have created the most powerful nation in the world."

"Not really. Antony was part of the Roman triumvirate. When word got back to Rome that he had thrown in his lot with Cleopatra, he was denounced as a traitor and Rome declared war on Egypt."

Carpo rolled his eyes. "Let me wager a tough guess here, Rome won."

Karen smiled and nodded. "Yup, they crushed them. The Roman navy burned the entire Egyptian navy in 31 B.C., at the Battle of Actium. It's still considered one of the greatest naval battles in history."

"Is that where Antony and Cleopatra died?"

"No, they actually escaped and retreated all the way back to Alexandria, where they survived for another year. The Roman legions didn't overtake Alexandria until 30 B.C. As they routed the city, Cleopatra was captured in her palace. Somehow word got out that she had been murdered, and in despair, Mark Antony stabbed himself. He was carried back to Cleopatra and died in her arms."

"What happened to Cleopatra?"

"She was placed under full-time guard in case she tried to commit suicide. Which she did after one of her attendants brought her a basket of fruit with a poisonous snake hidden in the bottom. She stuck her hand in the bottom of the basket and before the Roman guards knew it, Cleopatra was dead."

"That's true love, I guess." Carpo said. "What happened to The Cleopatra Bust?"

"This is where the story gets a little fuzzy. The bust was carried back to Rome and paraded through the streets in a triumphal ceremony. There's plenty of records of that. And we also know it was permanently displayed in the Temple of Saturn, a public statuary in the center of the Roman Forum. Legend holds that when the Barbarians overran Rome, they smashed the bust to pieces on the temple steps to symbolize the fall of the Roman Empire. Of course, that's what legend held until Frank got hold of it."

"How did his version go?"

"Pretty much the same until the Barbarians came along. He claimed the piece never was smashed on the temple steps; instead, it was carried away by the Barbarians and somehow protected through the centuries until the Nazis got hold of it."

Carpo shook his head. "It's still an incredible story. Frank must have embellished a lot on the relationship between Antony and Cleopatra."

"Are you kidding? That was ninety percent of his spiel. Frank was an amazing storyteller, especially with the parts about the love affair and suicides. He could make you feel like you had a front row seat right in Cleopatra's chamber when the snake bit her. I swear, the way he told it, you could picture Cleopatra wince when the fangs pierced her flesh."

Carpo nodded in the direction of the bust. "You said you rejected the piece because of the style of its hair. What's wrong with it?"

"It's difficult to explain—and, mind you, a lot of people think I'm dead wrong—but one of the ways we verify authenticity is by comparing styles. We look at what the styles were back then, in their sculptures, frescoes, or anything that reveals the fashion of the time, then we compare it to what the piece exhibits." Karen took a deep breath, checking to see if Carpo was still following. He nodded to show that he was. "Going by that, Cleopatra's hair is flawed in two very basic ways. First, she's missing her royal diadem, and that's a very serious omission if, as Frank claimed, Antony presented this bust as a betrothal gift. A diadem is the main feature that would have distinguished Cleopatra as a queen. And remember, at the ceremony, Antony had crowned her 'Queen of Kings.'"

"What does a diadem look like?"

"It was a flat, cloth band that was worn in the hair as ornament. It signified royal authority, much like a crown. In every picture we've found of Cleopatra, from other sculptures to cast coins, she is wearing one. Diadems were not prevalent until Cleopatra's reign, so its absence could mean the piece is actually older, which would normally increase its value."

"Yeah, I remember you telling me at the museum. In this case, it means the piece loses the Werner story."

"Exactly."

"What else is wrong? You said there were *two* inaccuracies."

"Keep in mind how detailed the hair is here in the front, all of those deep curls and intricate strands." She tugged him around to the back of the bust, nudging aside a few people in the process. She pointed at the curls of hair. "Now look back here. See how heavy the style looks in comparison? It looks more like a helmet of hair, compared with those realistic curls in the front. For a supposed High Hellenistic piece, it's completely wrong. It doesn't have as much realism as other works dated to 31 B.C."

"So she's having a bad hair day?"

Karen smiled and shook her head. "It would figure that even the Queen of Egypt couldn't get her hair right."

The time for the auction was approaching, so they joined the crush of people heading toward the bidding gallery in the back of the building. The room was filled with folding chairs, with a wide aisle up the middle to the podium. They took their seats on the left side of the room, about halfway down. The electricity in the gallery was almost tangible—excited whispers, creaking chairs, nervous laughter. Carpo soaked it all in, enjoying the suspense of witnessing a major event. Occasionally, a man or woman would enter the gallery and Karen would recite his or her name and relative position in the art world hierarchy. A few even recognized her, waving or giving a polite nod.

Carpo realized that Karen's appearance at the auction was

an important step toward regaining her respect in the art scene. While some undoubtedly considered her brazen for attending the auction, others saw her as the innocent victim of a media witch hunt. Carpo himself felt less self-conscious in public. After Tuesday's front page report and Wednesday's followup, his name had disappeared from the papers. He discovered that people either did not recognize him as the "fatal distraction journalist" or simply did not care.

If Cleopatra herself had appeared in the gallery, no more of a hush could have spread as when the bust was wheeled next to the auctioneer's podium. When it came to a halt, a smattering of applause broke out.

On either side of the stage, large boards displayed the bidding price, as well as the relative amounts in Japanese yen, British pounds, Italian lira, French francs, and German marks. Karen whispered to Carpo about the strategic positions of bidders within the room. Prominent buyers and purchasing agents were ceded the most favorable seats at the front of the room. The actual bidders were identified by the small wooden paddles they carried, each one containing a number. A paddle meant that a person was a registered bidder and had a bank account—checked over by Christie's—that could cover the price of a possible sale. Along both walls were facilities for telephone bids, where a spider web of fiber-optic cables relayed prices and bids to prospective buyers around the world.

The final late-comers were ushered to their seats before a tall man in a navy suit and red ascot tie took his position behind the podium. He tapped the microphone several times, then asked in a British accent whether everyone in the gallery could hear him clearly. Reassured that all could, he proceeded to lay out the rules for the bidding.

"On behalf of Christie's and the estate of Frank G. Werner,

I would like to welcome you to this historic auction of a High Hellenistic masterpiece, The Bust of Cleopatra the Seventh. My name is Peter Nathan, and I'll be conducting this afternoon's bidding."

He paused briefly to sip from a glass of water beneath the podium, then he removed a pair of half eyeglasses and perched them on the tip of his nose. "Without further hesitation, shall we begin this afternoon's bidding at twenty million dollars?"

Carpo expected the first bid to come slowly but a moment after it was announced a woman in a wide-brimmed hat in the front row raised her paddle into the air.

"Thank you, ma'am; I have twenty million here. Do I hear twenty point five million? Twenty point five, here," the auctioneer continued, pointing at a bald man in the third row.

Carpo watched the bidding proceed rapidly from all parts of the room; the ease with which people bid millions of dollars stupefied him. The pace was brisk until the auctioneer reached twenty-eight point five million, when a new bidder entered the contest. Karen leaned to Carpo and whispered, "Keep an eye on that man. He's the purchasing agent for the Sultan of Brunei."

Carpo edged forward on his seat for a better look at the man, but his features were concealed behind a white straw hat with a thin black band.

"Why hasn't he bid before now?" he asked.

"He probably wanted to weed out the frivolous bidders."

"Do you recognize any of the others?"

"The woman in the hat is an agent for the Getty Museum. The man farther to her right is a private collector. There's no way of knowing who's on those phone lines."

After the man in the white straw hat waved his paddle to

the price of twenty-nine million, the pace of the bidding slowed.
Now it was the auctioneer pushing the bids, his face flushed
red, brow glistening with moisture. The field had narrowed to
four potential buyers in the gallery and two more being represented by phone, all of whom he cajoled to raise their paddles.

"Twenty-nine and a half? Twenty-nine and a half? Do I see
a bid for twenty-nine and a half? There it is, I have twenty-nine
and a half." He pointed at a telephone bidder. "Let me see a motion for thirty million dollars? Thirty million? Thirty?" He nodded at the Sultan's representative. "Yes. Is that for thirty?
Thank you. I've got thirty million dollars."

As each higher bid was accepted, the crowd grew more and
more restless, every half million increase bringing collective
gasps of delight. It was like a heavyweight bout, each bidder
praying that his or her bid was the knockout punch; only, in this
contest the winner walked away with a prize somewhere
around two thousand years old.

"There's thirty and a half. Let me see thirty-one. Thirty-
one? Do I see thirty-one there? Sir? No? How about you,
ma'am? Yes? I've got thirty-one million dollars," the auctioneer announced, bestowing a warm smile on the Getty woman.
His attention turned to the right of the room as he pressured
the private collector with a bid of thirty-one and a half million
dollars. The man held perfectly still lest a movement show
agreement. When it became clear he was not going to budge,
the auctioneer shifted to the Sultan's man.

"Thirty-one and a half? Thirty-one and a half now?" he almost pleaded with the man.

"Fair warning," he stated to the room at large, telling them
the hammer was close to dropping. "Thirty-one going once,
thirty-one twice." He raised a shiny brass mallet as high as his

shoulder and glanced back at the Sultan's man, almost daring him to allow it to drop. The man still did not waver. "And thirty-one million dollars going—"

"Thirty-one and a half here," announced a low voice in the middle of the fourth row.

The room erupted in a roar of pleasure. People jumped up from their seats, eager to see who this newest, boldest bidder could be. Even Karen yelped with happiness, leaning into Carpo and shouting, "Who the hell is that?"

The noise hadn't died down before the Getty woman raised her paddle to accept the thirty-two million dollar bid, as if undaunted by the new challenger. The auctioneer turned to the man and asked, "Will you take thirty-two and a half, sir? Yes? Thirty-two and a half it is."

The auctioneer made eye contact with the woman, pestering her with taunts of, "Thirty-three, madam? Thirty-three? Will you agree to thirty-three?"

Carpo could see the edges of her hat brim shaking ever so slightly. He leaned over to Karen and asked, "What do you think the Getty's limit is?"

"I don't know, but I'll bet she's passed it."

"I've got thirty-three," the auctioneer bellowed after the hat brim dipped two inches in a signal of acceptance. He was back at the newcomer, who Carpo could recognize only from the neatly trimmed gray hair on the back of his head.

"I have thirty-three, sir. Will you go to thirty-three and a half?"

The man hesitated then dipped his head. More shouts exploded from the crowd. The woman in the big hat spun around in her seat, trying to catch a glimpse of her opponent. The look was an error on her part; it was the first time she had openly displayed surprise at a bid. Her invincibility shattered, she tried to regroup herself by motioning an acceptance of thirty-four million dollars before it had even been offered. The auctioneer yanked a white handkerchief from his pocket and dabbed it against his brow.

"We're at thirty-four and a half, sir. Do you bid thirty-four and a half? Thirty-four point five?"

A few scattered catcalls came from the crowd, as onlookers urged him to surpass the bid. Carpo wished he was seated in front of the man so he could see the expression on his face. After one more prod from the auctioneer, he lifted his paddle to the thirty-four and a half million dollar bid.

The support of the crowd shifted in favor of the woman, but this time she remained absolutely still. Even her hat brim had stopped trembling. The auctioneer, sensing that her resolve had evaporated, prodded the former bidders in the race and then the general audience at large.

"I've got thirty-four and a half million dollars here. Thirty-four and a half million. Anywhere? Sir? Madam? You've all had fair warning. Thirty-four point five going once. Thirty-four point five twice . . ." He paused dramatically as he hoisted the mallet high into the air, his eyes searching the room for any other bids.

"Thirty-four and a half?" he implored, then he released his wrist, bringing the mallet crashing loudly against the podium. "Sold to number six-four-three-one-two for thirty-four and a half million dollars. Congratulations, sir."

The noise in the room was deafening—shouts, screams, and applause. People raced forward, mobbing the man with handshakes and backslaps. The man struggled through the crowd until he reached the Getty woman. He shook her hand and then embraced her.

"Who is he?" Carpo shouted above the noise.

"I don't know. Let's try and get closer." Karen bolted ahead, plowing straight into the mob of people.

Within seconds, Carpo couldn't see her anymore. A surge from behind nearly lifted him off his feet. He spotted an open space along the side wall and leaned into it, deciding it was safer to wait until the crowd settled down a bit. All around him people shook hands and hugged each other, the record-breaking auction eliciting an outpouring of emotion.

From his perch, Carpo caught a glimpse of Karen maneuvering through the crowd. She was looking for him, standing on her tip-toes to see above the people. He waved with both arms but couldn't catch her eye. The victorious man was a few yards ahead of her, the circle of people creating a wave action that swept him, and Karen, toward the exit.

"I never thought it would go for that much," a voice said next to Carpo. The voice was familiar, high and marred with the trace of an accent. It wasn't distinctive, but for some reason, it needled Carpo's attention.

Carpo looked over his shoulder, pretending to check the wall for a clock. The closest person was a short, stocky man, perhaps in his early forties. He was standing next to a taller man, who looked to be a few years older.

"I'll say," the older man responded. "It went for a good five to ten million more than I was expecting."

"Yes, but I definitely think it was worth it," the man said. "Definitely."

Carpo snapped his eyes down and backed away from the men, a spasm of panic creeping into his throat.

The man's voice was unmistakable in both its pitch and accent—for Carpo, it was unforgettable. He forced himself to remain composed as he moved away, his knees turning to jelly, skin prickling.

He was standing next to Frank Werner.

# Chapter 17

"He's here! It's him!" Carpo exclaimed when he had finally reached Karen's side.

She was standing in a small group of people at the front of the bidding gallery, watching as The Cleopatra Bust was wheeled from the podium.

"Who's here?" she asked.

"Frank Werner, or the guy who said he was Frank Werner. The man who called me at the station last week."

Her face registered a look of shock, then her green eyes narrowed. She quickly put a finger to her lips and moved him away from the people. "There's a lot of people who know each other here," she explained once they had found a quieter spot. "Now, tell me where you saw him."

"I didn't see him, I heard him. Right over there, against the wall. I was waiting for the crowd to clear out and I heard him talking."

"You didn't see him at all?"

"Just a quick look, but if I see him again I'll recognize him." Carpo scanned the other side of the room for the two men. The gallery was much less crowded, but large pockets of people were still milling about. The men were not among them.

"This is a madhouse," Karen said. "Let's go downstairs and look for him at the exit."

They squeezed through the people and headed for the stairs, moving only as fast as the crowd permitted. Every so often, a person ahead of them would recognize someone else, trapping him or her for the few seconds it took the pair to reacquaint. All the while, Carpo kept his head and eyes moving, constantly scanning the crowd for anyone who resembled the man he had seen.

His news experience had taught him the importance of not just looking at his surroundings but *seeing* them. After his one quick glance at the man, he could recall several details unique to him. The man was short, maybe five foot six or seven, about one-hundred eighty pounds. He looked to be in his early forties, maybe even older, with gray, thinning hair combed across his large head. Despite his height, the man appeared very strong; a rippling jaw muscle, bulldog neck and a pair of thick veined hands tipped Carpo off to the obvious strength hidden beneath the man's tweed blazer and corduroy slacks. Beyond the muscles and balding head, the man's face was young, almost feminine looking. It was absent of wrinkles, liver spots, freckles, and other signs of aging. His soft, accented voice was a perfect match for the face but seemed awkward for the rest of the body.

When they reached the stairway, the going was even slower, the large crowd forced to converge in a double-line heading down the steps. Carpo continued looking back through the crowd, trying to suppress the sensation of panic whenever he thought of losing the man.

"Damn it, I can't see them anywhere," he said.

"Them?" Karen said. "I thought it was one person."

"No, he was with somebody."

On the first floor, Carpo stood against the wall and looked up the stairs, checking faces as they filed down the steps.

"Got them," he whispered to Karen. "Top of the stairs. Two men, both in dark overcoats. One of them is putting on his scarf right now."

"I see them," Karen said. A second later she added, "My god, Carpo, I know that man."

"Which one?"

"The shorter man, on the left, with the scarf. His name's Gabriel Adonis. He used to do restoration work for Frank."

"He worked for Frank Werner?" Carpo stared harder at the man, wondering if maybe it was the link he had been looking for.

"Yes. Come on, let's get out of here before he spots me."

They left the auction house and set out with a brisk pace down Park Avenue. After a few blocks, Carpo checked back up the street.

"I think we're okay. It doesn't look like they've even left the building yet."

"I don't want to chance it, Michael. Let's get a cab or something."

He scanned both sides of Park Avenue for anything yellow that moved. "They're all lined up outside Christie's," he said. "Let's cut over to Lex, we might have better luck there."

They crossed Park Avenue and headed east toward Lexington Avenue. The air was warmer than when he had arrived from downtown. He unbuttoned his jacket and loosened his tie. The temperature was probably only in the low fifties, but after all the excitement, he felt hot and sweaty. He reached into his jacket and undid his collar, freeing the perspiration trapped under his shirt.

"Are you sure that was the guy who called you?" Karen asked.

"Positive. That voice has haunted me ever since I found out Frank Werner was dead."

They reached Lexington and stood on the corner, looking up the avenue for a cab. Carpo glanced at Karen, noticing the stunned expression that paralyzed her face. Her eyes blinked rapidly and her mouth hung open a little, as if she wasn't getting enough oxygen. He wondered if it was from the fast walk. Or perhaps it was the shock of recognizing the man. Something about her expression bothered him.

His thoughts were interrupted by the skidding sound of tires next to the curb. Carpo smiled when he recognized the distinctive shape of a Checker Cab, the almost extinct taxi model with bumper seats and enough headroom for a professional basketball center.

"It's a Checker Cab," he exclaimed. "Every time I ride in one of these, it brings me good luck. Have you ever been in one?"

"Of course I have, Michael."

They hopped in the back. "Where are we going?" he asked her.

"I haven't even thought about it."

"What do you say we get some dinner and try to sort this all out?" She nodded in agreement. "Take us to West Broadway, between Prince and Spring, please," he shouted to the driver through the glass partition.

The cab roared into the middle of the street, the ancient springs in the wide back seat creaking with complaint.

"Where are we going?" Karen asked.

"To a little restaurant I know in Soho."

It was a little after six by the time they reached West Broadway. The sidewalks were crowded and bright, illuminated by street lamps and the neon glow from the windows of art galleries. The cast iron district was the heart of New York City's contemporary art trade, in direct counterpoint to the Upper East Side art and antiquities scene. The cab pulled into an opening at the corner of Spring and West Broadway. Carpo paid the driver, then they walked a few doors down to the small Italian restaurant, Vucciria.

It was still early evening, but the restaurant was buzzing with the trendy Soho crowd. Young men and women dressed in tight black dresses and black jeans were pressed three deep along the bar, sipping from bottles of imported beer. The restaurant was decorated like an Italian palazzo, its ambiance furthered by a cathedral ceiling and dozens of photographs of turn-of-the-century Tuscany. Karen looked around the room before giving Carpo an approving smile.

"What's the matter?" he asked. "Did you think I was going to take you to some pizza joint?"

"It wouldn't have been the first time," she said coyly as the maitre d' led them to a small table at the back of the restaurant.

After they were seated, a waiter stopped by with a basket of warm bread and offered to take their drink order. When Karen asked for wine, Carpo was presented with a thick book filled with labels from the restaurant's wine cellar. He flipped through the pages of the book, trying to understand the foreign writing on the fancy labels. About the only thing he could discern between the wine labels was "bianco" and "rosso."

"Would you like white or red?" he asked over the top of the wine list.

"Red sounds wonderful."

He raised the book high enough to cover his eyes, then he casually peeked at the tables surrounding theirs. The table next to them had a bottle of Tuscan red, Viticcio, standing in the middle. Carpo flipped through the book until he found its label.

The waiter returned and he ordered a bottle, thankful that his Italian lessons in college had at least taught him the correct pronunciation of the wine's name. The waiter nodded and left to find a bottle.

"I'm impressed," Karen said after he had left. The candle between them cast a flickering shadow on her face, drawing out the hazel glow from her eyes.

"There was no beer on the list, so it seemed like the next best thing to order."

"Come on, Michael, I never said you didn't have style."

"Oh, I can remember a few arguments that used to center on that topic," he said.

"I think we both said some hurtful things back then."

She glanced down at her menu, and Carpo noticed a splash of crimson on her cheeks. His comments had annoyed her; he suddenly regretted teasing her.

"So what looks good?" he asked, hoping the mention of food would brighten her spirits again.

"What doesn't?"

"Before you get set on anything on the menu, wait until the waiter tells us the specials. This place has some great ones."

The waiter returned with their wine bottle, holding it so that Carpo could read the label. He deftly uncorked it, then poured a few drops in Carpo's glass. Carpo felt the waiter and Karen stare at him with anticipation. He knew nothing about how to sample wine, so he decided to taste it like he sampled his coffee. He grabbed the glass with an exaggerated confidence, swirling it roughly around the crystal. He pushed his nose within the rim and took a deep sniff. The wine's strong bouquet caught him by surprise. He stifled a cough while he took a gulp of the wine.

"That's quite nice," he managed hoarsely.

The waiter filled their glasses as he recited an extensive list of chef specialties. After he left, Karen whispered, "How does he remember all of those? I can't remember any of the dishes he just told us."

"The pastas are gnocchi in venison sauce and a linguine carbonara. The entrees are grilled rack of lamb, grilled mahimahi with balsamic marinade, tuna carpaccio, and a pollo al forno. They can also fix up a grilled portabello mushroom for starters or a side course. And they have fresh broccoli di rappe, sautéed in garlic and oil."

"Thanks," she said with an exaggerated roll of her eyes. "I guess that memory of yours hasn't faded much since Georgetown."

"Not when it comes to food." He picked up his glass and dared another sniff. The acidic aroma had worn off a bit, rounding out to a nice, woodsy smell. "How about a toast? To getting our lives back to normal."

"I'll drink to that." She clinked her glass softly against his and took a drink. "Mmm, it's delicious. I didn't know you could pick wine."

"I can't. That couple over there looked like they were enjoying it, so . . . I thought it was worth a try."

Karen grinned. "I can't believe you, Michael."

"I'm knowledgeable about food. I know nothing about wine."

The waiter reappeared and took their orders. Karen

started with the linguine carbonara followed by the grilled mahimahi. Carpo chose the tuna carpaccio and the gnocchi.

After they had sipped some more wine, Karen asked, "How did you hurt your knee last night?"

"I was chasing that guy through Washington Square Park. He took a quick left, I took a quicker left and ended up eating shrubbery. I must have smacked my knee on the way down."

"Does it hurt?"

"Not too bad. Not as much as my neck, which a guard at the NYU Library did his best to twist off like a bottle cap."

"Did you get a look at the guy you were chasing?"

"Not really. It was very dark and he was wearing a big down coat and a fur cap. I got an idea of his general build, but I never saw his face."

"Do you think it was Gabriel?"

"You mean the guy I saw at Christie's?" Carpo thought about it for a second, then shrugged. "I guess they're about the same height and build, but I'm not positive. Tell me about him."

"He used to do restoration work for Athena Galleries. Frank mentioned him a few times—used to call him 'Gabe.' Apparently, he's a very good restorer."

"Does the museum use restorers?"

"Yes, except we call them conservationists. They're part of the museum staff. We rarely use outside people."

"So how did you meet him?"

"I met him at that first cocktail party at Athena Galleries." Karen lowered her head and stared into her glass. "He kind of walked in on me while I was . . . admiring a piece of sculpture."

"What do you mean 'admiring'? Were you combusting?"

She winced at the word. "No. There was a nice statue in one of the back offices at the gallery. I thought I was alone, so I reached over and touched it."

"So you were combusting," Carpo exclaimed happily.

"Would you stop with the combusting, Michael? Yes, I was touching it, but it's not like I was panting over the damn thing."

"What do you feel? I mean, when you touch them, how does it make you feel?" He held his breath after he asked it, wondering if he was probing something too private to ask.

Her eyes locked onto his. "I feel a lot of things. All the reasons I like sculpture are the same reasons why I like to touch it. It's three-dimensional and takes up space, so it has a presence that's tangible—unlike paintings or other two-dimensional media. I also like the materials: wood, stone, and bronze. They have strength, texture, even temperature. And sometimes sculpture has movement. It uses motion and realism to depict a moment forever frozen in time. Sometimes it makes me feel like there's a person there holding perfectly still so I can admire them."

"Your description reminds me of that poem 'Ode On A Grecian Urn' by Keats—the part where the young lovers are chasing each other, but they'll never meet because it's a moment frozen in a picture on the side of the urn. It's sad because their love will never be fulfilled, but they're also lucky because that moment will last forever." Carpo's eyes grew narrow, brows furrowed as he pondered something. "At the end, the urn recites its ode: 'Beauty is truth, truth beauty, that is all ye know on earth, and all ye need to know.' "

"That's a great description, Michael. My love of Greek sculpture is a lot like your Greek urn."

Carpo reached for the bread and tore a piece off. "I don't think I've ever touched a piece of sculpture," he mused.

"Most people haven't. It's one of the biggest taboos at the museum, and rightfully so; if everyone touched the statues there'd be nothing left. But I think it's such an amazing part of viewing sculpture, I can't imagine not doing it. We're supposed to wear these little white gloves when we handle pieces at the museum, but sometimes I just can't resist."

"What did Gabriel say when he caught you touching the statue?"

"It was a little awkward for us both. I think he apologized. We talked a little at the party. He seemed friendly. I think he was Italian, I mean actually from Italy."

"That would explain the way his voice sounds. Is that the only time you two ever met?"

"That's it. It wasn't long after the party that I started doing verification work for Frank, but I never met Gabriel again."

The waiter arrived with their first courses. Carpo's tuna carpaccio looked as if it had just been netted, the thin slices of fish pumping with sanguine fluids. Karen's linguine carbonara glistened in a mixture of heavy cream, butter, and chunks of prosciutto—enough cholesterol and fat in one serving to frighten off a convention of cardiologists. He smiled when he saw her dig into the plate without a concern in the world. She had always eaten every meal like it was her last supper, deserving of her total attention. It was something he admired about her, in stark contrast to the dining habits of most women he took on dates.

Between a bite of the carpaccio and a sip of the wine, he asked, "How can I find out more about Gabriel?"

She shook her head as she chewed. "His last name's Adonis. I've told you everything I know about him. Frank never made a big deal about him; he just mentioned the restoration work once in a while."

"Do you know where he works?"

"I haven't a clue. He must have a studio somewhere."

"Does the museum keep a listing of outside restorers? Maybe a file on them or something?"

"It's possible. I could certainly check."

"Ask around, too. I'm sure other people have used him, or at least heard of him. Especially if he was doing work for Frank."

"I'd rather not do that," she said. "It's bad enough I went to the auction today; they'll be dissecting that for weeks. If I start asking around about things that concern Frank, it'll just keep me under scrutiny."

"What about Athena Galleries then? There must be some record of Adonis there."

"Yeah, and how do we get it?"

"Do you have keys?"

"No. Frank and I were close but not that close."

"What about his sister? Mrs. Greenfeld? Maybe she'll let you in."

Karen's fork stopped halfway to her mouth, a ribbon of linguine dangling from the end. "How do you know Leslie Greenfeld?"

"I met her at Frank's wake."

The fork returned to the plate. "You were there?"

"Yes, for the whole thing. I even saw you there."

Karen wiped her mouth with the tip of her napkin, then went straight for the wine glass.

"Does that bother you, Karen?"

"No. I just didn't think anyone had recognized me. I was so careful. How could you tell it was me?"

"How could I tell?" Carpo gave a soft chuckle. "How could I not tell? From the way you wore that veil to the way you walked—of course I recognized you. What difference does it make?"

"It doesn't. I was pretty upset there, that's all." She shook her head adamantly. "Anyway, I don't know Leslie Greenfeld. Frank didn't get along with her, and I don't want to talk with her."

"Okay, I'm just brainstorming." He picked up his own wine glass and made little circles with it, washing the red wine up to the rim. "If this guy did restoration work outside the gallery, then the piece had to be shipped from his place back to the gallery, or maybe even directly to the museum. Right? That's got to leave a paper trail. Movers, insurance—there must be some record of that."

"That's an idea. I know of at least one occasion where a piece was shipped from a restorer straight to the museum. I'm not sure if it came from this guy, but I know where we keep the paperwork on it. I'll check it out tomorrow morning."

Carpo also remembered the list of names from Insect Warehouse. Gabriel Adonis's name was not among the twelve on the list—he was quite sure of that—but it didn't mean it was the wrong man. He might have used an alias or perhaps he hadn't placed his order yet.

He thought about showing the list to Karen, to see if she recognized any of the names. Instead, he asked, "Do you know what cochineal is?"

"Yes, I think it's a type of red dye."

"Yeah, but what is it used for?"

"I believe it has a lot of uses. At the museum it's used to match the patinas of old marble."

"It's used at the museum?"

"I don't know if it is anymore, but I'm sure it used to be. I studied about it in a restoration course in grad school. I think artificial dyes are used now."

"What's a patina?"

"It's the coloring bronze and some stones pick up as they age. Mostly it refers to bronzes; it's that greenish-blue color the metal gets when it goes a long time without being polished. In ancient bronzes, scientists can test the patina and date a piece from it. It's caused by natural oxidation and it's almost impossible to fake. That's why there are so few fake bronzes on the market. With marble, patina refers more to the coloring the stone gets over the centuries."

"So the cochineal is only used to match the patina on marble?"

"Marble and other porous stones. Sculptors used it to age the appearance of the stone. The cochineal was dissolved in a solution and brushed on the exterior. The stone absorbs the red coloring and looks older. Restorers often used it to match an existing patina." She broke off, frowning at him. "Why the sudden interest in cochineal?"

"It's something I came across while reading about sculpture."

"So you've been doing some homework."

"Just enough to know that sculpture is better off left to the experts," Carpo said.

The cochineal angle made it seem all the more likely that the man he had chased with the Insect Warehouse number was Gabriel Adonis. But something still bothered Carpo. Maybe it was the ease in matching Adonis to the entire investigation. It was all so obvious and simple, he wondered if he wasn't making some quantum leap in his deduction. As he mulled over the possibilities, the waiter appeared with their entrées.

They attacked their dishes with a ferocity borne of hunger meeting good cooking. Carpo's gnocchi was excellent, each tender morsel of the potato pasta dissolving on his tongue. Karen's mahimahi was expertly grilled, the balsamic vinegar adding a slight acidic flavor to the dish.

"This is perfect," Karen announced after they had eaten for several minutes. "I haven't had a meal this good in weeks. You must come here a lot to know so much about this place."

"No, I've never been here before," he confessed with a sly grin. "I heard some people talking about it at work and decided to give it a try."

The wine was starting to heat Carpo up; his cheeks and ear lobes felt numb. He looked across the table and openly stared at Karen as she concentrated on her meal. It reminded him of the good times they had shared—the first two years of their relationship—when they had been excited about life and enjoyed sharing it with each other. Then had come the bitterness of the third year and the final failure in the fourth. Night and day. One period so incredibly good, the other a series of failures stacked atop failures, like a house of cards, until everything came tumbling down. He swirled the ruby fluid around his glass, thinking of what might have been if he hadn't messed everything up.

"Hey? You doing okay?" Karen asked.

He flashed a little smile, unaware that she had been watching. "Yeah, I'm great," he mumbled. "I was just thinking about all this Frank Werner stuff."

When they were finished with dinner, both plates scraped clean of food, they leaned back in their chairs, wine goblets in hand, and enjoyed the narcotic effect of digestion.

"This has been nice, Michael."

"Mmm, for me, too. I'm enjoying your company."

"Feels a little strange though, doesn't it? I mean, being together like this?"

"I'd say this feels very strange. I never thought I'd get the chance to sit across a dinner table from you again."

Their table was cleared of everything but the wine bottle, the glasses, and the candle. The waiter popped up again and topped off their glasses as he recited the considerable array of desserts beckoning from the kitchen: canolis, zuppa di 'glese, tartufi de cioccolato, tiramisu, custard-filled eclairs, and fresh fruit. Despite the hard sell, Karen decided against dessert.

"I guess that leaves the choice up to me," Carpo said to the waiter. "I'll have the tartufi de cioccolato, with two spoons please, since my companion is sure to have a relapse of hunger once she tastes it. I'll also have a double espresso."

"And I'll have an espresso," Karen said as she planted a deft kick on Carpo's shin. He noticed that her foot lingered there for a second, giving a brush back and forth against his leg. It was so quick and delicate, he wondered if it had happened. He kept his eyes down in case it had not.

When the truffles arrived, they took turns plopping the powdered marbles of chocolate in their mouths. Carpo was especially thankful for the large espresso, scalding hot and very strong. They settled back against their chairs and watched each other over the candle, wick down to an inch of the silver holder, blue flame shimmering from side to side as it floated atop a puddle of wax.

Suddenly, the tranquility of the room was shattered by a sharp crack from the street, loud enough to rattle the restaurant's front windows.

Karen jumped up in her seat. "What was that?"

"I believe that is the first sign of the rain storm they've been predicting all week."

"Rain? We're in the middle of the coldest winter in history."

"We *were* in the middle of the coldest winter in history," Carpo said. "Right now, it's in the fifties—plenty warm enough for a little rain storm."

Karen excused herself to use the bathroom. While she was gone, Carpo flagged down the waiter and handed him his credit card. She returned just as the waiter brought him the receipt.

A serious look came over her face. "Michael, I've had a wonderful, wonderful time tonight. But I want you to let me pay for at least my portion of the meal."

"Not on your life."

"I'm serious, Michael. It's only fair. We're not dating, and I'm making good money at the museum. I don't want you to feel like it's your duty."

"Karen, thanks for the offer, and I really do mean that, but I want to pay. I've had a great time tonight, and it would make me even happier if you let me. So no more out of you, okay?"

"Deal," she said as she grabbed her coat from the back of her chair. "My god, we're one of the last ones here. I hope we didn't keep the waiter too late."

He held her coat as she slipped it on. "Or put too much of a dent in their supply of Viticcio," he said.

# Chapter 18

On the street, the thunder continued, sounding louder and louder with each concussion.

"We'd better hurry before this thing hits," Carpo said after one particularly violent snap of thunder.

Karen slid her arm through his as they walked up West Broadway toward Houston Street in search of a taxi. They crossed the wide, double avenue and walked another ten blocks before the first oversized drops of rain splattered against the sidewalk. Within minutes, the thunder cloud opened. Big drops slammed against the pavement so hard they seemed to ricochet back into the air.

The rain stung Carpo's face as they broke into a run, their chances of finding a taxi reduced to zero. Karen's hand moved down his arm until she was clenching his fingertips.

"Michael, I'm getting soaked," she shouted after another clap of thunder. "Do you live near here?"

"I'm on 12th Street. It's just a few more blocks. Let's try to make it."

By the time they stepped into the foyer of his building, the storm had relaxed into a steady rain, each drop adding to the roar of water pouring into the gutters.

"I think my suit's ruined," Karen said sadly as she inspected the black fabric. It was dripping wet; the water leaching muddy drops of color from the fabric. Her white blouse was plastered so tightly to her body, Carpo could see the goose bumps of her flesh poking through the fabric.

"Let's get you upstairs and dried off," he said, then added, "And I hope you don't mind stairs, because there's six flights of them."

They started up slowly, Karen plodding half a step ahead of him. On the third flight, Carpo almost toppled over when Karen turned back and took his hand. They climbed the remaining stairs that way, hand in hand, his body pumping into hers whenever their feet landed on the same step. Her slender hand felt familiar to him. He traced its outline with his thumb, remembering the shape of its bones and the soft grip of her palm. A few times he dared to glance down at it, reassuring himself that it was there, clinging to his own hand.

Inside the apartment, Carpo hung their coats up and put a kettle of water on the stove. "I'm making a pot of tea," he yelled from the kitchen. "Why don't you throw on a T-shirt and a pair of sweats until your clothes dry off?"

"If you have a robe, I'll put that on."

He went into his bedroom and grabbed the old terry cloth robe hanging on the back of the door. The fabric was soft and tattered from hundreds of washings. He hesitated a moment before carrying it into the living room.

Karen's eyes lit up as soon as she saw it. "This looks familiar," she said. She grabbed the robe and took it into the bathroom.

"You always gave me gifts we could both use," he called after her, happy that she had recognized it.

The robe was one of the first gifts she had ever given him. One night, she had searched his freshman dorm room for something to wear to the bathroom and discovered that he didn't own a robe. The next day she'd given him the blue robe as a present. Despite its threadbare appearance, the robe represented a memory Carpo was too scared to throw away.

He was pouring hot water into two mugs when he noticed her standing at the opening to the kitchen. Her wet hair was combed back in a neat ponytail, skin glistening and pink like she had just showered.

"That's beautiful," she said, pointing to the Rancilio coffeemaker on the countertop.

"I gave that to myself as a present two years ago."

"What does it make? Espresso?"

"Espresso, cappuccino, and American coffee. Do you want me to make you something?"

"No, I'm still flying after that espresso at the restaurant. Tea would be nice though. Michael, why don't you go change? Your pants are dripping wet."

"Okay." He handed her the mugs of tea. "I'll be right back."

He went into the bedroom and changed into a T-shirt and a pair of jeans. When he returned, she was sitting on the couch, the mugs placed on the coffee table by the couch. He noticed her casting glances around the room, as if she were trying to memorize the objects in it. There wasn't much to remember: coffee table, couch, side table, lamp, answering machine, and television. A small red rug was under the table. All four walls were empty.

"So this is where you live," she said, waving a hand around the room. "It doesn't look like you spend much time here."

"I don't. Basically, I just sleep here and make coffee."

"It could use a little, I don't know, brightening up. You barely have any decorations."

"I've been trying to cut down on my possessions, simplify my life. If I don't use something, out it goes."

"But what about your books? You used to have hundreds of them stacked all around your room at Georgetown."

Carpo smiled as he plopped down next to her on the couch. He nodded in the direction of his bedroom. "Simplicity didn't make it into the bedroom. They're all still there, gathering dust on the shelf."

She twisted her body around to face him, curling her legs underneath the robe. "I was thinking about that poem you talked about at the restaurant. You used to know so many of them. I always thought you were going to end up as an English teacher. I never even knew you were interested in journalism."

"I wasn't at the time."

"But how did you end up choosing it for a career?"

"I thought you knew the answer. At the museum you said I always thought I could save the world."

"Come on, Michael, I'm being serious. Why did you go into it?"

"When I started, I probably did believe I could do some good. I had this idea of the newsroom as a place where people cared about the city and tried to make it a better place."

"And you don't feel that's true anymore?"

"Let's just say, somewhere between the three-thousandth fire story and the five-thousandth murder story, I started to realize nothing was ever going to change." He scooped his mug off the table and took a sip of tea. "I was naive about it. Like anything else, news is a business. In order to survive, we have to sell advertising spots; to sell advertising, we need good ratings; and in order to get good ratings, we've got to keep our viewers. So every single night, we approach the show like its some sort of Broadway production. We promo it and hype it and distort it, just to get people to tune in. It's wrong, Karen. Inherently wrong. Sometimes it's even dangerous."

"Like how?"

"There've been a couple of times when we've done stuff I thought was completely unethical."

"Did you complain?"

"Yeah, I complained. It was sort of like spitting into the ocean, but I told them. Once I almost got fired because I wouldn't do what they wanted."

"What happened?"

Carpo set his cup back down. "You might actually remember the story. It was a big deal about two years back. I got a phone call from a guy who said he had some information Channel 8 would be interested in. It was almost like Frank's call last week: the guy refused to tell me the information over the phone and insisted on setting up a meeting. There was something about the guy's voice—the way he addressed me and the things he said—that made me feel like he really had something important. So I set up a meeting with him at a coffee shop near where I work."

"Did he have a good story?"

"He didn't just have a good story; he had concrete proof of it. The guy had a memorandum from his office that backed up exactly what he was claiming. The guy's name was Conductor Bob Martinez. Ring a bell?"

"You were the one who met Conductor Martinez? That's incredible. Were you nervous?"

"Not at the time because I had no idea how it was all going to turn out."

"What did the memorandum say?"

"Exactly what the inspector general's office backed up two months later. Metro North Railroad had received threats from a terrorist group that claimed it was going to blow up a commuter train. The scary part was, Metro North admitted in the memorandum that it had no plans for dealing with such an attack."

"I don't remember any of that; I just remember how the conductor died."

Carpo drowned a sigh in another sip of tea. "Bob Martinez was, understandably, paranoid as hell about coming forward with the information. He was two years from his pension, with a wife and two kids. He wanted to warn people that this threat had been made, but he insisted on remaining anonymous."

"Why did he call you?"

"Pot luck. He walked into the lobby of my building and chose my name off the masthead."

"Did you tell his story to the station?"

"Of course I did. A terrorist threat on the Metro North Railroad? That's a huge story, especially since the World Trade Center bombing was still fresh on everybody's mind. I showed them a copy of the memorandum and I told them about Conductor Martinez. They gave the story to Ed Thomas, this reporter at Channel 8 who I've butted heads with over the years."

"Don't tell me about Ed Thomas. He's the jerk who was hounding me up at the Met last week."

"The one and only."

"So far Bob Martinez sounds like a pretty normal guy. What made him snap?"

"Ed went live in Grand Central one night with the whole exclusive report. He showed the memorandum and told this great story using file tape of Metro North trains, even footage from the aftermath of the Trade Center explosion. It was a great story, an award-winner, until Ed gave out Bob Martinez's name on the air."

"Why did he do that?"

"I've asked him that about two hundred times since then. He claims he was establishing the authenticity of the document. Standing there holding a piece of paper with the Metro North seal on it, and he's worried about people believing him."

"I think I remember what happened now. Metro North fired the conductor, and that's when he flipped out, right?"

"Bob Martinez was a good man, a loyal father and an excellent conductor. He really cared about people's safety. When Metro North fired him, I called him and told him he could sue for his job back, or at least for his pension. But all Bob cared about was that the railroad had made his employee records public. He'd had a drug problem about ten years back and missed some work while he checked into a clinic. He said he could never live with his kids thinking their daddy had been a junkie."

"So that's what did it. I forgot why he killed himself. All I remember is that horrible picture in *The Post* after he jumped on the third rail."

"They made him out to be some kind of walking time bomb. He was just a guy trying to do the right thing. They basically killed him—Metro North and Channel 8 News. They trashed his name and reputation, then they acted all surprised when the guy leapt onto the tracks."

"So why did you get in trouble? You weren't the one who gave out his name."

"No, but I went on a little crusade to clear his name. I tried to get Channel 8 to report the truth about how we had made a mistake in giving out Bob's name. The execs wanted no part of it. When I continued making noise about it, they threatened me with a suspension."

"Michael, I'm sorry. That's a horrible thing to have to go through."

"I still get nightmares from it. I guess way down I think I could have done something to maybe save him. Or at least convince him not to kill himself."

Karen placed her hand on his knee. "Michael, you're depressing me."

"Yeah, enough. I'm getting too heavy."

"No, I think it's good you talk about it. I just thought you were happy with what you were doing. I mean, you must be good at it; otherwise, they wouldn't have promoted you twice."

A funny look crept over Carpo's face. "How did you know I got promoted twice?"

She smiled; the corners of her mouth heading into her reddening cheeks. "Oh, I have my ways."

"You checked up on me at the station?"

"No, nothing like that."

"Then how did you know?"

"About three years ago I was watching the news when the credits came on. Suddenly, your name's on the screen: Michael Carpo. What were you then? News Staff, I think. It was just for a second; I wasn't even sure if I'd really seen it. So I watched the next night and, sure enough, up comes Michael Carpo, News Staff. So I started watching Channel 8 News. Every so often, I'd see your position change. Next it was Production Associate; now I think your title is Newswriter."

"So you watched the news because of me?"

"Wipe that smirk off your face, Mr. Carpo. So what if I did?"

"It makes me happy, that's all. I always thought I was the only one looking out for someone."

"You checked up on me, too?"

"It was a little tougher, but every time I ran into a mutual friend of ours, I'd make sure the conversation shifted to what you were doing."

"You should have just called me," Karen said.

"After the way we broke up? I didn't think you'd ever speak to me again. Besides, if you'd really wanted to speak with me, why were you so snippy on the phone last week?"

"Let's just chalk that up to bad timing. First you dropped a bombshell by telling me Frank was dead, then you kind of surprised me at the museum."

"Phew!" Carpo made an exaggerated motion like he was wiping his forehead. "I thought maybe you were still holding a grudge."

Karen nodded her head solemnly. "I did hold a grudge Michael, for a long, long time. I was very angry at you. We were so committed that once you broke the spell, I wanted nothing more to do with you."

Carpo winced at the thought, as he did whenever he remembered the circumstances involving their breakup.

It had happened in late May of their senior year. Carpo had gone out with his roommates on a "guys' night out" type of evening. The next morning, Karen had shown up at his apartment to surprise him with breakfast. What she hadn't expected to do was surprise two people.

He would never forget the feeling of lying in bed with another woman and hearing Karen's footsteps coming up the stairs. The door had opened and Karen's face had gone cold, jaw dropping clear down to her chest. She'd never uttered a sound beyond the first horrible gasp. She'd looked between

Carpo and the strange woman, then turned and walked out. He had tried to run after her, but his nakedness had prevented him from leaving the house. Later that day, she'd ordered him out of her life forever.

"I was an absolute jerk," he said hoarsely, heart pounding at the memory. "I can't understand what spurred me to do that. I never, ever meant to hurt you."

She squeezed his hand. "Stop. We were both foolish. It was too intense at too young an age. We were like kids, Michael— little kids pretending to be grown-ups. If you hadn't cheated on me, I would have done it to you. It was bound to happen."

"Maybe so, but I still kick myself every time I think of it. I blew it."

"Yeah, sometimes I think of how it might have turned out if we'd met three or four years later." Karen's eyes focused on some spot on the far wall. "I wouldn't be mixed up in any of this business with Frank, that's for sure."

They sat on the couch for several hours, holding hands and talking about their jobs, lives, and the past. Through it all, Carpo had an eerie sensation he was revisiting one of the hundreds of nights he had passed with Karen at Georgetown. He would cook her dinner and they would sit at the table for hours: eating, talking, drinking wine, and smoking far too many cigarettes.

Now that she was there, sitting across from him again, he realized what he had longed for through the years. It was so simple and obvious, he nearly burst out laughing.

She was his perfect match, in every way imaginable. Even after six years of separation, Karen Blackwell knew him better than any other person in the world.

When he was struck by this realization, he was so overcome

with happiness that he reached out and hugged her, both arms wrapped tightly around her.

"Michael," she whispered, voice muffled by his shoulder. "What's the matter?"

He leaned back and looked into her face. He placed a finger over his lips to quiet her, then he reached across and placed the same finger on her lips. He touched them gently, tracing the outline of her mouth, admiring the shape and softness. His body trembled as her lips parted and gently closed around his finger, sucking its very tip. He put his hand behind her neck and drew her face to his.

Their first kisses were passionate but stiff, as if they had fallen out of practice after so many years. Her mouth was small and soft—he had forgotten just how soft—and her warm tongue darted against his, causing it to go numb. He savored each kiss, drinking in the sweet, undiluted nectar she was exhaling.

The kisses grew steadily longer and sloppier as they caught the rhythm of each other's mouth. His eyes were closed, attention focused on that one moist spot his mouth was encountering, ears roaring with the intensity.

Suddenly, she put her hands on his chest and pushed him away.

"Karen, I'm sorry," he whispered, fearing he had pushed her too hard. "Maybe I'm going too fast. This has been one hell of a nice night. I understand if you want to go."

"Six years, Michael. It's been six years." She shook her head from side to side in disbelief. "Do you think we're going too fast?"

"No, not for me. I'm still pinching myself. But I want us to feel comfortable. I would die if you regretted something tomorrow."

She reached down and took his hand, clasping it like she feared he was about to be dragged away. "The only thing I'll regret, Michael Carpo, is if you let me leave this apartment tonight."

Before he could answer, she took her index finger and mimicked his earlier motion by gently laying it across his lips. She slid her body next to his and undid the tie to her robe. He was surprised to see nothing but glowing pink flesh in the opening of the blue terry cloth. She pulled up his T-shirt and scooted right up against him, closer and closer, until there was nowhere farther to go.

Sometime during the night, Carpo was awakened by the lightning—quick, violent flashes that hit his eyes like the aftershocks of an explosion, lighting the desk, the bookshelves and Karen. Seconds later followed the thunder, loud blasts that shook the tiny apartment, rattling the windows of the bedroom. Karen stirred in her sleep, and he moved to her, cuddling her head in his arms until she stopped shivering. After the thundercloud passed, the rain continued. It fell long and steadily, scrubbing away the last bits of snow and ice that had clogged the streets of the city since early December. For the first time in months, the cold spell was snapped.

Carpo's mind was unaware of the changing landscape outside the window. His thoughts were within the room, focusing on the woman nestled in his arms. He caught glimpses of her peaceful face every time the lightning flashed. It was then that he noticed the wrinkles on her face. They were tiny marks—barely even deserved the title of "wrinkle"—but they had taken solid root in the corners of each eye. The marks were the first signs of age to tread across the landscape of her face.

Karen was a beautiful woman, would be for many more

years, but Carpo was mesmerized by these tiniest of intruders. Somehow, they made her face more beautiful than the perfection he had marveled at while at Georgetown. He felt a desire to watch her face grow older and older, until it was wrinkled with a lifetime of experiences. He wanted to watch the wrinkles appear and move across her face, like the expanding routes on a road atlas. At that moment, he knew more than anything else in the world, he wanted to grow old with her.

Carpo had gone to New York to forget Karen, to build an entirely new life, one that would totally block out the old one. He had moved to New York to be lost among its millions, believing that the larger the number, the greater the chance of anonymity.

But when he had learned that she was there, too, he had turned into a searcher. It seemed like he had looked into every one of the city's eight million faces, searching tirelessly until he'd finally stumbled across the only face in the city that meant happiness.

Just before falling back to sleep, Carpo thanked god. He wasn't a religious person—he never went to church or did much praying—but someone had given him a second chance. Something had allowed him another shot at the only thing in his entire life that had been totally right.

There, in the half-consciousness before sleep, Carpo swore to himself that he would never again let her out of his reach. Whatever it took, he would make it work. He knew there was no such thing as a third chance.

# Chapter 19

For the third morning in a row, the phone jarred Carpo from his sleep. He turned in his bed and found it empty, then twisted in the other direction and looked at his clock. It was already 10:00 A.M.

He untangled himself from the sheets and walked into the living room. Damn, he thought as he picked up the phone, it had all been a dream. "Hello?"

"Good morning, sleepy head," Karen's voice said in his ear.

Carpo smiled, reassured that the night before had been no dream. "Why did you leave so early?" he asked, the words distorted by a yawn.

"Some of us still have jobs, you know."

"Don't remind me."

"I've got some good news, Michael. I found an old U.P.S. label from one of Frank's sculptures. There's no name on it, but there's a return address. It could be from Gabriel Adonis's studio."

He switched the phone to his other ear as he grabbed a pencil from the end table. "What is it?" he asked.

"The address is 1356 Charity Street. It's in Pelham Manor, New York."

Bingo, he thought to himself, remembering that there was

a Pelham Manor address on the list from Insect Warehouse. "Karen, check at the bottom of the label, there should be a phone number."

"No, the only number here is the museum's."

"That's okay, I know how to find it."

"Michael, I want you to promise something," she said, urgency creeping into her voice. "Promise you won't go there. You don't know this man, and he could be dangerous. I don't want you to go up there alone."

He frowned at the piece of paper before him. Why was she suddenly so nervous about him looking into Gabriel Adonis? "It wouldn't hurt if I went up there and poked around a little."

"No. Promise me right now you won't go. Do it, Michael, or I'll get angry at you."

"All right, all right, I promise. Besides, how do we even know this is the right address?"

"I don't care. You take too many chances, Michael. Like the other night, running off after some strange man on the street. You still don't know what you're dealing with."

"Take it easy, Karen, I said I won't go. I have some errands to run today, anyway."

"Errands? Like what?"

He smiled; she knew him too well. She knew he would want to check out the address immediately.

"I've got to drop off my press pass at Channel 8 and then I have to go to the bank and cleaners. Stop worrying about me, okay? I'm not going to take any chances." He tossed the pencil onto the coffee table. "Besides, I've got a hell of a lot to stay healthy for now."

He waited for her to say something, but the line stayed curiously silent.

"Any regrets?" he asked, squinting his eyes while he waited for an answer.

"Not a single one. I woke up this morning happier than I've been in a very long time."

"Maybe we can have dinner again tonight?"

"I'd love to, just as long as I make it home afterwards. I'm exhausted. Why don't you call me when you're finished with your errands. We'll make plans then."

They said good-bye to each other and hung up. Carpo had considered saying "I love you" but decided it was still too early.

He looked around himself—the squashed pillows on the couch and the empty coffee mugs on the table—and broke into a smile. He picked up one of the pillows, buried his face in it, and inhaled. Her scent was still there, a sweet perfume that lingered in the fabric. It was real. It had happened.

He hugged the pillow tight and whispered: "I love you."

Carpo coaxed a small pot of coffee from the Rancilio; showered; and threw on some jeans, a T-shirt, and an old cotton sweater. With just a brief surge of guilt over breaking his promise, he grabbed the Manhattan directory and thumbed through the pages until he reached the Blue Section, which held the schedule for the Metro North Railroad. Pelham was about a twenty-five minute ride from Grand Central. Now he just needed to see if the address from the U.P.S. label was for Gabriel Adonis. He picked up the phone and dialed Channel 8's Assignment Desk.

A familiar, young voice answered: "Channel 8 News, this is David. Can I help you?"

It was David Brandt, the intern he had yelled at on Monday. "David, it's Michael Carpo calling," he said. "Is Sisco around?"

"He's here, Carpo, but he's in a meeting with Mr. Lipton."

The intern's voice sounded respectful, but Carpo still hesitated. He wondered if any hard feelings lingered with the intern. He decided it was worth a chance.

"Listen, Dave, I need to ask a favor, but it's got to be kept quiet. Really quiet. Can you help me?"

"Sure Carp'. What's up?"

"I need you to find the Cole's Directory and check the number listed for a street address. Get the directory for Westchester. If there's more than one, get the book that lists Pelham Manor."

"Hang on a second."

Carpo waited while the intern went to get the directories. The Cole's Directory was a reverse phone book, allowing a person to look up a street address and get the name and phone number of the resident. The books were invaluable in the news business because so often there was only an address to go on. The Assignment Desk used them the most since police and fire scanners usually only gave out the address of a suspected crime or fire. The Cole's Directory allowed the desk assistants and interns to look up the address, cross-check the phone number, and then call to see if something was going on.

"There's only one book for Pelham," David announced when he came back on the line.

"Okay. Now look up the name and number for a Charity Street, 1356 Charity Street." Carpo could faintly make out the sound of the intern leafing through the pages of the book.

"Got it. 1356 Charity. The phone number is (914) 732–1422."

"Is a name listed with it?"

"Yeah, G. Adonis. That's all it says here, G. Adonis."

"Good work, Dave. This really helps me. And let's keep it between you and me, okay?"

"I hear you, Carpo. I won't tell anyone."

He hung up the phone and went into the bedroom to get the list from Insect Warehouse off his desk. He already knew that Gabriel Adonis's name was missing from the list, but the Pelham Manor name contained the same telephone number as the Cole's Directory provided. The Insect Warehouse name was Gerald Applebaum. Close enough, he thought. Adonis must have formed an alias for the phone order from his real initials.

Carpo reached Grand Central Terminal by noon. The cavernous building was mostly empty, the time falling almost exactly between the two rush hours. He bought a round-trip ticket to Pelham and a black coffee at Zaro's bakery, then he wasted a few minutes at the newsstand, leafing through the newspapers to see if there was anything new on the official Werner investigation.

*The Daily News* held a small blurb on the case in its "City Section." It reported that police officials were delaying the release of Werner's autopsy report because of the revelation that the medical examiner had conducted an illegal interview with a TV journalist. The story did not mention Carpo by name, and it was buried at the bottom of a lengthy report on a possible serial killer preying on gay men in the West Village.

All it took was a few consecutive days of no leads for the press to bump a story aside. Even so, Carpo knew better than to expect the Werner story to disappear all together. When the autopsy came out and the papers discovered that the scream had been surgically carved into Werner's face, it would probably re-emerge on page one.

As small as the blurb was, Carpo felt bad about seeing Dr. Parkes's name in print. The medical examiner had put her career on the line to provide him with a major tip. He swore to himself that he would make it up to her once everything had passed. Somehow he would clear her name, and somehow he would show her that he hadn't gone to the papers.

Carpo bought the latest edition of *The New Yorker* for the ride to Pelham, then waited by the big board over the ticket windows to see what gate his train was departing from. He boarded the train as soon as it was posted. He took a seat next to a window, pulled out his coffee, and flipped through *The New Yorker.* He had taken out a subscription to the magazine while a sophomore at Georgetown, back when he used to be an avid follower of contemporary American literature. He still had his favorite editions of the magazine saved in a bundle in the back of his closet. It might be a good time to open another subscription, he thought. Maybe even crack the covers on a few of his old books from Georgetown.

Pelham was the fourth stop on the train, after 125th Street, Fordham, and New Rochelle. He found a pay phone at the station and dialed the number for Adonis's house. He let the phone ring thirty times, then hung up and dialed it again, just in case he had dialed wrong the first time. There was still no answer.

He walked out to the parking lot and joined a small queue for a taxi. He shared a rusted-out Peltown livery wagon with an elderly woman who smelled like peppermint lozenges. The woman barked orders the entire trip at a teenage driver wearing an oil-stained Skoal baseball cap on his head. The kid responded by turning up the volume on the radio until Carpo felt like the bass was lodged in his throat. The old woman was dropped off first. Carpo had the driver leave him at the top of Charity Street, about a hundred yards from number 1356. He jotted down Peltown's phone number for the return trip to the station.

The drive from the station had lasted ten minutes, but Carpo felt he had a good read on Pelham, an attractive town about fifteen to twenty miles outside New York City. Most of the houses had been built in the thirties and constructed in the same general style: sturdy brick exterior, painted wood shutters, two car garage, and meticulously manicured patches of lawn in front and back. It was suburban utopia; not a bad place to bring up a family, especially if you commuted to the city for work.

Carpo strode down the sidewalk lining Charity Street, trying to look like he was comfortable with the area. Pelham was the land of "Neighborhood Watch Patrol," as several signs warned along the way. Carpo tried to make it appear as if he had walked this stretch of pavement every day of his life.

Number 1356 was at the end of the street, where the groomed lawns ended in a dense patch of woods. The entrance to the driveway was blocked by an eight-foot wooden fence. In the middle of the fence was a small black sign with red letters that warned, "Private Property." Carpo continued past the driveway, noting the formidable stone wall circling the property. The wall was eight-feet high, and it prevented him from seeing what was inside. He guessed that the property contained maybe two or three acres. Over the top of the wall, he could make out the dark gray slate of two rooftops.

He walked to the end of the street and stopped, looking into the air as if the pine tree before him was the first he'd ever seen. He stared back the way he had come, made sure no one was watching, then stepped into the thin patch of trees beyond the road.

Once off the pavement he moved quickly, jogging through the woods until he reached the cool shade of the wall. He traced the wall through the woods, his feet sinking into the wet soil, creating sucking noises every time he lifted a shoe.

He walked along the perimeter until the slate roofs had

turned halfway around, then he started looking for a tree that grew next to the wall. He chose a thick-limbed elm with several branches reaching out over the top of the wall. He wedged his foot in a crook of the lowest branch and hoisted himself into the air. He twisted his way up, moving from limb to limb, until he had climbed about eight feet, even with the top of the wall. He held still as he clung to the tree's trunk and inspected the grounds, watching and listening for anything that might signal the presence of the owner.

From his perch, Carpo could see that the property was well landscaped and neatly kept. A gravel driveway ran from the wood gate on Charity Street, past a moss-covered stone house, to a large stone building near his side of the property. The edges of the driveway and wall were lined with flower beds, covered in black plastic for the winter. The lawn was ragged after the long cold season and saturated from the night's rain storm. Carpo noticed a woodpile next to the house with a small wheelbarrow leaning against it.

Despite the pastoral setting, it was apparent that someone had taken great pains to ensure the security of the residence. Carpo spotted two surveillance cameras mounted on top of the wall. The closest one made a slight buzzing noise as its lens swiveled from side to side. More ominous was the strip of razor blade wire curled over and over against itself on the inside edge of the wall.

Carpo studied the property for twenty minutes without seeing a sign of life. The house and barn had no lights on, nor was there any movement through the windows. The chimneys atop both roofs showed no smoke. The fence was closed and the driveway empty. Fighting back another rush of guilt, Carpo edged his body to the end of the limb, planted his foot on top of the wall, and pushed away from the tree.

He crouched there for a second, then stood and used the elm branch as a crude banister as he took a high, careful step over the razor blade wire. His crotch cleared the glimmering blades by less than two inches. He raised his other leg to step over the wire when his hand slipped off the wet bark. As he recovered his balance, his left foot lowered and the razor bit firmly into his shoelace.

Carpo flailed in space a few times until he grabbed hold of the limb. His trapped leg remained high in the air, bent at the knee like a flamingo's. He jerked on the shoelace a few times as he darted glances at the property that stretched before him. The wire blade remained firmly attached, but he noticed it cutting through the shoelace. He gripped the tree limb in both hands as he cranked his foot back and forth, sawing the shoelace against the blade. After several minutes, all while totally exposed to the house and barn—elm branch flapping up and down like a warning flag—the shoelace finally gave way. He stepped to the far side of the wall, lowered a hand to the edge, and jumped into the property.

He landed in the soft mud of a flower bed, his body concealed behind a patch of forsythia. He crept through the base of the bush, then waited in a tight crouch, eyes darting all around, while he plotted his next move.

The large building—it appeared to be a barn—was twenty yards from his position, the house twenty yards beyond that. He pushed himself free of the bush and sprinted onto the open lawn. He crossed the distance in sixteen strides, pressing his body against the wet stone of the barn. His bruised knee started to quiver, but he held absolutely still, listening for anything different. The only sounds he heard were the wind blowing around the corner of the barn and the far-off shouts of children playing.

Carpo stood and slapped the mud off his knees, then sidled along the edge of the barn, heading back in the direction of Charity Street. He passed two large windows, which he tried to peer through, but they were covered by heavy drapes and afforded no view of the interior. The front of the barn was outfitted with a double carport and a doorway. He peaked through the tiny windows in the garage doors; both were empty. He relaxed a bit, hoping that an empty garage meant an empty house.

He crossed the distance between the barn and the house in a brisk walk, his mind pondering several different excuses he might try if he was discovered on the property. He was lost? He had unwittingly arrived at the wrong address? He was selling magazine subscriptions? None of the excuses were half-plausible—why had he needed to climb the fence?—but he placed more stock in a lame alibi than in saying he was sneaking around the property.

He walked up to the front door and tested the knob; it was locked. He circled the house, ducking under each window and then carefully peering in, until he had a fairly good idea of what was inside.

The house was stylishly decorated by someone with an interest in antiques and works of art. Each room was filled with paintings and sculptures, the styles tending toward classical. The floors were covered with thick Persian rugs and bright Turkish kilims. The furniture appeared expensive and manly: oversized couch, sturdy Chippendale desk, dark paisley fabrics. Carpo also noticed an elaborate alarm system wired throughout the first floor; electronic motion detectors monitored each room, and several windows were wired to detect broken glass. He prayed he had not tripped any hidden alarm systems. He trusted a lame alibi even less if the police were to swarm onto the property.

Satisfied with the house, Carpo crossed back to the barn. It was a large structure, at least twice the size of the house, with what seemed to be a guest house or office above the garage. He approached the garage doors again and pushed against them. They vibrated slightly in his hand but didn't budge when he tugged on their handles. The door to the building was of the traditional barn-door variety, top half swinging independent of the bottom. He tested the knob on the top part; it was tightly locked, but his heart resumed its wild pounding when the knob on the bottom clicked and swung open.

"Jack-freakin'-pot," he whispered, his vision blurring from nervousness. If he entered the building, his crime jumped from trespassing to burglary. If he closed the door and left the compound, his crime would be nothing.

"And I'll still know nothing," he argued to his conscience. He pushed the door open a few inches and squirmed inside.

He stayed low to the floor and closed the door, pausing as his eyes adjusted to the darkness. A hint of light seeped through the heavy curtains, slivers of beams that captured the particles of dust floating in the room. Near the door, a tiny red light flashed on and off every time he moved. When his eyes grew more accustomed to the darkness, he could see it was a control panel for an alarm. The red light was flashing next to "UNARMED."

Carpo walked through an area that appeared to be a small living room. It was cluttered with a couch, several chairs, and a television set, all covered with white sheets. He walked through a doorway next to the couch. It led into a small bedroom and a bathroom. Both rooms were unheated and smelled of mildew.

He walked back to the living room and looked over each wall, searching for the way into the rest of the building. He found it opposite the bedroom, a small door that blended in with the rest of the room's paneling. He put his hand against it and felt a stream of heat pouring through the crack between the wall and door frame. There was no knob on the door, but it clicked open when he pushed against it. Beyond was a thin hallway leading to a steep flight of stairs. He started up them, grimacing every time a wooden step creaked under his weight. At the top was another door, this one metal, and he was relieved to find it also unlocked. He had come this far, it would be a shame to have to turn back.

Carpo opened the door and was momentarily blinded by bright light. He stood in the entrance, hands clamped over both eyes, while he waited for his pupils to readjust to the sunlight. It poured in through the north side of the roof, through a series of skylights.

He was standing in a huge loft, covering what he figured was the entire length of the barn. Between each section of skylight, rows of fluorescent and incandescent bulbs were installed. When turned on, the lights would easily brighten the loft during nighttime. Windows also covered both of the long side walls, providing unobstructed views over the wall of the surrounding neighborhood.

Once his eyes had adjusted, Carpo was amazed by the amount of dust swirling in the air. It was very fine and powdery white, almost like talcum powder; his nose itched every time he inhaled. The dust reminded Carpo of a grade school trip he had once taken to a lumberyard, where the sawdust was so thick in the air he had felt like he was going to choke. The dust coated every surface in the loft, and bigger particles were scattered on the floor. When he walked across the floor, his steps crackled as small pieces of stone and sediment burst underfoot.

Through the swirling dust and bright rays of light, Carpo spotted several figures standing in the loft. They were different body parts—torsos, heads, hands, legs—frozen in various positions of motion. He stared at the pieces, mesmerized by their ability to hold so still while appearing so real.

Carpo knew he had come to the right house. The link to Frank Werner was obvious. The figures were various pieces of sculpture in differing stages of completion.

He walked to the first object, a life-sized model of a foot wearing a primitive sandal, both carved from the same piece of ivory. The straps of the sandal pinched the sides of the foot, causing a hint of veins to swell under the skin. He brushed his hand over the foot. It was smooth and cool, the fine dust coating his hand, stinging the parts where he was sweating. He walked from sculpture to sculpture, circling each piece and studying its composition. Some were fragments like the foot, others were whole bodies. All of them appeared to be very, very old.

Carpo felt shaken by the figures. He had a sudden overwhelming urge to turn and leave, to spring back across the yard, climb the fence, and return to New York. Something in the room felt totally wrong, but he felt powerless to stop it. Instead, he moved on to the next piece of sculpture and then the one after that, until he had reached the far end of the loft.

There, the wall was covered by a thin sheet of plywood with hundreds of tiny holes drilled through it. The holes matched a perfect grid pattern with metal hooks inserted through some of them, balancing dozens of tools—hand drills, rasps, vises, hammers, and electric powered machines. Each tool was carefully displayed on the board, its exact size outlined in black pen and labeled by its proper name. Carpo was amazed by the number of names for chisels—flat chisels, pointed chisels, claw chisels, drove chisels, and rounded chisels—each type coming in various sizes.

Beneath the board was a long worktable, with rows of drawers underneath. Carpo opened each one and inspected the contents. One held screws, rulers, nails, nuts, bolts, and scrap pieces of metal. Another held various types of drills, power and manual, as well as a full array of drill bits. Like the tool board, the drawers were compulsively ordered. Each compartment was separated by thin slats of felt-covered wood that conformed to the exact shape of the tool. When he rolled out the drawers, the movement was silent, the felt material dulling even the rattle of the scrap metal.

The bottom drawers were larger and took Carpo longer to go through. There was a blue plastic case that caught his attention. It held a set of stainless steel surgical tools. They were small, razor-sharp instruments; some mirrored the shape of the large tools hanging on the tool board. Carpo lifted each one out of the case and admired it—the balance of the steel, the feel of the rough-etched grip, the sparkling blade. He removed the case and set it on top of the workbench. It would be useful when it came time to convince people about his discovery.

Carpo pushed the drawer shut and turned to the final compartment, on the lower right side of the workbench. The drawer was empty, save for a thin manila envelope. Carpo picked it up and undid the metal clasps. What he found inside the envelope did not disclose why Gabriel Adonis had murdered Frank Werner, however it explained a lot about why Karen had pleaded with him to stay away from the house.

The envelope held a set of four eight by ten color photographs, taken about five feet from their subject. The pictures showed the front, two sides, and back of a woman's head. The woman in the photo appeared to be in a sort of trance, eyes focusing on something off in the distance. Her face was poised and beautiful, its innate dignity accentuated by a slender neck.

The woman in the photos was Karen Blackwell.

Carpo wasn't sure how long he stared at the photographs. Five minutes, maybe longer. The photos were doodled on with a black grease pencil, tracing the outline of a faint crown that moved back behind her ears. In the pictures that showed Karen's face, someone had shaded the corners of her eyes, drawing them to a point so that she looked almost Asian.

It was not difficult to see what the markings and the photographs represented. Every picture corresponded directly to a view of The Cleopatra Bust.

# Chapter 20

"That bitch," Carpo said out loud. The long room swallowed up his words as if he had shouted them into a vacuum.

He folded the photographs in half and shoved them into the inside pocket of his jacket. When he stood up, they pressed out from his chest a little, but remained flat enough so they were not noticeable from the front. He closed the tab on the empty manila envelope and replaced it in the drawer. He took the case of surgical tools and threw them in the drawer, too. The unit was too bulky to carry with him. Besides, he already had all the proof he needed in his coat pocket.

He glanced around the room, making sure that he hadn't disturbed its general appearance, then crossed to the metal door. On his way past the side windows, he caught a glimpse of a green car in the driveway. It was a Mercedes sedan parked along the side of the garage. A split-second later, he heard the barn door slam downstairs.

Carpo raced back across the loft, searching frantically for a hiding place. He heard the door leading to the stairs push open, then heavy footsteps clomping up the stairs. On the same wall as the hanging tools, he spotted a door. He yanked it open and jumped inside, shutting it just as the door to the loft was thrown open.

Carpo ran his fingers wildly through his hair as he searched for a spot to hide. The room was a small closet, maybe four feet square and illuminated by a strange, ultraviolet light. Most of the space was taken up by an aluminum step ladder and stacks of rectangular wire cages. The wire on the cages was red and seemed to move back and forth, heaving like it was breathing. He moved closer to the cages and saw that they were filled with thousands of blood red insects crawling all over each other, struggling to get as close to the blue light as possible.

"Cochineals," he whispered as he moved a cardboard box out of his way. The box carried several blaze-orange stickers that read: "Caution: Live Insects. Keep Warm." On top of the box was a shipping label addressed to G. Appelbaum at 1356 Charity Street; it was from Insect Warehouse.

Carpo crouched in a corner and held the box in front of him. It was a feeble attempt at concealment, but he couldn't think of anything better. Outside the closet, he could hear someone moving back and forth across the loft, muttering something unintelligible. Even though he couldn't make out the words, Carpo recognized the voice; its familiar pitch and faint accent wafted between the cracks in the door.

The footsteps drew near to the closet and stopped. Carpo grabbed one of the heavy wire cages and raised it about his head, ready to smash it on the man's head if he entered. But as suddenly as the man had entered the loft, the talking stopped and the footsteps retreated.

He waited there for several minutes, the cage still above his head as he listened for any noise. Something brushed lightly against his neck, and he nearly screamed when he saw dozens of the scaly red insects crawling up and down his shoulder, scurrying toward the blue light behind his neck. The top on the cage had swung open and the insects were using his arm as a ladder to reach it. He dropped the cage and swatted the insects off his body. There were hundreds of them, crawling on the floor and scrambling over his foot. He had to get out of the closet.

Carpo stepped over the cage and pushed his ear up against the door. There was no sound from outside. A few of the insects had gotten under his pant legs; he could feel them maneuvering through the hairs on his ankles. He had to get out of the closet now.

He pushed the door open and stepped into the bright loft. It appeared as he had left it: dust devils swirling in the light, statues frozen in action, and the Pelham neighborhood outside the window. He took one step, two steps, then he heard the noise of someone breathing behind him.

He whirled and discovered Gabriel Adonis standing to the side of the closet door, a curious smile splashed over his young, hairless face. They stared at each other in silence for a few seconds before Carpo noticed the pistol gripped in the man's hand. It was a small silver gun with a mother of pearl handle. Carpo didn't know a thing about pistols or calibers, but the hole on the end of this one looked big enough to punch a lot of air into him. He raised his arms carefully above his shoulders.

"Michael Carpo, I presume?" Adonis said in a soft, almost polite way. "Or shall I just refer to you as Carpo?"

When he said Carpo's name, he pronounced each syllable distinctly. Car-Poe—the emphasis equal on both. "That'll do," Carpo said, eyes mesmerized by the black hole on the gun.

"I am surprised Ms. Blackwell did not accompany you today. She might have used her key to unlock my gate and saved you that perilous climb over my wall."

The man grabbed a metal folding chair that was leaning against the wall and carried it toward him. He closed the distance between them in three quick steps, his movements surprisingly fluid for such a short, thick body. He was dressed in a blue-striped oxford with charcoal gray pants, a large gold Rolex watch strapped to his left wrist, and fine Gucci loafers on his feet. As he moved, the scent of musk cologne spread in the air.

He laid the metal chair on the ground, then kicked it the rest of the way to Carpo. He gestured at the chair. "Please, make yourself comfortable."

Carpo picked it up, unfolded it, and sat down. Adonis moved closer, circling him, like a shark honing in on its prey.

"It was a bad idea to come here," Carpo said. His voice sounded tinny, unreal. "Maybe we can work something out. I could have Channel 8 do a story on you. Maybe get you some recognition for your art."

"Thank you. That is a kind offer," Adonis said, punctuating his statement with a squeaky giggle. "But I will have to decline. I am not looking for recognition."

The man seemed amused by Carpo's offer. His tone and body language relaxed. Even the tip of the gun lowered a bit. Carpo decided to try and keep him talking.

"But you must want some recognition," he said. "Everybody wants to receive honor."

"Mm-bah. Preposterous. No great artist is honored in his time."

"But isn't that why you faked sculptures?"

"Faked? I did not fake a sculpture. I have never faked a work in my life." Adonis ran a fat thumb across the top of the gun. "Every one of my pieces is a complete original. It is the collectors who are stupid. They hope so much the pieces are old, they are willing to believe anything."

"Most people would call that faking."

Adonis shrugged his wide shoulders. "I cannot be worried for the ignorance of people. You are no different, Carpo. You are terribly ignorant, especially when it comes to Ms. Blackwell. I watched you both enter your apartment. I can only imagine what she did to convince you to come here today."

The mention of Karen sparked a tiny surge of anger within Carpo. He wasn't sure if it was anger at Adonis for talking about her or anger at Karen. Either way, he coveted the emotion, holding it inside him and protecting it. Anger might be good, he thought. It might be useful.

"Why have you been watching my apartment?" he asked a little more strongly.

Adonis ignored the question. "I wonder about her sometimes, the way she acts with a man. I wonder if she uses her body and fondles . . . fondles like she does with one of my statues."

The man stepped in front of him and crouched until they were face to face, allowing Carpo to stare into his light blue eyes. They were a vacant blue, calm and emotionless. Carpo wished they were not so; he wanted them to be human eyes, eyes that displayed emotion and compassion.

"Does it bother you that she rejected The Cleopatra Bust?" Carpo asked.

Something happened, a quick flicker of emotion in the middle of each pupil. It was brief but violent, almost like a tiny bolt of lightning atop a tranquil sea. Adonis blinked twice, then recovered himself with a grin.

"I once thought Karen was different, but she is not so," he said. "She rejected The Cleopatra Bust because she did not understand it. In the end, she is like every other critic in history: she is unable to respect what is beyond her. She is the same as the ones who said Michelangelo was a fraud, who thought Donatello showed no promise, who laughed at Canova. She is no different, Carpo. She rejects and destroys anything she cannot comprehend."

Adonis resumed his stroll around the chair, the gun down at his side now. Carpo kept his head facing forward but allowed his eyes to wander across the loft, searching for an escape or a weapon. There was the grid of tools on the wall no more than ten feet away, an entire array of mallets, chisels, and hammers. A softball-sized chunk of stone was three feet to his left. There was also the metal chair in which he was sitting. All of the objects he could use as a weapon, be it for defense or attack.

"I am actually surprised she told you about the bust," Adonis said. "What did she tell you? What did she claim was wrong with it?"

"She said the hair was wrong for the time period. It lacked realism. She also said Cleopatra should have been outfitted with a crown of some sort. A diadem, I think it was called."

"Preposterous. Cleopatra's hair is perfect. And Mark Antony would never have allowed a crown to be placed on an Egyptian. Don't you see Karen for what she is? Don't you see her flaw? She cannot create, so she must destroy. Bernini could chisel right before her and she would object. If my Cleopatra is wrong, why then did it sell for so many millions. A record, the most ever paid! You saw those people yesterday, clamoring over it like a pack of wild dogs."

Carpo felt a chill run up his back. "You saw me at the auction?"

"Of course. Why do you think I permitted you to hear my voice? I have planned everything. Everything. Even waiting for you to arrive here."

"But why me? Why did you involve me?"

"Because she loves you," he hissed. "What better person to destroy her than the man she loves?"

"But I would never destroy Karen."

"Oh, but you already have, Carpo." Adonis smiled as he ran his hand over his thinning hair. "You and your television have compromised her reputation. That is what is important to a person like her. Reputation is her power."

Adonis shook his head in a solemn way, as if he were overcome with pity. "You are very naive, Carpo. Did you never see that she was a part of this? She was the way Frank and I got the pieces verified. She knew the stories were false; she knew I had carved all of those statues."

Carpo shook his head. "No, I don't believe you."

"I am sorry if I have destroyed your perfect views of her. As they say, ignorance is bliss. But I assure you, Carpo, she was a partner to all of this."

"Then why did she reject the bust? Why?"

"Because she got too big for herself. Frank plucked her out of obscurity at that pitiful museum. She was nothing there. *Nothing.* He took her and gave her my works and told her what to say about them. And they made her—my works *made* her career. Then, one day, she snaps her fingers and says no more. She sees my Cleopatra, my perfect Cleopatra, and she proclaims it wrong. Like she knows about such things. She tells Frank she can't approve it, can't compromise herself, can't jeopardize her *reputation.*"

"What about Frank? What did he say?"

Adonis's eyes narrowed, and his mouth set into an expression that was almost sad. "Frank was a fool. He allowed her to play him like an instrument. It must hurt you to hear this

Carpo, but she was very good at it. She used her body and feminine ways, rotting and corrupting his mind until he finally turned against me. We worked thirty years to build this, and he tossed it away for a woman."

"That's why you murdered him? Because he didn't side with you?"

Adonis's face cracked into a smile, his giggle tittering as high as a young child's. "I did not murder Frank; I immortalized him. If that fat bastard had died of a heart attack, they would have forgotten him in a day. But I turned him into something famous, something that was finally as stupendous as all of those ridiculous stories he used to construct. I made Frank Werner immortal."

"But why did you do it?"

"Simplicity, Carpo. Do you understand that word? People see something simple and they don't understand it, so they make it very difficult. Simplicity is beauty, remember that. What I did to Frank was simple, and it was beautiful."

"I don't understand."

"Frank was my next work of art, my next creation. So I make his body smooth like stone and I trouble over his face until it is interesting. Now do you understand? He was my sculpture."

"But why did you put him in the reservoir?"

"When I look at a block of stone, I read its contents. I study its texture, its shape, its cracks. They're all clues. I read them until I understand what the block of stone holds. When I see the form inside, when I understand its essence, I liberate it. I don't carve the stone into a sculpture, I chisel away the rock to free the form. With Frank, I do the same, but I do it in the reverse. Simple and beautiful. I have my sculpture—fat screaming Frank—so I return it to the solid. A blow torch on the ice, the water accepts the body and refreezes, and now the world can see in a solid what I see in a stone."

Adonis leaned forward, mouth just inches from his face, so close Carpo could feel the hot breath on his skin. "Do you understand now, Carpo? I am a god, a god like any worshipped on earth. That god formed us out of flesh, a medium that allows movement, emotion, and life. My medium is different, but the result is quite similar. I take a piece of rock, a substance strong enough to last for an eternity, and I mold it into a thing of beauty, a form that also depicts movement, emotion, and life. Flesh and stone—two materials from which life is formed."

Adonis raised the gun and pressed it into Carpo's temple. Carpo felt something relax in him, the hope drain out of his body. He closed his eyes and remained still, ready to accept it.

"No, no, Carpo, not like this," Adonis said. Carpo opened his eyes. "I must show you something first. Something simple and very, very beautiful."

There was a blur before Carpo's eyes as the gun raised up and then smashed down on his head. Too late for him to flinch, too late even to blink. Just a swish of movement, a glint of steel, and then an awful pain knifing clear through his skull.

He fell to the floor, hands grabbing for his head, balls of light flaring in his eyes like Roman candles. He could taste blood seeping down the back of his throat. His face hit the floor, nostrils sucking in the fine talc. He gasped, then coughed, then choked.

Adonis moved over him and smashed the gun down again on his head. Carpo put his arms up to protect himself, but they no longer responded. The light in his eyes grew brighter and brighter, and he felt himself falling inside himself, deeper and deeper, until the bright light exploded into a roaring sun.

As if from another hemisphere, Carpo heard two distinct sounds: a telephone ringing and a power tool running. The telephone was in the background, its tinkling bell eventually swallowed by the roar of the tool's engine.

It was an electric drill. It started from the side of the room and came close to him, buzzing around his face and neck like a manic bee.

Then there was no more sound. Only darkness.

# Chapter 21

Light. Dark. Light. Dark. Carpo blinked his eyes over and over again but couldn't make them focus on anything. Panic seized him as he thought, My god, I'm blind. But when he tried to reach for his eyes, his arms remained paralyzed at his sides.

For a moment he thought it had happened to him, the same fate that had been Frank Werner's. He remembered the sound of a drill being turned on and it coming closer and closer to his head, then the sound of a telephone ringing. Or was it the other way around? The last thing he remembered was a giant flash of light and then darkness.

But he couldn't be lobotomized. Not when his head ached so badly it brought tears to his eyes.

He rolled his head from side to side, feeling the bump on the back of it. Whenever the full weight of his head hit the bump, a sharp pain shot through his head, like someone was driving a nail into the center of his brain. He could feel the floor beneath him, its fine dust caking the inside of his nostrils, and he could still taste the sweet blood lingering in the back of his throat.

He tested his fingers, wiggling them up and down at his sides. He knew he wasn't paralyzed because he could feel the movement through his jeans. He could also feel a sharp sting at his wrists whenever he tried to lift his arms. After struggling for a few minutes, he realized why he couldn't see or move. His wrists were bound at his sides by some sort of tape, as were his eyes.

He rolled onto his stomach and bent his knees underneath him. His ankles were bound, but with a little squirming motion he was able to raise his torso into the air. When his head lifted, a wave of nausea came over him. He thought for a moment that he was about to be sick, so he slowly returned to the ground and waited for the feeling to pass.

In pieces, the afternoon came back to him. He remembered taking the train to Pelham and climbing over the wall. He remembered climbing the stairs, looking at the statues, even finding the photographs of Karen. He also remembered hiding in the closet, the feel of the cochineal insects on his body. It took him a little while before he recalled stepping out of the closet and hearing someone behind him. It had been Adonis, clasping a silver gun in his hand.

As each memory popped into his head, the next one came more and more easily. There was the conversation about Karen and the revelation that she had been part of the art hoax. Then Adonis had hit him with the gun. Once or twice? He remembered now: it was twice. He remembered that, and he remembered the noise of a drill, whirring with a high scream as it moved over his head. But what next? Adonis had captured him all alone in the loft and no one knew he was there. Why hadn't he killed him?

"Karen," he whispered in a panic.

Adonis might have assumed that Karen knew he was there. He might even have believed she had sent him. What if he had gone after her, realizing he could always come back to his prisoner in the loft? Carpo had to do something to warn her.

If I can't walk out of here, then I'll roll out, he thought to himself.

He raised his head a few inches off the floor, took a breath of cleaner air, and started rolling across the floor. After three full turns, his body collided with something hard and cold. He assumed it was a block of stone, maybe the marble base from one of the sculptures. He twisted his legs around the obstruction, then wiggled his body past. His lungs ached for more oxygen, but whenever he opened his mouth, the chalky air rushed in. His rolling was upsetting the thick dust on the floor. He imagined the room, obliterated by a swirl of heavy dust.

He began rolling again across the floor, bumping every so often into other objects. Some he could identify, like blocks of stone or metal tools, others he was unsure of. On just three breaths, he reached the far side of the loft. He sat up with his back planted against the wall, then leaned back and got his knees under him. Slowly, like a sail rising in heavy wind, he got to his feet.

Up high, the air was cleaner and he breathed deeply. He moved across the wall with little hops until he found the metal door. He leaned his body against it, but it was tightly closed.

With his hands still pinned to his sides, Carpo leaned forward and grasped the doorknob between his chin and breastplate. It took four tries, but he was able to twist his head to the right, turning the knob until it clicked. He pushed forward as hard as he could against the door. It swung away from him, catapulting him head first into the open space.

"Shit," he screamed as he rolled down the wooden steps. The wood was smooth and his clothes were caked with the talc, accelerating his body like a waxed surfboard riding down a monster wave. With each step, his body picked up speed, his grunts echoing in the hallway as he was struck high and low.

Near the bottom, a step crashed full force into his left side, producing a sickening crackle inside his body. He lay in a heap on the floor, lungs heaving against the pain of a busted rib.

It took a long time for his breathing to return to normal, but the pain stayed behind, burning his side like a hot ember held against him. He clamped his left arm down over the rib, bit his tongue, and continued rolling.

"Karen!" he screamed whenever the pain threatened to send him back to the darkness. He found that saying her name conjured up her face and made the next roll bearable.

Using his chin as a wedge again, Carpo undid the lower half of the barn door and pushed his way into the driveway. He fell to the macadam, screaming when the rib gave another sickening crack.

"Karen! Karen! Karen!"

He was sobbing now, but he forced himself to keep rolling, over and over, until it made him sick. As he retched on the pavement, his arm could feel the bump on his side where the bone was poking up. He wanted to stop. He wanted to give up. He didn't care anymore whether or not Adonis killed Karen.

"Karen! Karen! Karen!"

He felt the pavement slope downward and then the brightness of the sun evaporate from his eyes as he rolled next to the wall. A few more turns and he was against the wooden fence at the entrance to Charity Street.

"Karen!"

He put his back against the fence and leaned into it, the door giving a little from the pressure. He maneuvered his knees under him, then his feet. He pressed his forehead against the fence and pushed with all of his strength. It was bolted solid.

"Help," Carpo screamed. The pressure brought a flash of

pain to his head, but it was nothing compared to the pain in his side. "Help me, please. Someone come quick."

After each shout, he stopped and listened for sound. The street sounded empty. He remembered something Sisco had told him once, that people don't react to calls of "Help" as fast as they do to shouts of "Fire." Carpo leaned back his head and roared: "Fire, fire. Someone come quick, there's a fire."

Footsteps ran across the pavement. Carpo whirled toward them, lost his balance, and fell to the ground. Where were the footsteps coming from? Inside or outside the fence? He strained to pick up a noise but didn't hear anything else.

"Is someone there?" he asked weakly.

"Hi. What's your name?" a young voice called from the other side of the fence.

"Michael," Carpo gasped. "What's yours?"

"Robby."

"Robby, do you live near here?"

"Uh-huh."

"Is your mom or dad home?"

"Mommy is."

"Go run and get her. Okay, Robby? Go tell your mommy someone's hurt real bad."

Carpo heard the little footsteps run away from him. He put his head back on the pavement and concentrated on slowing his breathing. A few minutes later, he heard more footsteps, this time heavier and moving faster.

"Help me. Please help me," he shouted.

"What's going on?" a woman demanded, her voice unnaturally deep. Carpo could tell she was frightened.

"Ma'am, please help me. The wacko who lives in this house tied me up. Please open the gate and help me."

"How do I know who you are? You could be a burglar."

"Lady, look at me. If I was a burglar, I wouldn't be tied up."

There was a long pause—Carpo imagined she was peeking at him through the fence—then the woman said: "Hang on, I'll see if I can get it open."

He heard the fence creak as she pushed against it, but there were no sounds of it opening.

"It seems to be locked from your side," she said.

"Try to look through and see what's holding it. Maybe I can undo it."

He heard the woman step up to the fence and press on it again. "There's a post on the right side. It's got a sort of hydraulic arm on it. I think that's what's locking it."

Carpo pressed his body into the fence and squirmed upright. "Is it to your right or mine?"

"Uhm, my right. You go to your left."

He hopped along the fence until his thigh bumped into a metal bar. He followed it as it slanted away from the gate.

"Describe what this looks like," he said. "Can you see a release on it? Maybe a safety catch?"

"Hang on. Yes, it slants back to a post where a small box is. There's a chain hanging down from the box. It looks like it might release the bar."

He shimmied along the bar, his bare wrist at his waist rubbing the metal until he felt the box the woman had described. He twisted his body around until his fingers touched the box, then he patted below it for the chain. After he found it, he grabbed it tight and lowered his knees, bringing the weight of his body against it.

The chain didn't give until his knees were almost on the driveway. The box clicked and the metal bar clattered to the pavement, sending him back to the ground. Carpo heard the hinge on the fence creak, then he felt it bump into him. He rolled his body back up the driveway until there was enough room for the woman to get inside.

"Dear god," she said when she got a full look at him. She knelt beside him and started undoing the tape.

"Mommy, why's the man all white?" Robby said somewhere over Carpo's head. He could imagine what he looked like, clothes caked in the chalk dust.

"Robby, go home and wait for me. Understand? Go on, do as Mommy says."

Carpo heard the little boy's footsteps patter down the street. Within a few minutes, the woman had freed the tape from his eyes and wrists. He laid back and waited for his eyes to adjust while the woman went to work on his ankles.

"Are you all right?" she asked, her face registering concern.

"I think I've got a busted rib. Can you help me to a telephone?"

The woman grabbed him around the waist and helped him up. Using her shoulder as support, they walked out of the compound. Suddenly, Carpo's knees went wobbly, a nauseous feeling rushing over him.

"Stop," he gasped. "The other side. Move to my other side. You're bumping into my rib."

They hobbled down the road a few steps at a time. Carpo prayed the house wasn't far. He looked down at his body as they moved. His arms and legs were caked with the white talc, and he was surprised to see that his clothes were ripped, with splotches of blood staining the front of his shirt. He also tasted and smelled blood.

The woman looked at him, an expression of horror coming over her face. "Your nose is bleeding," she said. "I think I'd better call an ambulance."

They reached her house and she helped him up the front steps. "Go sit over there," she said inside, pointing at a couch. "I'm going to call for help."

"No, wait," he said, waving her back. His breaths were coming harder, needle-sharp gasps that contorted his face. "I've got to make a call first. Help me to the phone."

The woman started to argue, but Carpo held up a hand. He trudged into the kitchen, left arm pressed to his side, body doubled over with pain. The phone was next to the refrigerator. He dialed the number, thinking: Karen, Karen, Karen. As he waited for the connection to go through, he caught a glimpse of his reflection in a mirror across the room. His face was coated with dust, a solid white mask, except for two red trails forged by the blood dripping from his nose.

"Department of Greek and Roman Art," a female voice said.

"Connect me with Karen Blackwell. It's an emergency."

The line clicked as he was transferred to hold. A few seconds later, Karen's voice came on the line.

"It's me," he said, fighting down the urge to scream.

"Where have you been, Michael? I was starting to get worried."

"Can't explain. You're in danger. Go somewhere safe. Right now, get somewhere safe."

"What's the matter? Are you okay?"

"Can't talk. Please, Karen, go somewhere safe." He blinked his eyes a few times, a heavy feeling sweeping back into his head. The darkness was coming again; he could feel it sweeping over him like a tidal wave. He had to make her understand, make her see how much danger she was in.

"I'll stay here at the museum," she said. "There's tons of security."

He stumbled back against the refrigerator. The museum was no good; Gabriel would go there first. He tried to tell her, but all he could say was: "Safe. Get safe."

"Michael, what's wrong with you? Are you hurt? I'll come to you."

"No!" he screamed. "Get safe!"

He squeezed the phone in his fist, flashes erupting in his head. He turned to the woman who had helped him, eyes looking up at her, mouth open, like he was about to ask for something. Instead, his eyes kept moving, rolling right up inside his head, before he collapsed to the linoleum floor.

# Chapter 22

Carpo awakened to the smell of ammonia in his nostrils. He coughed hard, shook his head from side to side, then opened his eyes. He was lying on the couch in the living room. Two paramedics were kneeling over him, one of them waving smelling salts back and forth under his nose.

"Get that thing away from me," Carpo said. "I'm awake."

"Do you hurt anywhere?" the man asked, a young black man with round wire glasses.

"Everywhere."

"What's your name?"

"Michael."

"Michael, my name is Richard. Tell me exactly where you hurt."

"You point to a spot, it hurts," Carpo said, pushing himself to a sitting position.

"Stay down," Richard demanded. He placed both hands on Carpo's shoulders and tried to stop him from standing.

"Don't do that, it hurts. I'm okay."

"You're not okay. You've got a serious concussion and a broken rib." The paramedic ran his hand down Carpo's side, prying into his ribs. When his fingers touched the busted rib, Carpo screamed and swatted the hand away.

"If you know it's broken, then why the hell are you touching it?"

"Relax, Michael. I want you to lie back down and wait until we can get a stretcher in here."

"No thanks. I'm denying treatment." He swung his legs off the couch and stepped gingerly to his feet. The nauseous feeling swept over him, and he closed his eyes, waiting for it to pass.

"I'm warning you, that rib is in bad shape," Richard said. "You're going to have to go to the hospital for x-rays. They'll probably even admit you."

"Thanks for checking me over guys, but I'm not going to the hospital." Carpo turned to the woman. "Ma'am, may I please use your bathroom?"

The woman hesitated, looking between the two paramedics, before pointing to a door near the kitchen. Carpo limped into the bathroom and shut the door.

"First things first," he said as he twisted the knob on the sink. He filled the basin with hot water, then went at his face and neck with the bar of soap. After a few minutes of scrubbing, his skin returned to the surface, leaving a chalky film in the basin after it was drained. He dried off his face, then wet his fingers and raked them across his hair to straighten it. He dusted off his clothes and walked back into the living room.

The woman and the paramedics were standing as he had left them, debating some point in terse whispers. When they saw him coming, they stopped talking. Carpo could have sworn he had heard one of them mention the word "police."

"Listen folks, this has gone way farther than it should have," he announced as he approached them. He hoped they were only talking about the police and had not already called them. Paramedics were no problem; police would be a major one. "Ma'am, if you would call me a cab for the train station, I'll be on my way."

The woman stared at the paramedics again until Richard nodded. She turned and headed into the kitchen.

"Michael," Richard said. "I think we should discuss what's going on here."

"There's nothing to discuss. It's all been a big misunderstanding."

"But you're in real bad shape."

"I'm fine," Carpo said, then added, "And I'm refusing treatment." He knew there was nothing they could do if he refused medical aid.

The woman returned to the living room and sat on the couch while the paramedics started packing their equipment. When they were finished, she waved Richard into the kitchen. Carpo could hear her voice breaking apart as she pleaded with him to stay until the stranger was gone. He felt bad for causing her so much anxiety. Without her help, he'd still be lying hog tied in Adonis's driveway.

A horn sounded from the street. Carpo walked to the window and pulled aside the curtain, spotting the Peltown taxi idling outside the driveway. The woman came out of the kitchen, hands kneading.

"Thank you for your help back there, ma'am," he said. "I really appreciate it."

She nodded at him in a dazed way, as if she were terrified at having helped him. Carpo walked out of the house and hobbled down the front stoop, his left arm resting snug against the broken rib to keep it from shifting. He was forced to move slowly, relaxing only after the cab was headed toward the train station.

In many ways, it was the pain that kept Carpo going. The

concussion made it difficult to think straight, clogging his brain with a drugged sensation, but whenever he felt like he was about to nod off, the sting of the rib burned off the haze, keeping him awake and preparing him for what he still had to face.

He made it to the train station, bought a ticket, and boarded the next express to the city. It didn't even occur to him to pick up a telephone and call the police. There were too many things to explain, too many things that still didn't make sense. Besides, it was simpler this way. It was him against Adonis—one on one. Simple and beautiful.

He was the first one off the train when the metallic scream of the brakes let up, signaling that they had pulled into Grand Central Terminal. He jogged to the far side of the station and crossed into the subway. He bought a token from a vending machine and ran to the Lexington Avenue line platform.

As he waited for his train, he fished a quarter out of his pocket and dialed the museum. It was after five, so he wasn't surprised when a recording answered. He dialed Karen's extension and waited through a dozen rings until her voice mail came on. He hung up and took out another quarter. Again, there was no answer. He saw a headlight cutting through the dark tunnel. He slammed down the phone, then hopped aboard a number six local heading uptown.

He slumped on the hard plastic bench, his breath coming in painful wheezes. His adrenaline was gone, all burned up. He noticed passengers recoil from him, a few even moving to the opposite side of the train. He couldn't blame them; he knew what he looked like. He just shut his eyes and concentrated on controlling his breathing.

At 86th Street, Carpo hopped off the train and started jogging again—up the stairs, west on 86th Street. He passed a pay phone on Madison and considered calling the museum again, but he'd spent his last quarter in the subway station. He hunched back over his rib and kept going.

At 5th Avenue he turned south. The museum loomed in front of him, enormous and busy with people. As he sprinted up to the entrance, he noted with strange fascination that it was finally warm enough for the tourists to linger on the steps. He dodged between them and pulled open the door, skipping past a guard, who shouted: "It's five-thirty, sir! The museum has just closed!"

He cut straight across the Great Hall, running toward the thin hallway Karen had used to reach her office. Several guards in starched blue uniforms heard the shouts and spotted him running.

"Hold it there," one of them ordered.

Carpo whirled and held up his right hand like something was in it. "Don't come near me or I'll blow this place up!"

The guards halted together in a pile and stared at his hand, wondering what it contained. Carpo cradled it to his stomach and kept running: through the Medieval section, the area with the wooden saints, then the Hall of Armor. He kicked open the door at the end of the gallery and started up the stairs toward the Greek and Roman section. A woman was walking down them, carrying a large carton of books. Behind him, Carpo heard a guard burst through the door.

"I need to borrow these," he said as he grabbed the carton from the woman. He tossed it over his shoulder down the stairs. The books rained down on the approaching guard, knocking him to the ground. "Thanks," Carpo said as he passed the woman.

He continued up the steps three at a time, until he spotted the placard that read: *"Department of Greek and Roman Art."* He jumped through the door. The book-lined hallway was pitch black and silent. He glimpsed into each office he passed; all were empty. At the first lighted one, he poked his head inside and demanded: "Is Karen Blackwell still here?"

A man in a tweed coat and cloth tie was sitting inside, puffing on the end of a briar pipe. He looked up at Carpo with an expression of mild annoyance. "Haven't seen her," the man said with an affected British accent.

Carpo felt a tug on his elbow, then his body was snapped back against a bookcase. It was the guard from the stairs. The man snapped a grip like a plumber's vise onto his arm and said: "Game's up, pal. You've gone far enough. Now come on with me."

The British man poked his head out of the office. "What's going on here?"

"Sorry for the disturbance, sir," the guard said. "This guy just ran past us at the front."

"Wait, you don't understand," Carpo said to them both. "Karen Blackwell is in trouble. She's right there at the end of the hallway. Please, go see if she's okay."

"Shut up," the guard ordered. "Shut up or I'll take you out of here on my shoulders."

"Make him check," Carpo pleaded with the British man. "She's in trouble, right down there. Go check on her."

"Have it your way." The guard threw a long arm around his neck and wrenched it into a headlock. Carpo felt his neck make an ugly ripping sound, but the only pain he felt was in his rib.

"Please, no," he gasped. "Help her."

"Michael, what's going on out here?"

It was Karen, leaning out of her office, body shielded by the half-open door. The guard looked from her to Carpo, then released his grip. "You know this guy?"

"Yes, I do," she said, then turned to Carpo. "What's wrong with you?"

"Are you all right? Are you alone?" He searched her face for any sign of trouble, but it appeared composed.

"I'm fine," she said. "Why are you creating problems here?"

"Problems? You don't even know what I went through today." He brushed past the guard and started toward her office. "Your little friend Adonis is a —"

"Stop!" she shouted. "You're not allowed back here."

"What do you mean?" Carpo said with surprise. The guard clamped back onto his elbow, preventing him from moving farther down the hallway.

"Guard, don't let him back here," she said. "I barely know this man."

"Karen, what the hell is going on?"

"I'll escort him out, ma'am," the guard said. He clamped his hold extra tight on Carpo's elbow. "Now then, we're going nice and peaceful, or should I put the neck hold back on you?"

"What's wrong with you?" Carpo screamed down the hallway, but Karen was already gone, office door closed and deflecting his shouts.

Carpo realized what was wrong with her. Her calm and composed look had been just that: too calm and too composed. She should have been furious with him for creating such a scene at the museum. And no matter how angry she was, she would never allow a guard to carry him out.

Carpo relaxed his entire body, allowing his knees to buckle and legs to sag onto the floor.

"So you still want to be difficult," the guard said angrily. "Have it your way, pal. It's just going to hurt that much more."

The guard released his grip on Carpo's elbow and bent

over to pick him off the ground. At the exact moment Carpo felt the grip loosen, he planted his legs firmly on the carpet and rammed his shoulder up. The move caught the guard by surprise, creating a few inches of space between them. It was enough. Carpo swung both hands into the man's chin, snapping his head into the bookcase. The guard released Carpo as he tried to break his fall. By the time the guard got back to his feet, Carpo was ten steps down the hallway.

He arrived at Karen's door a split-second before the guard and opened it. The guard crashed into him from behind, falling on top of him. The added weight made his rib feel like it would explode. Just when he thought he would pass out again, the guard rolled off him.

Carpo stayed on the floor, eyes clenched tight as he moaned in agony. He opened his eyes, amazed to see the guard kneeling next to him, both arms high above his head. Looking back in the other direction, Carpo saw Gabriel Adonis sitting on the couch, hand wrapped around his silver gun, its small black end pointing alternately between Carpo, the guard, and Karen.

They remained frozen for a few moments, the only movement in the room being Adonis's gun. It flicked from side to side at them like a serpent's head.

"Are you all right?" Carpo asked Karen. She nodded, but he could see that her mask of calm had melted into a flush of panic. "Sit tight, we'll be okay."

"I would not count on it," Adonis said, voice high and steady, eyes dead. "You escaped once, Carpo. It will not happen twice."

There was a soft tap on the door to the office; the silver gun froze. After a second knock, Adonis looked at Karen and whispered: "Ask who it is."

"Who's there?" she called.

The muffled voice of the British man came through the

door. "It's me, Karen. John Marshall. What's going on in there?"

"Tell him to come in," Adonis whispered.

"Come in, John."

The door swung open, and the man peeked around the door.

"Oh dear," he sputtered when he saw the pistol.

"Join us, Mr. Marshall," Adonis said. The gun started weaving between them again, making an added stop on the British man. "Perhaps there are others in the hallway?"

"No," he answered.

A walkie-talkie on the waist of the guard made a static noise, then squelched: *"Jared, where are you? What's your status?"*

The guard reached for the unit. The silver gun flashed at him, stopping his head.

Adonis flashed a smile at him. "Okay, Jared, nice and easy." He motioned with the gun for the guard to pick up the radio. "Why don't you tell your friends that you have apprehended the intruder and are bringing him down?"

"They'll want to send someone up here," Jared said.

"Just say you have everything under control, then turn off the radio."

The guard removed the unit from his belt. "Percy, it's Jared. I've apprehended the subject and I'm bringing him down."

*"Good job. What's your location?"*

"Yeah, I'm bringing him now, Percy."

*"Copy. What's the location, Jared?"*

"That's enough," Adonis said. "Put it away."

The guard looked up at him, the unit shaking in his hand. His eyes grew wide and crazed as he shouted, "Greek and Roman, Percy. Help me!"

"No," Carpo screamed, but his voice was blotted out by the bark of the gun.

The bullet caught the guard in the throat, splattering flecks of blood on the wall behind him. Karen screamed and clamped her hands over her eyes; Carpo stumbled backward away from the guard. Jared blinked with disbelief as he looked down at the blood streaming from his shirt collar. His hands went to his neck and tore at the fabric. Adonis brought the gun up and aimed it, slowly this time, shutting one eye as he stared down the short barrel. The next shot caught Jared in the face, silencing the gurgles from the hole in his neck.

"Dear lord," John Marshall said as he sank to his knees. "Lord have mercy."

The gun flicked among them again, its transitions no longer smooth. The expression of control had left Adonis's face; his forehead glistened pink, eyes finally showing emotion.

"Damn him," he shouted. "Damn you all. I'll use this again. I swear I will."

Carpo stared at the blood pooling on the carpet, his mind strangely occupied with wondering how the janitors would remove the stain. Oddly, the fear and worry in him had evaporated. Even his rib had stopped hurting. He looked at Adonis, noticing the man's jaw muscle flexing as his teeth mashed together in anger.

A whimper came from Karen. Her hands still covered her face, body shaking with tiny convulsions. Carpo stood and moved next to her, pulling her hands away from her face.

"What the fuck are you doing?" Adonis howled, a glob of spittle flying from his lips. "Get away from her."

When she felt Carpo's hand, Karen recoiled, then stared at him with a questioning face. He rubbed her cheek and whispered: "I love you."

"I said get away from her. Sit down or you are dead."

Carpo turned to Adonis, a smile creeping over his face. The little man actually appeared comical, all red in the face and shouting. In contrast, Carpo had never before felt so calm, so sure of what he was doing. "What are you going to do?" he asked him. "Shoot us all? One by one?"

"I'm warning you, Carpo, I'll . . ."

Adonis's voice broke off at the sound of footsteps in the hallway. He leapt off the couch and shoved Carpo aside, then grabbed Karen by a fistful of hair. A guard burst through the door as Adonis put the pistol to Karen's head.

"Move and she dies," he said to the guard.

"Take it easy," Carpo ordered the guard, as much as he ordered Adonis. The gun pressed into Karen's temple, shattering Carpo's calm. "Everyone just relax."

"Fuck you, Carpo," Adonis screamed, a vein bulging from his forehead.

"You can't escape, Adonis. There's nowhere to go."

"Fuck you, fuck you, fuck you!"

The gun pushed hard into her face, Adonis's finger tugging ever so slightly on the trigger. Carpo raised his hands in a gesture of submission, his eyes riveted on the movements of Adonis's finger.

More footsteps echoed through the open door. Adonis yanked Karen in front of his body and pushed her into the hallway. The footsteps stopped.

"Get me out of here safely and you'll live," Adonis whispered to Karen before addressing the guards in the hallway. "Move and the girl dies."

Karen pointed at the end of the hallway, away from the guards, where a red fire exit stood. Adonis wrapped his arm across her chest and pushed her toward it, their jerky movements down the hall making them look like a pair of drunken waltzers weaving across a dance floor.

"No, Karen," Carpo screamed as Adonis pulled open the door. "Don't go with him."

Before she could answer, Adonis draped his thick arm over her face and pulled her into the stairwell. The heavy door slammed with a metallic clang.

"Call 911," Carpo shouted at the guard. "Get the police and an ambulance. There's an injured man in the office."

The guards rushed into the office, joining the one already kneeling at the side of his dead partner. Carpo tapped the closest man on the shoulder. "Give me your radio," he said. "I'm going after them. I'll tell you where they are."

The guard removed the heavy plastic unit from his waist and handed it over. Carpo took it and ran down the hallway toward the fire escape.

# Chapter 23

Carpo burst through the red door onto a steep metal stairway built within a fire-resistant, concrete shaft. Each landing was lit by a pair of spotlights that cast a long V-shaped shadow across half the passageway. He leaned over the banister and peered down the thin space that went straight to the ground floor, five flights down. Far below he heard scuffling, then a shouted curse.

He started down the stairs, taking them four at a time. Each time his left foot landed, a prickly sensation shot up his side, like a current of electricity. He clamped his left arm hard against the rib and ignored the pain.

At the bottom of the stairs was another metal door with a sticker that said "WARNING: OPENING DOOR WILL TRIGGER ALARM." The door was open and swinging insanely on its hinges, as if a strong wind were gusting against it. A red light swirled atop the door, showing that the alarm had been triggered.

Carpo found himself at the back of the museum, on a small macadam path that wound its way through thick shrubbery. The path disappeared in the uncertain darkness of Central Park. Thirty yards down it, he could make out the forms of Adonis and Karen.

He raced in their direction, walkie-talkie still clenched in his right hand. He held his breath as he ran, trying to make his steps as silent as possible. He gained quickly, mostly because Karen was putting up a struggle. Adonis was in front of her, dragging her down the path by a handful of hair.

Carpo was within ten yards of them, timing out his long steps to tackle Adonis, when the walkie-talkie squelched in his hand. Five yards away and Adonis was turning. Two yards and the pistol was rising. He was almost there, arm outstretched with the radio, diving at the shadowy figure. He caught a glimpse of the silver pistol rising just as he crashed the radio onto Adonis's skull. A split-second later, the gun went off in his face.

The light and sound were overwhelming. His ears roared with deafness, nostrils filled with the acrid smoke. He fell to the ground with Adonis, eyes searching for him through the burning tears. He felt Adonis squirm beneath him, maneuvering the pistol for another shot. Carpo smashed the walkie-talkie down on the smaller man's head, again and again, each blow bringing splotches of red to the surface of the man's scalp.

The gun was up, its dark center pointing into his chest, when he slammed the radio against Adonis's wrist. There was another explosion, then the pistol clattered to the ground.

Adonis pushed free of Carpo and stood in the path. He made a grab for Karen but then turned and slinked off into the darkness. Carpo tried to get up, but his body wasn't responding. He rolled onto his back, eyes closed, analyzing each part of his body for a gunshot wound. His rib felt like it was sticking out of him—a quick feel with his hand proved it wasn't—his head ached from the concussion and exertion, and his kneecaps jerked around like pistons. But beyond those physical symptoms, he seemed to check out okay. Both bullets had missed him.

He rolled onto his stomach and got his knees under him. He was surprised to see Karen next to him on the ground, thin hands clutching her chest, where spidery lines of crimson flowed from between her fingers.

"Karen," he gasped as he rushed to her. Her eyes were very wide and her face looked pale. He pried the fingers away from her chest and ripped open her shirt. A small hole, perfectly round, had pierced her chest, just below her bra. He clamped his palm over it, trying to stop the blood.

She sat up and calmly brushed the hair out of her face, her fingers leaving a smudge of blood on her forehead. She gave a nervous smile and said: "Michael, I don't feel so good."

"Please, please, no!" he screamed.

His hand went to her back and found where the bullet had exited. A gaping, uneven hole had blown out the flesh above her shoulder blade. The stream of blood was much thicker there; huge black globs dropped out of the wound. He squeezed his hands on both sides of it, compressing her upper body, desperately trying to keep the life inside of her.

"Michael, I . . ." she started to say, but a rough cough choked off her words.

He held her close, squeezing, squeezing, always squeezing. He pushed his face into her neck and kissed her, feeling the warmth, smelling her.

"I . . . I'm sorry, Michael. I'm so sorry."

"No, don't say that," he said angrily. "Don't you dare say that to me."

"I didn't know what I was getting into. Frank tricked me. They wouldn't let me out."

"Stop it. Please, stop it. Don't say any more."

"I called Gabriel's loft. Thank god I called it." She rubbed a hand against his cheek; her fingers felt as cold as ice. Her words came out like harsh croaks as she strained to catch her breath. "I'm so . . . happy he . . . didn't . . . hurt you."

"Hang on, Karen. Damn you, hang on." He shook her hard, hands still squeezing both sides of her. She stared back at him, the hazel eyes starting to go a bit glossy.

Suddenly, Carpo was crying, sobbing like he hadn't since he was a child. "Please don't leave me, Karen. Please. You're all I've got. You're my second chance. I'll never get another. Never."

A police officer appeared from the fire escape and ran toward them. He looked at them, saw the blood, and shouted into his radio for an ambulance.

It seemed to take forever. All the while, he held her tightly, brushing out the blood that had caked in her long hair, kissing her face and neck and shoulders. He cried without shame or control, convulsive sobs that reverberated down into his busted rib.

There were a couple of times when he thought she had left him; quick, hard seizures froze up her body. Each time he hugged her close, pleading with her to stay with him. Over and over he told her that he loved her, that she couldn't die on him, that she was his second chance, that he'd never get another. Somehow she held on.

When the paramedics arrived, they had to pry his hands off her body; he didn't hear them asking him to let go of her. When he did release, she reached for him with fear, as if his contact was the only thing keeping her going. He held her hand as the paramedics went to work, squeezing it insistently, like an auxiliary heart pounding within her palm. The paramedics worked around him, sticking needles in her, shining light on her face, packing her with gauze.

More police officers arrived, and they were able to back in an ambulance from the other end of the path. They brought out a stretcher and put her onto it, fastening a Velcro belt around her waist and legs.

When they picked her off the ground, Carpo tried to hang on and follow, but his legs quit working. He had just enough sense to remember to release her hand before collapsing.

After Karen was rolled into the back of the ambulance, the siren going and vehicle pulling away, the attention turned to him. The paramedics took his pulse and shined a bright light in his eyes. They felt around his body, poking here and there until one of them found his rib.

"I'm okay, I'm okay," he told them, but nobody seemed to listen. He recognized one of the paramedics who had worked on Karen—a wiry guy with a long blond ponytail—and tugged on his shirt. "Tell me, is she going to be okay?" Carpo asked.

The man looked at Carpo with a blank face like he didn't get what he was talking about, then he nodded and said: "Oh yeah, don't worry, bud. She should be fine. It was close, but it totally missed her heart."

A cop walked over and kneeled next to them. "Can I talk to him for a minute? Just a few quick questions?" he asked the paramedic.

"Go ahead, he's not too serious."

The cop turned to Carpo. "Did you see where the perpetrator went?"

"He kept on this path," Carpo said, trying to picture what direction the path went into Central Park. "South, I guess."

"What does he look like?"

"He's wearing a blue-striped shirt and gray pants. He's

got a balding head. And his scalp's all torn up. I whacked him with that." Carpo pointed at the bloody walkie-talkie on the ground.

"Is he armed?"

"I don't think anymore. He dropped the gun somewhere over there."

Suddenly, the radios on the hip of every officer blared: *"Report of a 10–39 at the Central Park Zoo. Officers responding exercise extreme caution. Suspect is in vicinity of shooting at Metropolitan Museum."*

"The Central Park Zoo," Carpo said out loud. Of course, he thought, if the path headed south, it had to intersect with the zoo.

The radios crackled again. *"Suspect has entered the Tropic Zone exhibit. Building is at southwest corner of zoo. Proceed with caution."*

A troupe of officers raced down the path, while the one talking to Carpo got on his radio and gave the description Carpo had given him of Adonis. The paramedics continued working around him, one of them strapping a clear plastic mask over his face that flooded his lungs with pure oxygen.

"Hey, is this guy okay?" the cop asked the long-haired paramedic. "Can I take him with me for a little while?"

"He's got a concussion and broken rib, but there's not much we can do for him here." The paramedic shrugged. "If he says he's up to it, fine. He should stop by a hospital later for a few x-rays."

The cop turned to Carpo. "What do you say, guy? You feel well enough to come ID this perp?"

"Sure."

The cop got back on his radio and barked some orders. Within a few minutes, a squad car backed down the path the same way the ambulance had come. The paramedics wrapped him in a wool blanket and helped him to the cruiser. Carpo got into the front passenger seat; the cop got in behind the wheel.

"We're on our way," he informed someone on the car's radio.

The scene outside the Central Park Zoo was like no other crime scene Carpo had ever visited. Dozens of police cars, ambulances, and unmarked cars were parked on the sidewalk lining 5th Avenue, their red and yellow emergency lights reflecting off the buildings across the street. A large crowd of people had gathered, and several cops stayed behind to control them. Live TV trucks and freelance station wagons double-parked behind the official vehicles, and reporters and photographers rushed toward the police barricades outside the zoo.

Carpo's squad car found an opening a block above the crowd and jumped the curb. They sped down the sidewalk until they reached the entrance to the zoo. An officer with a fluorescent orange vest made them stop. When Carpo was identified as an eyewitness, they were waved through.

They drove past a row of large brick buildings until they reached the zoo's central courtyard. Most of the space was taken up by a large pool of water. Carpo could make out several dark forms skimming beneath the surface of the water. Along the edge of the pool was a row of white-whiskered animals. They were sea lions, lined up along the railing, watching the action as intently as the humans outside the zoo fence.

The officer parked the car and walked over to Carpo's side, helping him from the seat. "You sure you're up to this?" he asked.

"Yeah, I'm okay. Where do we go?"

"The perp's in there." He pointed to a circular wooden

building with a sign on the front door that read "The Tropic Zone."

They crossed the courtyard, Carpo leaning on the officer for support. At the door to the Tropic Zone, they approached an officer who appeared to be in charge of the scene. He was older and had several brightly colored bars under a shiny badge. His nameplate identified him as Sgt. William J. Corsaro.

The officer escorting Carpo talked quietly with the sergeant, explaining that Carpo was an eyewitness to the crime. Sergeant Corsaro looked Carpo over as the man talked, then nodded at him to approach.

"How're you doing there, fella?" he asked.

Carpo shivered a bit. "A little cold, but I'm fine."

"We're going to take you inside there, okay? But it's very important you stay close. Understand?"

Carpo didn't understand, but he nodded to show he would stay close anyway. The sergeant turned and escorted them through the entrance of The Tropic Zone.

Inside, the building was black and humid, the air thick with the odor of rotting topsoil. It was so humid, Carpo could feel a layer of mist settle on his hair and clothes. They walked along a narrow trail, then crossed what appeared to be a wooden bridge. Above them stretched an elaborate canopy of lush trees and wiry vines. The sounds of running water, rustling trees, and bird screams filled the air. Something whooshed past Carpo's head. He was amazed to see a brightly colored bird fly past, its long plumed tail darting among the trees. Between the slats in the bridge, he could see long shadows floating like logs in the fake river. He realized the shadows were crocodiles.

They stepped off the bridge and headed up a concrete stairway. Sergeant Corsaro held onto his elbow, as much to steady him as to make sure he didn't disobey his order to "stay close."

It was a like a dream, the dark forest and his aching body only adding to the surreal qualities of the building. At the top of the stairs another officer stopped them. He shined a flashlight into all of their faces and said: "Be careful. They still haven't caught the snake."

Adonis was there, lying on the concrete floor, his cold blank eyes staring unblinkingly past them.

"Is he dead?" Carpo asked shakily.

"Yeah, he died a few minutes ago," the cop with the flashlight said.

"Is he the guy from the Met?" Sergeant Corsaro asked.

He stared for a long while, heart hammering as he waited to see if Adonis would ever move again. Finally satisfied, he said: "Yeah, it's him."

The sleeve of Adonis's shirt was rolled high above his biceps, the fabric shredded as if it had been done quickly. Carpo was amazed at the size of the man's upper arm. The muscle was tensed in a permanent contraction; it held the bulk and definition of a bodybuilder's arm. Several long, jagged cuts were evident in Adonis's wrist. They grew deeper and deeper as they moved up his arm to the elbow. The cuts were no longer bleeding, which seemed strange until he remembered that the man was dead.

Carpo looked up, and for the first time he understood what had caused the cuts. Above the dead man's head was a glass case with its side smashed in. Adonis must have punched his fist through it.

But The Tropic Zone, Adonis's exposed arm, the glass case—none of it made sense to Carpo until he spotted the plastic sign hanging on the wall next to the case. In neat, black letters, it read: "Egyptian Cobra."

# Chapter 24

After he had identified Gabriel's body, Carpo was led back to the squad car and driven outside the zoo's front gate. The officer who had escorted him asked him to wait there until the body was removed from The Tropic Zone. The man had left the car running to keep it heated, and he poured Carpo a cup of lukewarm coffee from a thermos in the trunk. Before he left, the officer told him not to speak to the press until he'd had a chance to question him some more.

As soon as the officer left, a tiredness descended on Carpo like he had never before experienced. The heater cast a steady flow of warm, dry air over his face, opening his pores and, for the first time since that morning, relaxing his body. He shivered and wrapped the wool blanket close to himself, enjoying the warmth captured by the thick fabric. The coffee was good, too, very sweet and diluted with a large dose of cream. His eyes grew more and more relaxed, until they were closed. His head bumped against the car's window, sliding down the glass until it was nestled against the soft padding of the door.

A hard rap on the window made him sit upright. Carpo rubbed his eyes and looked at his watch, surprised to see that ten minutes had passed. His breathing had fogged over the window; he fumbled with the handle to roll it down. Ed Thomas was standing on the other side.

"Carpo. Great! What luck to find you," the reporter announced vigorously. "I've been searching through every police car for you."

Carpo flashed a tired smile. The knock on the glass had dragged him from his nap, but it hadn't cleared enough of the fatigue to make him feel like talking.

"What's going on in there?" Ed asked, pointing over his shoulder at the zoo. "Does it have anything to do with the shooting at the Met?"

"I can't really say, Ed. You'll have to wait until the cops make a statement."

"But weren't you just inside there? I heard you were helping out the police. What were you doing?"

Ed's whining voice started to grate on Carpo's nerves. He took a slow drink of coffee, then said: "Yeah, I was in there. And yes, I saw everything. I was even up at the Met."

"You were?" Ed's eyes grew wide, his upper lip quivering with anticipation. "Hold on. Don't say a thing. I'll be right back."

The reporter scurried off into the darkness. Carpo rolled his window back up and leaned his head against the door's padding, trying to find the position he'd had before. No sooner had he found it when the same obnoxious knock jerked him upright. He located the handle and rolled the window down. Ed was there again, this time accompanied by a WIBN cameraman.

"Okay Carp', listen up," he said. "They're throwing to us live at the end of the six o'clock show."

Ed reached into his pocket and pulled out a leather case

holding his IFB—interrupt from broadcast—earpiece. He slid the molded rubber piece into his ear, then withdrew another case, smaller and round, from his pocket. The case was a makeup compact. He dabbed powdered rouge all over his face, then he pinched his cheeks vigorously until the skin was bright red. Carpo smiled at the reporter's antics, finally understanding why the reporter's cheeks always looked so flushed on the air. Ed inspected himself in the compact's mirror, primping his hair and running his tongue across the front of his teeth. When he was satisfied with his appearance, he grabbed the microphone from the cameraman.

"Is the mike on?" he asked the cameraman. "They're coming to us in about a minute. Can you frame those ambulances behind me into the shot? It looks more newsy. Now, I'm going to do a little lead-in, then we'll pan over to Carpo and do a little q-and-a, then we'll pan back on me, nice and tight, and I'll wrap. Got it?"

"Hang on, Ed," Carpo said. "The cops told me not to—"

"Don't bother me, Carp'," the reporter interrupted. "I've got to come up with my lead. Just answer my questions and you'll do fine."

The camera man flicked on the light above the camera, white-balancing the unit against the side of the squad car. Ed stood with his hand over his eyes, lips mouthing possible leads for the story.

Carpo sipped his coffee as he watched Ed's preparations. It was ten minutes before seven, so they were throwing to Ed right before the sports. Carpo estimated that the shooting had happened a half-hour earlier, meaning that Channel 8 was probably one of the first stations to go live on the story from the field. He could imagine the newsroom right now, bustling with activity as the writers hammered out last minute changes to the copy and the production assistants rounded up file tape.

"Ready?" Ed asked suddenly. "Here they come. Five, four, three, two . . ."

Ed stood still, face frozen with anticipation as the anchor toss was broadcast into his earpiece.

"That's right, Maria," he said in his lowest, most breathless reporting voice. "The showdown with police started some thirty blocks north of here at the Metropolitan Museum of Art. A source tells me a gunman broke into the world famous museum and took several employees hostage. The gunman, who remains unidentified, allegedly shot and killed at least one employee before he fled to this location, here at the Central Park Zoo. Details are sketchy, but it seems the gunman was shot by police or turned the gun on himself. With me right now is an eyewitness to the entire ordeal."

The camera panned to Carpo, who squinted painfully in its bright light. Ed's microphone followed the camera's movement, stopping just an inch beneath Carpo's chin.

"Now sir, you said you saw everything that took place." Ed's voice was softer as he addressed Carpo, as if he needed to reassure this timid witness that it was his civic duty to tell the world what had happened. Carpo guessed that Ed was calling him "sir" so that nobody would know they worked together. Maybe Ed had forgotten that his picture had been on the cover of *The Post* just three days before.

"Yes, I saw everything," Carpo said.

"Were you also an eyewitness to the museum shooting?"

"Yes."

"Tell us, sir, is the gunman dead?"

Carpo paused for a moment and tilted his head away from

the bright light. He wanted a better look at Ed's face; it was a moment he never wanted to forget.

"Sir, I asked if the gunman was dead," Ed said.

"No comment."

Ed blinked hard. "Excuse me?"

"I said, no comment."

"Could you tell me what you saw then?"

"I'm sorry, I can't do that." Carpo turned to the camera and flashed a polite smile. Its wide lens stared back, reflecting a tiny, distorted picture of his face. It was hard to imagine the lens was broadcasting his face into every apartment in the city.

"Carpo," Ed whispered ominously, his air of confidence melting. "Would you please tell the people what happened in there?"

Carpo turned to the camera again and flashed another polite smile. "I'm sorry Ed, but I tried to tell you a minute ago, the police told me not to speak to the press. You'll have to wait for their statement, just like everybody else."

Ed snapped the microphone away from his chin. The cameraman, unsure of where to go, swung the lens back and forth between them. When Ed started speaking, the lens focused on him. Carpo could see the side of the cameraman's face, fighting against laughter.

"That's about as much information as we have right now. I'll be out here until I learn more and bring it to you live. This is Ed Thomas reporting live from the Central Park Zoo in midtown Manhattan. Let's go back to Maria and Matt in the studio."

Ed stayed focused on the camera lens for a few seconds. When he was sure the station was no longer broadcasting him, he threw his mike on the ground. "Turn that fucking camera off. Carpo, what the fuck were you doing?"

The cameraman turned the light off, returning Carpo to the darkness. He blinked his eyes to readjust them.

"You're fucking crazy, Carpo. Do you know how many people watch the six o'clock broadcast? Do you know how bad that made us look? Made me look?"

Ed stepped away from the car, mumbling to himself. After a minute, he stepped back to the window.

"Okay, okay, you got your way on the live shot," he said. "Maybe I was a little pushy. But damn it Carpo, I've always been straight with you. Just give me a quick interview on tape and I'll leave you alone. I'll use the interview in my package for the ten o'clock show."

Carpo looked into Ed's face and gave it the same polite smile he had given the camera and its half-million viewers. "Sorry Ed, but the advice I gave 'the people' holds true for you, too. You'll have to wait for the police to make a statement."

Ed leaned his head through the car window, close enough for Carpo to smell the putrid stink of cigarettes on his breath. "Maybe I should spell things out loud and clear for you Carp'. Give me the interview or you'll never work another day at Channel 8."

Carpo reached up and pinched the man's earlobe between his thumb and forefinger, twisting it until the reporter squealed. "Let me spell it out even louder and clearer, Ed. Get out of my sight before I make you so ugly, you'll have to do radio."

He gave the earlobe an added twist, then shoved the man's face out of the car. From the corner of his eye, he saw Ed stomp off in the direction of the live truck, hand cupped protectively over his ear.

Carpo rolled up the window and pulled the blanket around him. His rib was aching terribly, and he wished the police officer would return to take him to the hospital. It took a while for his nerves to settle back down; it took even longer for the sluggish fatigue to return to his eyes.

He had just dozed off again when there was another rap on the window, this one softer and less persistent. Carpo reached for the handle. As he rolled the window down, a soothing voice floated inside the car, bringing a genuine smile to Carpo's face.

"How're you feeling, little brother?" Major Sisco asked.

"I'll live, Sisco. Hey, what brings you out in the field tonight?"

"Case you haven't noticed, this is the story of the year. Lipton wants the first half of the ten o'clock show to go live from up here. I thought I'd better help set up for it."

"But who's running the Assignment Desk?"

"One of my assistants."

Carpo's mouth flew open. "You're trusting the night desk to one of your assistants?"

"I've got to start handing over the power some time. So I hear you and Ed are still getting along famously."

"Did you see him interview me?"

"No, but Ed sure filled me in on it. He must think he's pretty damn powerful around the station if he's going to start firing people."

"Sorry about that. The cops asked me not to speak to the press. He didn't seem to care when I told him."

"Not to worry, Carp'. How are you doing for real?"

"I'm a little banged up, but I'll be fine. Karen got shot by that guy up at the Met. I'm going to see her at the hospital as soon as the cops finish with me."

"How bad is she?"

"I don't know, but she looked real bad."

"Be careful, Carp'. She's still a suspect. A friend of mine

downtown says they think she was part of some sort of fake art scam."

Carpo averted his eyes. He knew they would lie as bad as any lie he said out loud.

Sisco must have sensed his discomfort because he leaned through the window and patted his shoulder. "Don't you worry about that now though. You go see her at the hospital and straighten out the loose ends in your life. When things get back to normal, I want you back with us at Channel 8."

Carpo noticed the officer emerging from the zoo gates to drive him to the hospital. He turned to Sisco, shaking his head from side to side. "I appreciate the offer, but I don't think so. I'm not going back."

"What? Why not?"

"Some things never change. Ed Thomas will always hype and distort stories. Bill Lipton will always be a bully. I think it's time for me to find a new line of work."

"Don't make that decision yet, Carpo. Let's go out for lunch next week. I want to pitch a new position for you at the station."

"It'll never get Lipton's approval."

"I've got news for you buddy, some things do change. Lipton got bumped to an executive position at the mother station. He's moving out to Chicago next month. Ed's on his way out, too."

Carpo groaned. "What position did he get?"

"He's not getting a new job. He's getting fired."

Carpo sat up in the seat. "They're firing Ed Thomas?"

"No, Carp'. *I'm* firing Ed Thomas.

Carpo flashed a suspicious grin at the Metro Editor. "What's up Sisco?"

"You're looking at the new executive producer of Channel 8 News. Pinkney sent out the memo this afternoon."

"Congratulations." Carpo extended his hand to Sisco. "You deserve it."

"I'm going to be making lots of changes in the newsroom. I'm bringing in some new people, and I'm shuffling the reporter line-up a bit. You know, I think you might look good in front of a camera."

Carpo's eyes grew narrow. "What are you talking about, Sisco?"

"I'm saying I think you might make a good reporter someday."

"When did you say you wanted to have lunch?"

Sisco erupted in a loud chuckle. "Whenever you're ready."

The door to the driver's side opened, and the officer slid into the car.

"I've got a great idea for the May sweeps piece, Sisc'. The gullibility of the modern art buyer. We can ride the wave caused by this scandal."

Sisco dropped his hand onto Carpo's shoulders and gave him another pat. "Take the weekend off and call me Monday morning."

"I'll see you next week," Carpo shouted after him. Sisco waved and disappeared into the crowd of people.

The officer threw the car into reverse and backed off the curb, spinning the steering wheel until they were facing down 5th Avenue. They threaded through the parked cars and started south. Carpo shifted in his seat, feeling the heaviness against his side.

"Hang on a sec'," he said to the officer, holding up his empty Styrofoam cup. "I want to throw this out."

Before the officer could answer, he made like he was getting out of the car. The officer pulled over immediately and Carpo stepped out. He jogged to the wire trash bin on the corner. As he did, he reached inside his jacket and pulled out the four photographs of Karen posing as Cleopatra. He crumpled them into a tight ball, shoved them into the bottom of the cup, and tossed it in the trash. A brief feeling of guilt swept over him, but before he could change his mind, he jogged back to the car.

"Thanks," he said to the officer once he was back inside.

The officer flicked a switch on the dashboard, and a light started revolving on top of the car, its flashing strobe cutting across the buildings.

Carpo pressed his face to the window and watched as they zoomed past Central Park, the strobe capturing the dark shadows and lighting them for just a moment.

# Prologue

The wonderful thing—the thing that never ceases to amaze me—is the fact that people will do anything to avoid looking me in the eye.

When I make my rounds on the street, strolling in a manner that I imagine as forceful, people try their damnedest to shake off eye contact. They look past me, above me, even straight through me, as if I'm some inanimate being, an essence, apparition, barely a presence. Even when they approach me head-on, when a glance in the face is inevitable, they allow their eyes to go soft-focus, as if they were off somewhere in a daydream or a trance.

When I was younger, it used to really bother me.

Back then, I used to interpret those lowered, inhospitable eyes as a sign of disrespect, a deliberate disregard for myself as a human being. Those dodging eyes were a signal that I didn't warrant their attention. I wasn't intelligent enough, handsome enough, witty enough, important enough. I wasn't good enough.

Especially in the eyes of women.

The women, they seem to do everything in their power to guarantee no chance encounter with my eyes. They might stare off into the distance, eyes positioned a half-inch over my shoulder, as if they're checking for the street sign down the block. Some might keep their eyes focused on the pavement, as if a hidden obstacle threatened to suddenly appear before them. Others might peer into their hands, perusing a newspaper or a magazine. The ones really adamant about not seeing me might place an object between their eyes and mine: a pair of reflective sunglasses, a raised hand, even an extreme squinting of the lids, as if it were necessary to repel the snow, rain, heat, or gloom of night.

When I was younger, such women made me very angry.

So angry, in fact, that I often did things that would demand their attention. Sometimes I would act like a crazy man, shouting all kinds of gibberish as I lurched down the sidewalk. Other times, I would exhibit a posture that can be interpreted only as menacing: fists and jaws clenched, eyes narrowed, upper lip curled with contempt. I would say things too. A whispered "bitch," a snarling "fuck," even the hissed "c" word, the most despicable word on this planet to a woman's ears. But I learned very quickly that when you act that way and say those things, people remember you. They remember your face and the way you acted. Especially the women.

Now I enjoy my anonymity.

Actually, I rely on it. To be anonymous means I have the opportunity to study the women, to inspect each one like a show judge, appraising their every feature: hair (color and sheen), clothes (quality and label), body type (fat, thin, or middling), smell (perfumed or natural). Most of all, I judge the women by their eyes. I search and search each day, looking into the faces of each woman who passes, until I spot the one particular woman who is worthy of the grand prize.

Believe it or not, today I was in the presence of two such women.

One lives on 12th Street, between Second and Third avenues. She's a spicy little number: pretty face, long black hair, big chest, and a narrow waist. When she walks down the street, she moves kind of like a fashion model, a jaunt to her step, so those tits of hers bounce up and down. I'm sure she's aware of all the men staring at her. They whistle at her and shout crude things, which I'm positive she can hear even through the headphones of her Walkman.

When I saw her, I didn't ogle those tits. I was waiting for a glimpse of her eyes.

They're a magnificent set of dark brown, wrapped in oval eyelids, like the shell of a toasted almond. When she squints, those lids wrap around her brown eyes like a pair of soft hands, as if they were being presented to me.

I know a fair amount about this woman. Her name is Irene Foster. She's twenty-seven years old, single, no children. She lives in building number 228, apartment number 6E. Her phone number is 555-0554. Her checking account at Citibank is 43110213, with a balance of $6,256. If there were any more money in there, I might start wondering how she supplements her $600-per-month scholarship money from New York University. You see, she's a graduate student in art history.

I know a lot about the other woman too. Her name is Adelle Simms. She's a thirty-six-year-old resident nurse at Cabrini Medical Center, the place where I went to get stitches after a dog bit me in the ankle last year. Adelle is married with two children, twelve-year-old Brent and nine-year-old Lizbeth. Her husband is Doug Simms, a boorish-looking certified public accountant at Walker, Thomas, and Barth. Adelle and her family live in a tiny apartment on East 8th Street.

Unlike Irene Foster, when Adelle Simms walks down the block, men never ogle. She's built like a cement igloo: five foot two in heels, and tipping the scales at one hundred and eighty pounds. When she moves she waddles, sending uneven tremors through her dimples of cellulite. But there is something about Adelle's eyes, a pair of melon-brown beauties with a dot of light in the center, an uncontainable glimmer of excitement, that intrigues me very much.

You may wonder how I know so much about Adelle and Irene. The simple reason is that I have spent time in both of their apartments, making small talk with them, cracking jokes and saying "not a problem, ma'am," whenever they said "thanks." Both of these women have stood before me and met my stare. By doing so, by making eye contact, they have sealed the contract and sealed their fate. They are among the chosen ones upon whom I will someday bestow the ultimate prize. Me.

# One

On the last Saturday of an unseasonably warm May, some-where between eight-thirty and nine o'clock at night, Michael Carpo began his Black Magic ritual in the kitchen of his one-bedroom apartment on 12th Street.

Black Magic was the house blend at Java The Hut, a small-time coffee dealer just around the corner on Second Avenue in the East Village. The blend was a potent mixture of Colombian and Sumatran beans, double-roasted for added kick. Every Saturday evening Carpo ground a one-pound bag of Black Magic, refilling an old Medaglia d'Oro espresso tin that he kept in the refrigerator. The can lasted exactly six days, from Monday morning to Saturday evening, when Carpo would knock the remnants into his Rancilio coffee-maker and brew his final pot of coffee for the week.

The ritual carried almost a religious significance to Carpo, mostly because he did not drink coffee on Sundays. After feeding the addiction for six straight days, the day of abstinence was important to him; somehow it proved that he was still his own master.

Carpo poured a handful of the dark, waxy beans into a Braun grinder and pressed the on button. The beans disinte-grated in a silvery whirl as an ear-throttling screech rose from the machine. He closed his eyes and concentrated on counting slowly to twelve. One Saturday he had forgotten to count and his coffee had turned out the consistency of talcum powder instead of the desirable size of gritty sand. His Rancilio coffeemaker had backed up twice that week, sending cascades of steaming brown water onto the kitchen floor.

By the count of four, the screech softened, the resistance easing on the two steel blades. In its place came another noise, a strange one, far off at first but growing steadily louder. He ignored it as he focused only on counting to twelve, but by the time he reached ten, the noise took a disturbing turn: shrill, with the hint of an echo. Carpo's eyes flew open and he forgot the twelve count, the coffee beans, and the consistency of the grind.

*It sounds like a scream,* he thought. *A human scream.*

His hand flew off the power button as if it had scorched him, and the screech of the grinder subsided. Carpo held perfectly still, holding his breath as he listened for the strange noise. The clock ticked off seconds on the wall over the stove. Water plinked into the sink. The refrigerator motor shifted to a higher gear.

Then he heard it again, from out on 12th Street: a woman was screaming for help, and screaming as if it weren't going to get there in time. Carpo slapped the coffee soot from his fingers and ran for the bedroom.

It was a clear, still night; both windows facing 12th Street were open, the shades halfway drawn. As Carpo drew closer to the street, the woman's voice became sharper, each scream dividing into separate, intelligible phrases: "Help me! Please, someone! Please, help!"

The window screen darkened the already dark street, reducing everything to shadows and blur. Carpo spotted a commotion across the street. A woman stood on the sidewalk, arms waving frantically, as if she were trying to flag down a rescue plane. Carpo squinted through the screen but he was unable to make out her face. Suddenly, a man in a long black trench coat burst from the shadows. He shoved the woman aside and sprinted toward Third Avenue.

*What's happening,* Carpo wondered. *Is it a mugging? A slashing? An attempted rape?*

His first concern went out for Candi. Often she walked home along 12th Street, when her shift had ended at Little Poland. *Could the woman be her?*

"Help me!" the woman screamed. "Please, someone!"

The telephone was in the living room, on the table beside the couch. It occurred to Carpo to use it before running downstairs; he knew he shouldn't rely on neighbors to call 911. But there wasn't time for it: to call and give his name and explain what he had seen on the street. Not if someone was in trouble. Not if it was Candi.

*Please God,* he thought as he unlocked the door and raced down the stairs, *please not Candi.*